Without Due Caution

Meredith Ryan Mystery
Book 5

Thonie Hevron

ROUGH
EDGES
PRESS

Rough Edges Press
An Imprint of Wolfpack Publishing
9850 S. Maryland Parkway, Suite A-5 #323
Las Vegas, Nevada 89183

roughedgespress.com

Paperback ISBN 978-1-68549-267-0
eBook ISBN 978-1-68549-266-3
LCCN 2023937928

Without Due Caution

California Penal Code 192 Manslaughter

Manslaughter is the unlawful killing of a human being without malice.

(a) Voluntary—upon a sudden quarrel or heat of passion.

(b) Involuntary—in the commission of an unlawful act, not amounting to a felony; or in the commission of a lawful act which might produce death, in an unlawful manner, or without due caution and circumspection.

Chapter One

Monday, March 5, 2:00 PM

"YOU OWE ME." RAUL ESPARZA'S EYES NARROWED ABOVE THE grimace lines on his face. Prison hadn't improved his demeanor. His hair had grown longer and was peppered with gray. He'd maintained his fit physique in the seven years since she'd seen him. "I saved your life."

"I don't owe you anything." If anyone deserved incarceration, it was the man in front of her. He'd killed without remorse. One of his victims had been her husband, Richard Taylor. Still, Meredith Ryan's conscience tugged at her. She couldn't admit he was right. "I paid my debt at your sentencing."

"If I hadn't shot Giroud, you'd be dead." His voice was steely. "And you know it."

"You brought me down here to remind me?" She gripped the phone, her eyes on Esparza through the pitted plexiglass, each in an adjoining cubicle. Esparza, like every other inmate, was looking for a deal with the outside. They were at San Quentin, which housed the most serious convicts. The stench of institutional hopelessness permeated everything. Salt air pocked the concrete walls that surrounded the prison. Walls that were three and four stories high surrounded her when she came in the gate. Cameras ensured nothing was secret. When she parked, she put her firearms in the car's locked safe. She didn't want anyone touching her guns.

"Wait." He sighed a breath of resignation. "I'm just reminding you that it's because of me that you're breathing."

"Number one, you killed my husband." Meredith hissed into the phone. "Two, you aided in the murder of my brother." The metal chair screeched across the worn linoleum as she stood. The brother after whom her son was named. "No, I don't owe you anything." She stretched to hang up the phone.

"No. Wait." Esparza closed his eyes and bowed his head.

Intrigued by his unusually obvious desperation, she sat down. "You've got one minute. Astonish me."

Esparza looked up, searching her eyes. What made this man call her? What was he looking for? Trust? She and Nick had treated him fairly but firmly after he'd shot Judge Stephen Giroud. He'd saved Meredith's life by stopping Giroud's assault. She and her partner, Nick Reyes, had spoken up for him at his sentencing. While the judge dialed his prison term down to life, he'd never entertain the possibility of parole.

Esparza's gaze was unflinching. "I need you to find someone."

"Are you kidding me?" She wanted to reach over and wrap her fingers around his neck. Good thing the plexiglass was in place, for her sake. "Nick and I put our reputations on the line for you. It's because of us that you didn't get the death sentence." Wasn't anybody afraid of the death sentence? Is it worse than life in prison? "What makes you think I'll help you?"

He rubbed his eyes. Esparza was a hard man. Whatever he wanted carried a major price tag on his ego.

She glanced at her phone. If she left now, she could beat commute traffic back to her office in Santa Rosa at the Sonoma County Sheriff's Office. But she stayed anyway. "What?"

"I need your help to find a young girl." He hesitated, searching her face for a reaction. When he saw none, he continued. "My niece, Esme, is missing."

"Missing or runaway?" The law enforcement definition of both had been a powder keg issue in the past two decades. By definition, a missing person's disappearance is unexplained, whereas the runaway has a motive to vanish and doesn't want to be found. A missing designation would infer a lost or abducted person and initiate a search. A runaway was merely a delinquency matter. The frequency of juveniles who simply ran away made police skeptical to classify them as missing. After several high-profile "runaway" kids were found to have been kidnapped and murdered, federal and state laws tightened. Sometimes these laws were perceived as obstacles to doing police work, but on the rare occasion that a truly missing child was found, those concerns were put into perspective.

"She may have run away, but I believe she was manipulated or coerced."

"What makes you think this?" She'd heard it before from many family members who refused to believe their child was unhappy at home.

"Let me start at the beginning."

"Before I hear this story, tell me: Have her parents reported it to the local police?"

"You know how seriously cops take runaway reports." He waved the thought away, a convict unwilling to trust the police even though he'd once been a cop. "She's living with my aunt for now. A nice lady, but not too savvy about the horrors of the street. Esme's mother is my brother's wife, Teresa. She lost custody of her last year because of one too many drug convictions. Esme had a tough time."

"Where's your brother?"

"Dead. Stabbed by a gangster in Soledad three years ago." Esparza's shoulders drooped at his loss. "My sister-in-law went off the rails after Arturo died. She and Esme moved up to Sonoma County to live with my aunt in Rohnert Park. Auntie threw the mom out because Teresa got herself drugged up most of the time, and wouldn't get off the junk. Esme's only thirteen, but she's turned into a handful, too. Running away two or three times. The school called in the county to take her away."

Meredith wanted to move the story along. "And she ran away from the foster home."

"No, she never got placed. She left from my auntie's house." He laid his hands flat on the shelf, grounding himself. "She's a good kid, just a little confused. An "A" student, in spite of her flaky home life. Auntie told me Social Services wanted to keep her with family, so they left her with her. Then, she disappeared from school three days ago. Left her phone and backpack in her locker."

"A teenager without her phone is alarming, for sure." It didn't sound right. The investigator in Meredith knew a report on Esme would be easy to find. "Why're you telling me this?" She knew where he was going.

"I need someone to find her before something bad happens. It has to be someone I trust. The cops won't look for her."

There it was, laid out on the table. The prisoner and the cop. The murderer and the law enforcer. He'd slain her husband, but he'd also killed the man intent on murdering her. Meredith had to admit there was a shred of something between them. But *trust*? Obligation? Responsibility? Duty?

A shred.

She would make a few inquiries.

Chapter Two

BORED AND WISHING SHE HAD HER PHONE, ESMERALDA VELA Alfaro picked at her sweater. Even if it was an old hand-me-down iPhone 7, she missed scrolling through her social media. Her mind wandered as she waited. She pictured the apartment building on Yulupa Avenue in Santa Rosa, where they used to live—her mother, Teresa, and her. Next door to Michael and Sofia. A quiet suburban apartment neighborhood in a tranquil wine-country area.

They'd only been in Santa Rosa less than two years. Esme had settled in nicely. She'd gone to a decent middle school, gotten good grades, and made friends in the brief time she was there. That was, until Teresa got into trouble six months ago.

One afternoon, her mother had gathered her up and run out of their apartment with few of their clothes. In a panic, Teresa moved them in with her auntie in Rohnert Park. Then her mother was arrested and had to go to jail. Her sentence was court-ordered to rehab while Child Protective Services removed her from her mother's custody. CPS placed Esme with Auntie Almita officially.

She'd been at her auntie's apartment long enough to know what she was in for. She liked the school she'd been attending, but sleeping on the family couch was tiresome. She had no privacy. Even though she couldn't talk to her mother, Esme had begun developing a plan to get away. She'd even made a few experimental forays overnight, staying with school pals.

With the help of her friend and next-door neighbor, Sofia, she decided to drop school, get a job, and when her mother got out of rehab in a month, they could rent an apartment of their own with her earnings. Sofia had suggested her father, Michael's, cleaning business. Without a school-dispensed work permit, she'd have to work on the sly. This limited her opportunities to earn money.

Earlier today, at the school lunch break, Esme had called for Michael to take him up on the offer to work for him. Sofia answered and said that her father wasn't home yet. She offered to pick Esme up at school and bring her back to a house on Aston Avenue to wait for Michael.

Esme didn't much like most men but especially Michael. Trust wasn't in her heart after the parade of strange men her mother brought into their lives. She'd seen how they pushed her mother around, so she found ways to hide and stay out of range of wandering hands.

Sometimes Michael was too bossy, and other times was overly affectionate to Sofia, touching her in ways Esme thought were too personal. But Sofia didn't seem to mind. Esme figured it was okay as long as he didn't bother her.

Esme loved Sofia. The young woman felt like a sister. To Esme, a girl who'd spent her life isolated from family and repeatedly moved away from the few friends she made, Sofia became someone special. After CPS took Esme away from her mother, she and Sofia talked on the phone every chance they got. Sofia encouraged her plan of finding a place of her own for her and her mother.

At first, Esme was uncomfortable around Sofia. The vivacious blond girl with the cutest pixie cut—ever—was shorter by seven inches than Esme's five foot ten. And Sofia was older. Esme had never pinned Sofia down, but figured she was at least eighteen years old. She didn't go to high school or college. She seemed to have a charmed life.

To Esme, Sofia grew to be almost as precious as her mother. Esme hoped her friend would be the means to reunite with Teresa. She crossed her fingers and said a prayer that Sofia would talk Michael into finding her work. It was up to her. Her mom couldn't hold a job for long. That was just a fact. She was sick most of the time, so Esme felt it was down to her to find a place to live—and pay for it.

Even though Esme thought Michael was paranoid, like her mother got sometimes, she wanted to stay on his good side. Sofia promised she'd talk to him first, then Esme and Michael could make arrangements.

So, she did what Sofia told her.

Before she left school, she put her phone and backpack in her locker. After the last bell, she went outside and stood at the curb, waiting.

Chapter Three

Monday, March 5, Noon

THE AIRPORT PA SYSTEM BLARED PASSENGERS' NAMES WITH A warning their plane was about to depart. The tall, slump-shouldered man with kinky curly blond hair pushed his way through the slow crowd with the disdain of a city slicker walking through a cow pasture.

Mikhail, or Michael, as he was called in the states, hated touching strangers. He knew how unsanitary Americans were. When he got back to Rohnert Park, he'd have to shower, not only to rid himself of American germs, but to wash away the shame and disgust he felt after his meeting in LA. He'd show them. His brothers had it all wrong. He would make his branch of the family enterprise profitable. They'd see. He would succeed, and then, he'd be in charge of all the brothers.

There were four of them. He was the last to leave home. He remembered his father standing with an arrogant attitude at the airport curb as Michael unloaded his suitcase from the Aurus. Michael eyed his father's car with the intention of returning to Moscow and buying one of these luxury SUVs for himself. Not feeling any particular affection for the old man, he still remembered his last words. "Make us proud and profitable, Mikhail. We're counting on you." There had been no tender embrace at his departure.

That was two years ago. In California, he met up with his brothers in Los Angeles. Michael had created a small cluster of domestic helpers, culled mostly from the streets of San Ysidro. Mexican women seeking a better life flocked to his promises of work and pay. Through his brothers' connections, he placed the women in homes where no one would ask questions. This trip yielded two more homes available for housing women workers. A woman acted as overseer, while a trusted man ferried them to their work assignments. That was the blueprint for his further houses in the northern part of California.

This had been a working trip, meeting with his brothers and discussing expansion plans or making excuses, while adding women to the new houses for his enterprise. Still, he fell last in the family business profits column. Something needed to change.

He texted Yevgeny, his driver, where to meet him at the front door curb. While he waited, he went over some of his better expansion ideas. He would branch out into the sex trades to bolster his profit margin. Keeping the domestics was essential. Even though they didn't generate the revenue he hoped for, they were dependable income.

He hoped to find a half-dozen girls to start up an escort business. Santa Rosa wasn't a high-powered corporate area, but now the pandemic was waning, and there were social activities, especially around the wine industry. Escorts would grow in demand. Sonoma County's other cash crop was marijuana cultivation, but those creeps didn't go for women like other businesses. The deal with the Sonoma crowd was to have class products to offer. These professionals wouldn't go for a meth-using bleach blond with no teeth. They'd want something special.

He considered some of the two dozen girls he had in his three Sonoma County houses. There were two girls who might work well into this plan. He'd have Sofia train them on how to improve their appearances and behave in public—and private. He'd tell Sofia to be on the lookout for more girls to add to his stable.

The germ of an idea took root in his brain. Maybe he could even find a naive leading citizen who he could film in the act—then black-mail. Now that would make some serious cash.

Chapter Four

Monday, March 5, Early Afternoon

IN THE CAR, ON THE WAY BACK TO ROHNERT PARK FROM SAN Francisco Airport, Michael called Sofia. He told her that he was coming back.

But she had even better news. "Remember Esme? That sweet Mexican confection from Yulupa? She called for you. She wants to take you up on your promise of a job."

"A job?" Yes, he remembered her. Tall for a young girl. She'd been twelve or thirteen then. Long, dark hair, and deep brown eyes set in a lovely oval face. Full lips, too. Some of those Hollywood bitches would give anything for lips like hers.

He'd made the offer to the neighbor kid months ago, but never thought she'd take him up on it. "I'll find her a job." He smiled to himself. If he sealed the deal with Esme, she'd be the newest star in his stable.

Then he remembered what had made him hesitate over the offer all those months ago. "What about the girl's mother? I remember she was a druggie, but she watched out for the girl."

"Yeah, a righteous pain in the ass." She laughed. "Well, it seems that momma has been court-ordered to rehab. When she gets out, she and the girl want to find an apartment. It's a cinch that momma can't —or won't—work to support them. Even the kid knows that. It's why she quit school and wants to earn cash to put a roof over their heads."

He thought for a moment. "Too bad Esme has her mother for baggage. I'll put the girl to work, but the mom, no way. She's too burnt out."

"I have no clue where the mom is, but Esme will be waiting for you at Aston Avenue."

"Aston?"

"Yeah, I was going to pick her up at school, but I ran out of gas. But she figured out where the house was and knocked on the front door. Can you believe it? Sharp little cookie, huh?"

"Why the fuck don't you keep an eye on the gas gauge? You should've been there to pick her up. What if something happened to her?"

"No worries. Bernardo just called. She wasn't very cooperative with him, but when I described her over the phone, we figured out it was her."

"You could've called Bernardo to pick her up at school."

"She wouldn't have gone with him. Besides, it's irrelevant now. He's watching her. He'll bring her over when you give the word."

Michael sighed while he played a chess game in his head with lives. "Hold her there until I say. Bernardo can bring her over to the Burton House then."

"Okay." Sofia sounded expectant. "By the way, Esme told me she'd never had sex before."

A world of possibilities burst open in his imagination. This could be monumental for the beginning of his empire. "Okay," he said. He didn't want to sound too excited about this prospect. He knew how jealous Sofia could get. "I'll stay at the Burton house for a day or two. And tell Bernardo not to touch her."

At her squeal of delight that he'd be staying with her, he disconnected. Michael didn't have a home. He kept most of his few clothes at Aston Avenue, but he chose not to set up a "home" anywhere except Russia. All three of his brothers had settled in Southern California and were doing well. They had roots in the community, including women. One was even married.

That wasn't for him. His plan was to make a bundle of money here, then go back to his private sector hometown outside of Moscow. Hopefully, his father would be in the dirt by then, and then he could take over the old family businesses. Or maybe he'd retire. He shrugged mentally as he considered his future. There were many possibilities, beginning with a thirteen-year-old Mexican girl.

Michael's phone rang. The caller ID said it was Teo, his oldest brother. Wishing Teo would drop dead, he debated whether to pick up or not. He answered it as they drove over the Golden Gate Bridge. The afternoon was cool and blustery, puffy clouds scudding across the crystalline sky.

"I've been thinking about our last conversation, little brother." Teo never bothered with banalities. He had a purpose for his call, and he jumped right into it. "I'm not sure your idea of diversification will work, given the logistics. Your houses are too spread out…"

"No, Teo. They're in just the right locations. Far enough…"

"I'm coming up there to take a look. In fact, I'm getting on a plane in twenty minutes. Pick me up at the airport in San Francisco. I should land around three PM."

"There's no need for you to come up here." Michael's heart pounded. He hated his brothers' interference. They didn't trust him to do this. "I've told you how it all works. What are you going to look at here?"

"Everything. Just get me a hotel room and a car. I'm not staying in any of your brothels."

"Hotel room? How long do you plan to stay?"

"A few days. When I'm satisfied, I'll leave. Get me a *nice* hotel. A *nice* hotel, you hear me?"

Teo disconnected before Michael had a chance to protest again.

This would mess everything up. He'd have to hold off with the Mexican girl until Teo left. It would be just like him to take her for himself. No, he'd keep her under wraps.

On his phone, he tapped the icon for Bernardo. "Listen. Keep the girl there until I tell you. It may be as long as three or four more days."

Bernardo whined, but Michael had heard it all before. He spoke over the complaints. "Do what I say. I'll send someone over with cash for the week. Just keep her there and alive. And don't touch her."

And now, to call Sofia and fill her in. He'd be spending time with Teo instead of her.

Chapter Five

Monday, March 5, Afternoon

"RAUL'S GOT BALLS; I'LL SAY THAT FOR HIM." A LATE WINTER GUST blew in petals from the plum tree in their backyard. Nick nudged the door shut after Meredith entered the kitchen.

True. "He loves his niece. It speaks well for him that he cares enough to want her safe."

Nick's face twisted in a sardonic smile. He thumped a pair of grocery bags on the kitchen counter. "Like he's reformed or something?" It didn't matter if Raul Esparza reformed, got religion, or repented his ways. He was never getting out of prison. Sentenced to sixty-five years to life for the hired murders of Stephen Giroud's ex-wife and Richard Taylor, Meredith's husband, Esparza would never draw a free breath. That didn't count the murders that prosecutors couldn't find enough evidence for charges against him, like Meredith's brother, David.

Meredith shrugged.

Nick stopped pulling groceries out of the bag and stared at his wife. "What are you thinking, Meredith?"

She pursed her lips and leaned against the counter.

"You can't be serious. What if he has another motive?" Nick's stomach muscles clenched. He dreaded what she wasn't saying. He knew what was coming. This woman he knew so well and loved so much, in spite of her hardheaded determination when she made up her mind. And she had. "Damn. You're going to help him."

Her eyes widened, the picture of innocence, but he could tell she was already embarking on a plan. "It won't hurt to ask a few questions."

Meredith never asked just a few questions. She was either all in or not. "This is a bucket of shit, Meredith. Don't go there." Once he told her what he thought, she'd do what she wanted anyway. He should've been smarter about this. The beginnings of heartburn roiled in his gut.

"Okay, wait." He raised his hand like he could stop what was happening. "Wait just a minute. Think about this."

"I thought about it all the way back from San Quentin."

"Meredith, you don't have time to go on some fishing expedition for Charles Manson. You've got the sergeant's exam next month, and Davy is starting preschool. The bedroom flooring goes in next week. That's in addition to your regular hours in VCI." VCI stood for Violent Crimes Investigations in the Sonoma County Sheriff's Office, where Meredith worked as a detective.

Meredith sighed and finally met his gaze. "I know. But I can ask around. Not make a big deal about it. Just get a bit of info to pass on to Esparza."

"He guilted you out, didn't he?" Damn that man. It pissed Nick off that Esparza would play on a scrap of Meredith's gratitude for the two seconds of his life that the criminal ever showed a conscience. The detectives' testimony about his action during his trial had repaid that debt.

She waved the notion aside. "Don't get your panties in a bunch. It's not a big deal."

Nick stopped at this stupid white man's phrase. Then he pushed onward. He had to. Esparza took advantage of her good nature or played on her guilt. Whatever the manipulation, it worked. "This has the potential to be a cluster fuck, Meredith. You have jurisdictional issues, logistics, and staffing problems. Who are you going to go to when you have an actionable piece of info?"

"I'll go through Rohnert Park Department of Public Safety. They took the initial report. If I get any intel, I pass it on to DPS. I'll call Deb, fill her in, and offer to help. She's still in detectives." Meredith shrugged. "They find her, the agency looks good. If I don't turn anything, no one's the wiser."

There was a point with his wife where you stood on the edge of a cliff, leaning. Mere had already jumped. She was going to do it. "I can't help you. I don't have the time," he said quietly.

"I didn't ask for your help." She looked shocked at his refusal. He couldn't remember the last time he'd said no to her. But she shouldn't have been surprised. He'd made it clear how he felt about Raul Esparza. Her involvement in this runaway kid would lead to nothing but trouble.

"Good." Nick bent to shove a carton of milk into the fridge. He pushed it a little too hard and caught it before it fell over. What happened to the discussion? They usually weighed the pros and cons of any endeavor together. Had she just decided on her own? His heartburn churned. What was this about? He decided on another tack. He'd be reasonable. "Meredith, what happened to talking things over?"

"I told you what I wanted to do when I got home." She crossed her arms over her chest. "You said you weren't going to help. I didn't feel like there was room for discussion." She turned to leave, then stopped and faced him. "Besides, I don't see this as a favor to Esparza. It's about a missing thirteen-year-old girl."

Crap. When she put it that way, it made him feel like a jerk.

Chapter Six

Monday, March 5, Noon

ESME'S LIFE WAS DIFFERENT NOW. SHE'D MADE A CHOICE THAT HAD altered her future. She looked back at it and tried to figure out when it had all gone wrong. It began after she'd decided to quit school and go to work. Her friend Sofia was going to pick her up, and the adventure would begin. Three days ago. She lay on the filthy carpet and re-traced her mistakes.

Esme had waited on Snyder Lane sidewalk for Sofia. Disappointment growing, she walked up and down the street, eyes straining in the sunshine for her friend's blue Corolla. After an hour, Esme decided something must have come up. She counted out her change and had just enough cash to catch the northbound Santa Rosa bus in thirty minutes. She'd see if anyone at the Yulupa apartments knew where Michael and Sofia had gone.

Sofia hadn't said they'd moved from Yulupa, but she assumed they must have. No one answered the door at number 15.

It had taken Esme all afternoon at the Yulupa apartment complex, hanging around the parking lot and laundry room. She finally found someone who knew—and was willing to tell her—where on Aston

Avenue the pair had moved. A single-story yellow house down a long gravel driveway behind a brown one in the middle of the block.

She'd hoped to find them nearby. She had no idea where Aston Avenue was. And she'd run out of money. Against her instincts, she had no other recourse—she hitchhiked to Aston Avenue in the hopes she could spot the house by the description. Her ride dropped her off at the intersection of Santa Rosa Avenue and Aston Avenue near the Sonoma Fairgrounds in Santa Rosa. The two blocks to Aston were a short walk. Once on Aston, she searched for Michael's new place. She was told it could be seen from the driveway off Aston.

The neighborhood was past decline, with a pair of newer apartment houses interspersed with cheaply built one-story homes decades old. Weeds grew between the cracks in the asphalt sidewalks, and bright blue tarps flapped in the breeze on several roofs in anticipation of a coming rainstorm.

There it was, in the middle of the block. The houses looked abandoned except for a weathered trampoline between them. Not able to put words to the dread she felt, Esme thought about her purpose. Why was she here? She had to make some money to get a place for her mother and her. Finally sucking up her nerve, she knocked on the door.

It took three tries to get someone to answer. A Mexican guy with reddened eyes and a wife-beater T-shirt, holding a half-empty bottle of Modelo, squinted against the late afternoon sunlight.

In Spanish, she asked for Michael.

"He's not here."

"What about Sofia? Is she here?"

The man glared. "No one here by that name." He turned, shoving the door to close it behind him.

"Wait." Esme stuck her forearm against the door's peeling paint. "She's his daughter."

He turned back to glare at her, his eyes revealing the delight he'd take in messing with her. "He doesn't have a daughter."

"But…" The malice shocked her. It occurred to her how much she didn't know about life. Sure, her mother had done things that Esme didn't understand, like selling furniture, and disappearing for days at a time without a word. But surely, there were people out there who did the right thing for the right reasons. She had to find a way to be with her mother. Teresa needed her protection, and no one else would do it. Her father, Arturo, was dead and buried three years ago. He'd been in prison and hadn't lived with Esme and her mother for two years before he went to prison. She hadn't any real memories of him. Her uncle, Raul, was also in prison, and according to her mother, was not ever going to get out. Arturo's sister, Almita, threw Teresa out of her apartment. Her mother, Teresa, was in rehab currently, but Teresa had told her those places were the worst. She had to try to find something lasting—for her mother. "Can I wait for him?"

The man looked at her like she'd said she was from another planet. Then, with a curious smile that looked a lot like a shark, he stepped back. The hand with the beer swept a welcome gesture. "Sure. Come on in."

She looked past him into a dark room with windows and curtains shut. It was impossible to see inside. Maybe this wasn't such a good idea. "No, I'll wait out here."

"Oh no. If the cops drive by here and see you sitting on the porch, I'll get in trouble." He swallowed the last of his beer and tossed the empty over Esme's shoulder. A drop landed on her shoulder. She smelled the sour odor and decided she couldn't wait for Michael. She turned to leave.

He grabbed her by the arm and pulled her into the darkness.

Chapter Seven

Friday, March 2, Night

ESME'S FIRST NIGHT AT THE ASTON HOUSE WAS LIKE A BAD DREAM. The Mexican guy threw her on a broken-down sofa that reeked of unwashed body odor. She couldn't miss his leer as he duct-taped her wrists.

She had messed up. She shouldn't be here. This was a mistake.

Then after the man had tossed her aside, he was on his cell phone. He spoke in muffled tones but in English and mentioned Michael's name. He said something about Sofia, too, but when he walked into another room for privacy, she couldn't hear anymore.

While he was in the next room, she saw an opportunity. She stood, planning her path to the front door. She stumbled over a partially full beer carton. A strong hand shot out, grasping her arm to keep her from falling. "No, you don't, sweetheart."

There was another man inside.

He pulled her to his chest, inhaling her scent like a starving man smelling food. His hands moved over her shoulders and downward. She felt his excitement rising against her. Filled with revulsion, she pulled away with all her strength. This time she paid attention to the alarm bells going off inside her brain. She didn't know why, but this felt horribly dangerous.

"Bernardo. Forget about that. You got work to do." Bernardo released Esme, and she collapsed to the floor with relief. The other man stood next to Bernardo, and they both watched her crumple to the filthy carpet.

The other man was clearly in charge because Bernardo did as he was told. He continued, "We keep her here for the weekend. Tie up her ankles and put her in the back room. The boss has plans at the other house. They won't be ready for this one until early next week."

"I don't like it," Bernardo snapped. "It's dangerous. Maybe somebody saw her coming into the house."

"So what?"

"So what? Calling in the fucking cops?" Bernardo's body shook as he faced the other man. "I can't go back, Isaac. I can't go inside again."

Isaac put his palms on Bernardo's chest to calm him. "Nobody's going to call the cops." He glanced around. "Have you seen this neighborhood? That's not going to happen."

Bernardo took a deep breath, and his shoulders slumped with the effort. "You're right, Isaac."

Isaac turned to walk away but stopped to pat Bernardo's shoulder. "Just follow the boss' orders. Do what you're told. That's all you have to do."

Chapter Eight

Tuesday, March 6, 9:00 AM

DEB LANG PUSHED A CHAIR INTO HER CUBICLE AND WAVED A HAND for Meredith to take a seat. The two women had caught up with each other on the way up to Deb's second-floor office. Conversation was easy for these two detectives who'd shared academy time and parallel career paths at different law enforcement agencies. Deb was on track to be the department's first female Hispanic sergeant, and Meredith worked detectives for the sheriff's VCI. Meredith had supported Deb the year before, during, and after the break-up of Deb's first marriage. Deb had organized Meredith's baby shower for Davy's arrival.

Deb brought them to business. "What brings you to the Friendly City?" Rohnert Park's tagline was "The Friendly City." There had been times in recent history when contentious politics and minor crime waves had turned Rohnert Park into the butt of jokes because of its nickname.

"I'm interested in a runaway juvenile report your agency took in the past week. The girl's name is Esme or Esmeralda Vela Alfaro.

She's thirteen. I don't have her date of birth." Meredith pulled out a notebook.

"Okay, let's see what we can find." Deb was a tall, lean young woman who favored weight rooms and ironman competitions. Deb had beaten all but two of the men in the academy academics and came in first in Physical Training. Meredith was always just a little intimidated by her athletic prowess. While a runner and a gym rat, Meredith couldn't compare to her friend. Her long legs gave her height over five foot ten, but she lacked Deb's stamina. With shoulder-length brown hair, blue eyes, and a sprinkle of freckles over her nose, Meredith looked every bit of her Irish heritage.

Deb swung her chair to face her computer monitor. Seconds later, she read from the screen. "Esmerelda Vela Alfaro, known as 'Esme', DOB 02-27-2008. Address on Adrian Drive, this city. Hmm, three reports this year. Most recent runaway case taken 03-03-2021."

Meredith jotted it down. "Anything interesting in the narrative?"

Deb scanned the report, then read it out loud. "Vela Alfaro was last seen at Lawrence Jones Middle School on Friday, March third, at the end of school. Says here her aunt told the officer that she hadn't been upset or angry when she left for school. My officer spoke to the girl's counselor. She's considered a good student. No behavior problems."

"Hmm. What made the officer consider her a runaway instead of missing?"

"He says, 'Based on the interview with the aunt and school counselor, there was no specific reason for her to leave. The aunt said she'd been emotional over the situation with her mother but hadn't made any explicit threats to run away.'" Deb turned to Meredith. "Kids do this all the time. Sounds pretty cut and dried to me." A sliver of defensiveness crept into her tone.

Meredith realized Deb would need convincing. A tacit law enforcement loyalty to their agency permeated the profession. Meredith considered her approach. "It bothers me that a kid who decides she can't face her troubles takes off without her phone."

Meredith felt Deb's probing gaze. Her friend was thawing.

Deb asked, "How did this come to your attention?"

Meredith laid it all out. Deb, of course, knew of Meredith's horrible encounter seven years ago with an obsessed judge—the one that led to his death at the hand of his own hired thug, Raul Esparza.

Deb blew out her doubt. "He's preying on your sympathy as a mother, Mere. There is no debt to pay. You did what you could at his sentencing." She eyed her friend. "He got a better deal because of your testimony. I'd say you're even."

"It's not about keeping score." Meredith put a hand on Deb's arm. "It's about a thirteen-year-old girl who is missing under unexplained circumstances."

"Unexplained?"

"What teenager goes anywhere without her phone?"

Deb's daughter was eleven. She'd relate. Shrugging, she said, "Okay, that's weird, I'll grant you."

"The phone and her backpack were left in her locker at school."

Deb scanned a page of the report and summarized it off the computer. "Right. The principal opened the locker and turned the contents over to the aunt."

"Might be something on the phone that'll help find her." Meredith shook her head. "Dunno. Maybe I should go ask the auntie."

Deb's lips pursed with concentration. "We could."

Meredith straightened as she realized Deb had included herself.

"You *espeak espanish?*" Deb asked, with an exaggerated Mexican accent. She'd spoken Spanish at home growing up.

"Some." Living with Nick, she'd learned to speak the basics, but could understand much more.

"I'm betting auntie doesn't speak English so good." Deb opened a drawer and reached for her holstered handgun. "And there might be more to this story."

"Like, what if she's not a runaway?"

Chapter Nine

Tuesday, March 6, 11:00 AM

ESME'S AUNT, ALMITA ESPARZA PACHECO, OPENED THE DOOR OF THE third-story apartment. The building had been built in the fifties and probably hadn't been painted since. The short, homely woman in a rumpled house dress and apron showed no surprise at the two cops and showed them in. A cumin-infused pot of something simmered on the stove, filling the room with its spicy aroma. The living room and kitchen were immaculate and orderly. Religious pictures hung from the walls alongside cheaply framed family photos. The older woman motioned for them to sit on a worn, shapeless sofa. Deb was adept at establishing the reason for their presence. The older woman's rigid posture softened as the conversation progressed. Meredith marveled as her friend worked the older woman.

Deb only translated when something directly pertained to Esme came up. Meredith understood enough of the language to know her friend was determining the groundwork of an investigation. All information formed a foundation for a case.

What a lovely clean home you keep.

Thank you. I was a housekeeper for many years.

In the US?

Yes. Before that, in Michoacan.

And you're living here with how many family members?

Nine. My husband, his sister, her husband and their two daughters, and my two granddaughters. Esme makes nine." Almita glanced over Meredith's shoulder to a wall clock in the living room. *My granddaughter Isabella will be home from school soon.*

All of you in two bedrooms?

"*No, Esme and one of the girls, usually Isabella, sleep on the sofa.*" Almita's face crinkled with a sad smile. "*It's not as crowded as it sounds. During the day, all the adults are working, and the kids are in school. I stay home to cook and keep the house.*"

It was a story Meredith had heard and seen often. Many immigrant families shared homes to ease the financial burden. It was common for several generations to live together. Mexican families often relied on grandparents for help to raise young children. Auntie appeared to be the family matriarch.

Almita stood, excusing herself to stir the pot on the stove. Deb kept up the patter, asking about the food. *Tinga. It will be the evening meal.* Almita turned off the stove and returned to the living room. It was early in the afternoon, and she had already moved slowly, her shoulders slumped. Meredith wondered what her morning had been like.

The front door burst open, and a pudgy, dark-haired girl with braids burst into the room. She threw her bookbag on a chair and ran into the kitchen. Despite the dramatic brows, mascara, and lip gloss, Meredith put her age at twelve. A year younger than Esme. Very possibly a *confidante*.

Almita reprimanded her sharply. "Isabella. *Tenemos invitados.*" We have guests.

Despite their gender, Deb and Meredith were easily pegged as police officers. A quick look was all the police warranted. Pulling open the refrigerator, Isabella said in English, "Okay, *abuelita*. Let me get a glass of juice first. I'm thirsty."

Almita stood, her voice firm, still in Spanish. "*Son la policía,*

Isabella. Ven aquí de una vez." They are the police, Isabella. Come here at once.

In English, the girl said, "Police, huh?" Isabella straightened as the refrigerator door slammed shut. She played the game of innocence well and made an effort to sound relaxed. "Is this about Esme? Have you found her?"

Deb took the lead, staring hard at the girl. "Not yet. We're looking for her."

Isabella sniffed and walked over to her grandmother. The older woman looped an arm around the girl's waist. Isabella's bravado shrunk under Deb's scrutiny.

"Can you help us?" Meredith spoke up. "Maybe there was someone she was hanging out with or talking to online?"

The room was quiet.

Meredith broke the silence. "Please, Isabella. It's important we find her to be sure she is safe. Do you know where she is?"

The girl looked away. "No."

Meredith pressed her. "She could be in danger, Isabella."

Isabella's dark eyes clouded with doubt. Her swagger slipped away. "I can't say. I promised."

"Promises like that could get Esme in big trouble." Deb's voice held an authority that made the girl wince. "We need to know she is okay."

"She said she would be fine…"

"She may think she's all right now." Meredith tried a softer tone. "Sometimes trouble can sneak up on kids like Esme. Will you help us, please?"

Isabella looked at her feet for what seemed like minutes. Even at twelve years of age, she must have heard whispers about the dangers. Finally, she spoke. "Esme told me she was going to get a job. She wanted money to pay for her own apartment so her mother could come live with her again."

Deb's lips relaxed in an effort to set the right tone to elicit help from someone so young. This culture wasn't known for trusting the police. "She's only thirteen. She can't get a job legally."

Isabella exhaled the burden of her secret. "She said she knew a man who could fix it for her." Meredith's mind soured with the thought of a man finding a job for a thirteen-year-old girl.

"Did she tell you where she would meet this man?"

Isabella stared at Deb, her eyes reflecting her fear over a betrayed confidence. Almita understood enough that her embrace became the hold of a reprimand. "*Diles lo que sabes.*" Tell them what you know.

Red tinged Isabella's ample cheeks. "I don't know. She wouldn't say."

Almita gripped the girl's shoulder while hurling machine-gun-speed threats in Spanish.

Deb stood, calming Almita and extricating Isabella. "Thanks for your help, Isabella. One last question: Where is Esme's phone?"

Almita threw her hands up, the situation beyond her comprehension, her granddaughter a stranger. She shook her head, her eyes drilling Isabella, forcing the truth from her.

The girl's voice was barely audible. "Yes, she had a phone, but she left it in her locker."

Meredith looked at Deb. "Didn't the school give it to the aunt?"

"The report said the phone was left with her guardian, Almita." Deb spoke sharply to the older woman, who stood and hurried to an end table. She retrieved the cell phone and handed it to Deb. Deb dug around in a pocket and produced an evidence bag. She dropped the phone in it and wrote the case number and date on it.

Meredith tapped Isabella's phone number into her own contact list. She looked from the girl to Almita. "Thank you both for your help. We'll be in touch if we have any information for you." Meredith knew how hollow the words were to families in this situation, but she had to offer something.

In the car, Deb snapped. "We've lost two days. If that bumbling patrol officer had done his job, we could've had this girl back home safely."

Meredith sighed. "This could be anything. Human trafficking, porn, work slavery, prostitution." She looked at her friend behind the wheel. "We need to make this case a priority."

"We'll start with the phone, the call history."

"Can you get a subpoena for a GPS triangulation history?"

"I'll do what I can. I'm not sure I have enough probable cause for that." Deb's fingers tensed on the steering wheel, knuckles whitening.

Meredith had an idea. "Don't you have a guy from your agency on a task force through the DA's Office? Drugs? Human trafficking?"

"Oh yeah, Rogers. And it's drugs. I'll get in touch with him to see if he's got any local addresses on his radar. If he is, we can narrow it down with footwork. Then, we'll use his intel for the subpoena—if he's willing to share. But we need to go through her phone call history on the off chance that a call will tell us where she is. We can do it at the office."

Meredith clicked her seatbelt, noticing a new feeling of foreboding.

Chapter Ten

Tuesday, March 6, 12:30 PM

Rohnert Park Department of Public Safety, or DPS, was a square, four-story concrete building at the end of a cul-de-sac in the middle of town. Deb steered their unmarked Ford sedan through the security gate and parked among the other vehicles. The Investigations Bureau was on the second floor. They took the stairs, and Meredith was pleased that she could keep up with the Ironman veteran. Deb wasn't even breathing hard when they entered the Investigations Office. They were alone in the room.

"I'll open a supplemental report on this missing person and log the phone into evidence. That will make this an official case. The sergeant is a real stickler for following the rules." Deb crossed her eyes in a comical commentary about the brass, but Meredith knew the benefit of coloring inside the lines—especially these days—in this profession. Doing the job the right way was good insurance to keep a cop from ruining a career.

Meredith had a few calls to make too. She rummaged around in her jacket pocket for the right phone. Many cops carried two phones, one department-issued, and their own personal cell. Using the work phone for case-related business made pictures or videos, recordings, or phone calls easier to find. These were also considered official records and potential evidence, thereby making them able to be subpoenaed by the court. Meredith still shivered at the thought of defense attorneys listening to her conversation with her three-year-old on the phone. That was more of a deterrent than department procedure.

Using her work phone, she first contacted her sergeant, Craig Bennett, and filled him in on the missing person. She added that the lead detective had asked for her assistance. She provided the RPDPS case number and told him she'd be in the office the next morning. Bennett was an agreeable boss but no pushover when it came to bending the rules. By the nature of the job, deputies had to be able to run solo, make the right decision in a hot second, and not rely solely on backup. In some remote areas of the county, backup could be an hour away. A certain amount of independence was expected, but clear standards and expectations were in place. The sheriff's office had tightened up policy and procedure by necessity in recent months. Civilian oversight and media coverage had scrutinized all law enforcement. Meredith didn't mind the rules and had played it straight with Bennett since his arrival six months ago. He'd returned the respect.

Deb typed a paragraph, tapped a button to save it, then closed out of the case. She punched four digits into the landline on her desk and spoke quickly. When Meredith got off the phone, Deb said, "I'm going to track down Rogers. He's in the office somewhere. You want to come?"

"No thanks. I've got a phone call to make."

Meredith liked working with Deb. It had been almost eight years since their academy time together, and she'd forgotten how attuned Deb was to her. It was almost like working with Nick again, with a few obvious differences. Meredith had worked well with the other detectives until her current partner. Meredith's previous sergeant had permanently paired her with Jerry Peters. Peters was a decent enough guy and a good albeit plodding detective, but his negativity made him difficult to be around. In any space he occupied, he sucked the energy dry. Deb was a breath of fresh air.

Meredith waited until she heard the elevator doors close to open her personal phone and press the icon for Nick's number.

"Hey."

"Hey, yourself." Meredith heard her son Davy chattering in the background. She checked the digital clock. It was just after one PM. "You've got Davy already?"

"Tina broke a tooth," Nick sighed. Their neighbor Tina handled daycare. "She had an emergency dentist appointment, so I picked him up. I'll catch a few more hours of sleep when you get home."

She weighed how long it would take to go through the call logs on Esme's phone versus how much sleep Nick would get before he had to get to work at nine PM.

Damn. He needed sleep. A patrol sergeant had to be rested to perform his job. There was no choice. Deb would have to go through the phone log by herself. "I'll be home soon. I'm in Rohnert Park now."

"With Deb?" Nick's voice deepened. "You're working Esparza's missing kid?"

"I'll fill you in when I get home." She said a hurried goodbye and disconnected before he could protest.

Meredith waited for Deb to return to tell her she couldn't stay. Her friend was disappointed but understood Meredith's priorities. "I'll let you know if I find anything useful." Deb leaned a hip against her desk. "I'd like to find a number for the mother. I'll bet the girl's headed wherever mom is."

"We can only hope so."

Deb frowned. "Unless mommy's pimping her out."

The sad thought had rolled around in Meredith's head, but hearing it said made it more of a possibility. What detour had Teresa Alfaro taken that ruined so many lives? Meredith got the addiction part. It was the reason for the need to escape that she considered. What grief could be so painful for which a mother would sacrifice being with her child?

She would do anything for her son. Anything. Then, Meredith

thought about her own mother. Her husband abandoned her and left her with two children to raise on her own. Even while wrestling with debilitating bouts of depression, her mother still went to work to put food on the table. She had put her children first. Teresa hadn't.

Dang. She wished she could stay and help find Esme.

Chapter Eleven

Tuesday, March 6, 2:00 PM

NICK'S DISPOSITION SUFFERED FROM A LACK OF SLEEP. BEFORE THE call from Tina, he'd only been in bed for three hours. He checked the kitchen clock with resignation. He wouldn't get any more sleep before he had to go in to work. He knew his wife. Meredith was like a terrier with a bone when she got a case. Even though this case wasn't hers, she'd do whatever she could to help find Esparza's niece.

And why? Nick searched his soul for a feeling of obligation to the imprisoned ex-cop, Raul Esparza. On orders from an obsessed judge, Esparza had killed Meredith's first husband in a calculated hit-and-run collision. Then they discovered something even more alarming. They discovered a similar killing of the judge's ex-wife one year earlier in the central coast area of California. The original agency, Paso Robles PD, couldn't find enough evidence to charge him until almost a year after the incident. Early in the investigation, Esparza was a person of interest even though he was employed as a patrol officer by Paso Robles PD. The lieutenant Nick and Meredith had interviewed over the case emphasized how dangerous he was. The

Paso Robles Police Department was in the process of firing him for brutalizing an arrestee.

Nick had to admit Meredith would be dead if Esparza hadn't shot the judge while he tried to push her off a balcony to certain death below. The man had an attributable body count on his back, probably more than they knew.

Irked that Esparza would use such a feeble manipulation, Nick wondered why she couldn't see through this. Granted, a thirteen-year-old on the streets could certainly be in danger, but it shouldn't have been Meredith's concern. Someday, Meredith might learn she couldn't save the world. But not today.

Davy's squeal shattered his irritable ruminations. "Mama, Mama, Mama." The three-year-old trotted to the back door and threw himself at his mother as she opened the door. Their garage was on the ground level below. Meredith routinely parked her dear decrepit Subaru in the garage and walked up the outside back stairs.

"How's my little man?" Meredith dropped her briefcase on the counter and swept him into her arms. She wrinkled her nose. "Oh, Buddy. You need a bath."

"He's been playing with the new puppy at Tina's." Nick tried to keep the annoyance out of his voice. "It's bath night anyway." He sounded defensive, even to his own ears.

"You look tired." She put her son down, and he ran out of the room, making barking noises. Her husband was tall at six-foot-three. His dark wavy hair and smoky brown eyes attracted her, along with his broad chest and muscular shoulders.

"I am." He dialed down the terseness. "I was counting on you to take him so I could get some more sleep."

Meredith squinted at him like he'd spat serpents from his mouth. "Tina's issue was unplanned. I'm sure she would've postponed breaking her tooth to fit your schedule if she could've."

Nick held his breath. This wasn't going well. "Look, I didn't mean to snap at you. I'm just tired." He rubbed his face with both hands like that might make him more alert.

"Well, I'm here. You can go to bed now." Turning, she picked up her briefcase and started to follow their son as he ran down the hall. "I'll read to him, then make him dinner."

"Wait." He put a hand on her arm to hold her back. "Did you find the girl?"

Her deep brown eyes widened. "No. Actually, she may be in more danger than I thought."

Damn. Nick looked away, feeling the heat in his cheeks. But he had to ask. "Is Deb working on it?"

"Yeah. I was helping when I called you." Davy charged back into the room, and Meredith sat at the kitchen table. He dove into her lap, still making puppy noises. "The girl left her backpack and cell phone in her locker at school. When Deb and I interviewed the aunt, a cousin told us Esme was going to meet a man to help her get work. She wants to get a place to live with her mother."

"Not good. Especially without her cell. You have no simple way of tracking her down."

Meredith's shoulders loosened, her tension evaporating as it usually did when the two discussed a case. They were good together as cops and honest with each other as a couple. Sometimes she thought being people should be easier than being cops, although it often wasn't. "Deb's going through the girl's call log. She's hoping to get a line on the mother. She might know where her kid is."

"Maybe you can triangulate her movements from the cell." He shrugged. "I don't know if it will help if the girl hasn't met up with the guy who promised her work."

Meredith looked away. "It's in Deb's hands now. She's working on getting a subpoena for the GPS coordinates for the past week."

A glimmer of relief sparkled in his mind. "I'm glad to hear you say that."

"Why? Because she's Raul Esparza's niece?"

Nick ground his teeth to hold back his initial remark. "No, because it's not your case. It belongs with Deb in Rohnert Park. Besides, I worry about you getting in trouble for going off the reservation."

Again, the brown eyes settled on him. He felt two inches tall. "I told Bennett what I was doing. He cleared me for this afternoon to help Deb."

"You told Bennett everything?"

"Why do you care so much?" Meredith stood, a hand gripping her son's arm, ready to leave the room. "Are you jealous?"

Jeez, when did she get so snarky? "No, no." Nick grimaced. Jealous? "No, but Esparza's taking advantage of you. That pisses me off." He hated sounding like her boss. He didn't want to sound like—or be—Meredith's supervisor. Being cops together was hard enough, but the real work seemed to be allowing her to be free of his mentorship.

Meredith straightened, her spine rigid. "You're wrong, Mr. Overprotective. Even if he was, it's my choice. I'm a big girl."

Davy stood still as he looked from mother to father. He hadn't often heard his parents speak with such tension.

"Now, why don't you go back to bed?" She turned and left, dragging her confused son with her.

Crap. Me and my big mouth, Nick thought.

Chapter Twelve

Wednesday, March 7, 8:30 AM

"My sergeant made a phone call. Looks like you're officially helping out." Meredith heard the enthusiasm in Deb's voice over the phone the next morning. They'd helped each other in the academy but hadn't worked together since. Meredith was pleased. She'd not had a partner she'd enjoyed working with since Nick.

"No kidding?"

"Really." Deb laughed. "We're down three investigator bodies right now. The two other guys have big cases, so I'm it. I convinced him this girl could be in big trouble, and time is crucial."

"Right. You get through that call list on Esme's phone?"

"Not yet. I had to finish a report yesterday and ran out of time. This is where you can help."

"You want me to come to your office? I'm leaving my house in Petaluma now." This transfer of assignments wasn't unheard of in law enforcement. It just didn't happen very often. Usually, it involved arrangements for task forces or special incidents. For a single deputy to assist was unusual. Meredith felt a little special.

"Yeah, the sergeant wants you to work my hours."

Meredith's pulse quickened. A challenge that felt scary. The office hours were easy. The real challenge was finding the information that would lead to the girl and get her home safely. "I'll be at your office in fifteen minutes."

TRAFFIC MADE it closer to twenty minutes before Meredith walked in the front doors of DPS. The City of Rohnert Park was one of a few hybrid public safety models in the nation of law enforcement and fire services, wherein each sworn officer was trained in both fields. Meredith always felt a little off-kilter in their building, like they all knew something she didn't. They did, in fact, know how to fight fires, treat the sick and injured, and rescue kids who get their heads stuck in a railing. She didn't.

Deb met Meredith in the lobby and waved her into the elevator, not bothering with a greeting. The detective picked up right where she'd left off last night. "I got the subpoena for the phone company. It's at the courthouse, waiting for a judge to sign. When I get it back, I'll send it off to the phone provider."

Meredith nodded. "I've been thinking. Maybe we can get a jump on the phone numbers if we collect a few. For sure, I want to get the mother's number. Maybe the aunt has it. We already have the aunt's and cousin's. Maybe Isabella can help us with numbers of friends, so we don't waste time tracking them down."

"Oh, good idea." The doors opened to a hall that led to Deb's office, a large 30'-by-40' room divided by portable partitions into six desk spaces. One entire wall was simply windows overlooking the employee parking lot and the commuter train tracks that bordered the DPS property.

"Did you run the mom?"

"Yeah. No warrants. She's on probation out of this county."

"Good. I'd like to read the mother's pre-sentence probation report. We should be able to gain insight into her actions. It takes a serious addiction to choose using over your own child."

Deb had cleared a space on the desk in the next cubicle. A

monitor and keyboard, tablet, and pen lay ready. So was Meredith. "I'll call Probation. What's the case number?" All reports had case numbers assigned. With privacy concerns so prominent these days, case numbers offered a link in the progressive chain of an investigation. Should the state audit the Sonoma County Probation Department, the release of information to Rohnert Park's missing juvenile case could be tracked. Meredith sat and punched in the phone number.

After her introductions, Meredith said, "I'd like to talk to the probation agent for Teresa Alfaro."

Meredith heard muffled tapping on a keyboard. "The agent is Shane Eberling. He's in the field now. Do you want to leave a message on voicemail?"

"I'd rather leave it with you. Will you take the information?" Meredith appreciated technology but knew that sometimes calls with a human element were answered quicker.

The expected response was less than enthusiastic. "Um, okay."

"Teresa Alfaro. Do you need her date of birth?"

"No, I'm sure there aren't two Teresa Alfaros. What number can he reach you at?"

Meredith provided the DPS investigations phone number and her department cell.

"Okay, I'll give him the message…oh." The woman didn't try to hide her surprise.

"What?"

"I pulled up Alfaro while we were talking, and it just so happens that Shane is at the halfway house where Alfaro lives now. He's there for someone else, but—"

"Can you get hold of him?" Meredith stood and swung an arm over the office partition to get Deb's attention. "Can you tell Shane to wait there? We can be there in fifteen minutes."

Deb's eyes widened, but she gathered her phone and slipped her holster onto her belt.

As she disconnected, Meredith heard the woman say, "I'll try."

Deb was already in the hall when she shouted over her shoulder. "We'll take my car."

Chapter Thirteen

Wednesday, March 7, 8:30 AM

IT WAS THE SIXTH DAY, NEAR AS SHE COULD TELL, THAT ESME HAD been tied up and held in this stinking rat hole. She'd been in the dark literally and figuratively and had difficulty telling when it was nighttime. But she knew one thing: She needed to get out of there. She had been left alone for long periods of time. Bernardo fed her a Carl's Junior hamburger and water once or twice a day and let her go to the bathroom afterward, but other than that, she'd been ignored. Tied up and tossed in a corner like so much trash, they left her alone.

Once on the first night, when she thought no one was around, she'd tried yelling. Bernardo hustled into the room and kicked her in the ribs until she stopped. They hadn't gagged her, but the ropes were tied tightly around her wrists and ankles so she couldn't walk. She'd have burns from struggling against them. Even though she knew it was futile, she had to work at them. She had to try to get free.

She didn't dare think about what could be in store for her. But she knew it wouldn't be good.

Then at what looked like late afternoon of the sixth day, the two men came into her room. Bernardo squatted to her feet. In the shadows of the darkened room, she made out his glare. He pulled something out of his pocket. She heard a snick. From the depths of her memories, she searched and finally identified the sound. It was the sound her father's pocketknife made when he opened it.

She kicked out, her feet smashing into Bernardo's knees. The knife fell to the floor. He shouted at her in Spanish as he fell over. Isaac laughed and gave him a hand up.

"You think it's so funny, then you do it." Bernardo spat out the words as he straightened.

"Sure, buddy." Then to Esme, he said, "I'm going to cut the rope off your feet. No need to kick. All right, girlie?"

Esme didn't feel the need to say anything to these two thugs.

Isaac knelt, felt around, and came up with the pocketknife. A swift sawing motion and her ankles lurched free. She sighed, relieved that she was at least partially released.

"Stand her up."

Bernardo shifted gingerly, poised to dodge any resistance she might offer. He leaned over, grabbed her upper arm, and yanked her to her feet. Three or four days of being tied up, and allowed to walk only to the bathroom and back, took its toll. Her legs buckled beneath her.

"Get her. Hold onto her." Isaac shouted at Bernardo.

Bernardo whined his excuse and stepped behind her. He slipped his arms under hers and half carried her to the living room.

Isaac said, "Take this piece over to the Friendly City. The boss is there waiting for her." Isaac slapped Bernardo's shoulder. "And no touching."

"Three fucking days I babysat this bitch. Now you're saying I can't even—"

"That's exactly what the boss said. No touching." Isaac shook his head. "If you don't like it, you take it up with him."

A torrent of expletives in English and Spanish followed, but Isaac ignored Bernardo's temper. Isaac disappeared into the next room and materialized seconds later with car keys in his hand. "Here. Take the truck."

Bernardo snatched the keys from Isaac's fingers.

"You'll need to tie this one up again," Isaac said to Bernardo. He gave Esme an appraising glance, as if he approved of her resistance. "You're going to get your wish. You'll be with your friend Sofia in a little while."

Mystified at his comment, Esme wondered if Sofia had befallen the same fate as she. Melancholy enveloped her as she guessed that Sofia wouldn't be able to save her.

What had she done?

Chapter Fourteen

Wednesday, March 7, 9:00 AM

BERNARDO DRAGGED ESME OUT OF THE OLD PICKUP TRUCK KEEPING a one-handed grip on her arm. He stood her on the driveway and pulled a gym bag out from the jump seat. He pushed her up the slight rise of the driveway to the front door. He pushed the doorbell several times, grumbling with impatience.

Esme didn't care what he said or how irritable he was. She just wanted to see her friend.

The door swung open with Sofia standing on the threshold. She glanced out at the neighborhood and pushed Bernardo's hand away from Esme. Sofia grabbed her friend's reddened arm and pulled her into the house. She shut the door on Bernardo.

In the living room together, Sofia said, "Esme, my sweet girl. What have they done to you?" Sofia embraced Esme in a fierce hug.

Delighted with the warm welcome, Esme melted in Sofia's arms. "I'm okay. They didn't do anything really bad."

Sofia held her friend away to inspect her. "Look at that." She inspected the rope burns. "They're not too bad. We'll clean them up and put medicine on them."

Esme nodded.

"But right now, you need a shower and a change of clothes." Sofia didn't ask. She told. Given her seniority in years, she never had any trouble giving Esme orders. Secretly, Esme was grateful for this guidance. She felt loved when Sofia told her to do something that would benefit her. She couldn't have picked a better sister. She'd often wanted her mother to offer her this kind of help.

Sofia walked down the hallway and opened a closet door. After pulling out a towel and washcloth, she called out to Esme. The carpeted hallway offered four doors. At the end, Sofia opened a door to a bathroom. Hair dryers, flat irons, lotions, and cosmetics lay across the counter. Pushing the towel into Esme's chest, she said, "Take a shower and wash your hair. Shampoo is in there. You'll feel better. I'll find you some clothes, and then I'll make you something to eat."

Sofia was right. The shower felt magnificent. Afterward, she toweled herself dry, applied lotion on her arms, and looked at a pile of clean clothing waiting on a small table behind the door. Finding a pair of flip-flops, sweatpants, and a T-shirt that fit her, she combed out her long damp hair. She looked in the mirror. She felt better than she had in days, but the dark rings under her eyes gave away the fact that she hadn't slept well.

A rhythmic beat thrummed in the room. She opened the door to the frenetic beat of techno music vibrating the walls from an adjoining bedroom. She walked past it to the living room in search of Sofia. Two young women sat on a couch playing video games. One of them eyed her with suspicion while the other tapped on a console, staring glassy-eyed at the television. Another girl curled up in a chair, hunched over a phone.

Sofia stood at the stove in the kitchen. Esme hadn't remembered until now, but Sofia liked to cook. She was good at it, too. The heady aroma of frying bacon reached her. "Oh girl, that smells fabulous."

"Good. It's not much of a banquet, but I remember you like bacon. I'm making you some eggs, bacon, and a slice of toast."

Esme's stomach growled in testimony of her hunger. She sat at a table which had been set with a fork, a dinner knife, and a tumbler of orange juice.

After the meal, Esme sat back in the chair. Her stomach was full for the first time in six days. She drank the last of the orange juice, savoring the sweetness of the liquid. Sofia took the tumbler to the sink, rinsed it, and put it in the dishwasher. Then she sat down at the table and reached for Esme's abraded wrists. From a pocket, Sofia pulled out an ointment tube. "This will help heal these awful wounds. How..." She stopped like she knew the answer. "You must be tired."

Esme nodded. She finally felt she could sleep. She was safe with Sofia.

Yet something was a little off. This house didn't feel right. It was nothing she could put her finger on, but she couldn't resist asking. She didn't want to put Sofia on the spot, so she decided to be clever in her questioning. "I've never seen a closet with so many toiletries. There must be enough for the whole county."

Sofia smiled. "Not quite, but we don't skimp on personal hygiene products for our girls."

Esme didn't know what that meant. Was she now one of 'our girls'? There were more questions. "How many people are in this house? I don't see any men. Are there just females here?" It wasn't like a family.

"You are safe, Esme." Sofia patted Esme's hand. "It's just women here. Bernardo stays in the garage, so no men in the house until Michael comes. But neither of them stays here."

Esme nodded with relief.

"Look at you, sweetie. You're falling asleep sitting up. You need a nap. I had a mattress moved into my room until one of the other girls leave."

ESME ALLOWED Sofia to steer her to a bedroom. The girl was too tired to see anything but the twin mattress on the floor next to a queen-sized bed. Blankets had been piled in the middle with a pillow on top.

After she spread the blankets out and dropped the pillow at the top of the mattress, Sofia hugged her friend. "We'll talk more later this afternoon. Right now, you need sleep."

Esme dropped to the mattress and fell asleep before she could draw the blankets around her.

Chapter Fifteen

Wednesday, March 7, 9:30 AM

THE SOBER-LIVING FACILITY, AURORA HOUSE, MADE ITS HOME IN A historic two-story building in west Santa Rosa on Highway 12 near Brush Creek Road. The highway was a main artery from the Sonoma Valley to the county seat of Santa Rosa. Bisecting Santa Rosa, east to west, Highway 12 traversed some of the high-dollar real estate in the area. To the south, Montgomery Village featured small, post-World War II bungalows. North were the bucolic hillside neighborhoods of Montecito and scenic Brush Creek. Less than four miles to the west was downtown Santa Rosa; to the east was the exclusive retirement community of Oakmont.

Routinely congested traffic passed by this century-old stone structure on a four-lane highway without any regard for the anguish that the walls contained. Originally built in 1909 as a boarding house for immigrant laborers, it had passed through the years as a hotel, speakeasy, tuberculosis sanitarium, bordello, and topless dance club. Finally, in 2010, the California Human Development Corporation bought and converted the structure into a residential treatment center for women.

Teresa Alfaro had been court-ordered to six months of rehabilitation at Aurora House. The judge cut her a break when he took the probation officer's recommendation in consideration of the sad fact that Alfaro had lost custody of her daughter. Rehab instead of jail was a meager consequence compared to losing your child. With Teresa nearing the end of her term, Deb and Meredith hoped she might help them find Esme.

During the ride to Santa Rosa, Meredith texted Isabella asking for the contact information of Esme's friends. Then, on the unit mobile data terminal, Meredith found a booking photo of Teresa Alfaro. She sent it to her own phone and then studied it. Esme had her mother's dark eyes and high cheekbones. Meredith scrolled through jail photos noting the progression from early arrests when she was an embarrassed but pretty young woman to later, a tired, worn-out junkie. If Esme took after her mom's early years, she'd grow into a beautiful woman. Meredith hoped she'd get to Esme in time to save her from her mother's fate.

The winter afternoon had warmed, as it often did in Sonoma County. At Aurora House, rose bushes budded out, and bright orange geraniums bloomed in the front yard of the striking quarried stone edifice. The setting was inviting. Meredith wondered if the management made the effort to keep up the grounds to appease the neighbors. So many of these establishments faced residents who didn't welcome them. It was as if Aurora House was a woeful reminder of the bad hand that life could deal anyone.

As they drove into the parking lot at the rear of the building, Meredith reflected on the reality of the residents' suffering. No matter what the success statistics said, this place was a miasma of torment, misery, and occasionally, hope.

Even as the detectives got out of the car, the traffic noise couldn't compete with a woman's screeching coming from Aurora House. Inside the back door, a pudgy, middle-aged white man in a blue dress shirt and khaki pants stood, trying to calm a hysterical black female. "Shantelle, you knew one more dirty pee test would send you back," Shane Eberling said, in a shame-on-you tone. He was a parental figure castigating a child for a violation she knew was wrong.

Meredith had dealings with Eberling before. He was the kind of guy she'd walk around the block to avoid. He was an old-school P.O. who offered no mercy to violators. He wasn't so much by-the-book as he was the guy who used the book to flex his power.

"It ain't mine." The woman's volume lowered, her lip quivering. "You bulls do this shit all the time. You just wanna roll me up."

Eberling glanced over at the detectives on the porch and grimaced. "You made good time. I thought I had a few more minutes to manage this one." His head cocked toward the Black woman.

Deb put her hands on her hips. "We'll wait."

Eberling reached into his back pocket for a pair of handcuffs. "Shantelle, you are under arrest for violation of your probation terms."

"Ah, man," the woman wailed. She eyed the two detectives and recognized a lost battle. She put her hands behind her and hung her head.

"Would one of you gals mind searching her? I always like to use you if I can."

Meredith stepped to Shantelle and began a pat search. With few places to hide contraband or weapons, Shantelle's T-shirt and sweatpants made the search easy. Meredith was glad Eberling chattered with Deb. She wouldn't need to make small talk with this small mind.

Eberling took Shantelle outside and placed her in the backseat of a county pool car. He closed the door to lean against it. "Thanks for showing up, ladies." He nodded toward his unwilling passenger. "I'm sure you two are the reason she didn't go sideways. Now, what can I do for you?"

Deb looked to Meredith. "Meredith, you want to fill in Mr. Eberling?"

Meredith told a concise story of their case. She ended with, "Teresa Alfaro, Esme's mother, is here. Her sentence will be up in a week." Meredith took a second to pause and give the moment the gravity it deserved. "We want leverage. Any background info you can give us to get Alfaro's cooperation in finding her girl."

Eberling sighed, his fleshy lips pressed together in a particularly unattractive manner. "I don't recall anything off hand that would help. I'll look her up." He retrieved a tablet from the trunk, and spent a moment logging on, searching, and scrolling. "Hm." He eyed the report. "It looks like she was selling herself for drugs." He looked up with the sadness of the real world in his eyes. "If she'd sell herself, she'd sell her kid too." He closed the tablet with a huff. "Admin just assigned her to me. Her P.O. went out on family leave recently. I haven't gone over her file yet." Meredith suspected he'd seen her probation termination date and decided to let it expire without any interference from him. "I've seen her around in the past few months, but I didn't get a read on her. I figured on meeting her today, but Shantelle's pee test came back dirty. That's the priority at the moment."

"Okay with you if we shake the tree and see what falls out?" Meredith liked to maintain cooperation between agencies. The terms of Alfaro's probation made his permission unnecessary—she was subject to search by any law enforcement officer. But Eberling was here, and it didn't hurt to be courteous.

"Sure." He slid behind the wheel. "You turn anything interesting, drop a dime, will ya?"

Chapter Sixteen

Wednesday, March 7, 9:45 AM

DIANA VERGARA, THE ON-DUTY COUNSELOR, LED THE DETECTIVES TO a day room on the first floor. Two women outfitted in colored T-shirts and gray sweatpants, exactly like Shantelle, lounged on a sofa watching a raucous game show on a flat-screen TV. A third woman, a skinny, dark-haired Hispanic, sat at a table playing solitaire with a deck of cards. As if in a uniform, this woman dressed the same as the others. Meredith saw the resemblance from Esme's school photo. The cheekbones, the jawline. Yes, this was Esme's mother.

"Teresa," Vergara's voice rose over the television. "Police here to see you."

Teresa Alfaro's attention swiveled from her card game to Deb and Meredith, then back, her face blank. Meredith figured she'd ID'ed them as cops as soon as they entered the room. She wasn't going to make this easy.

Deb took the lead. "Teresa Alfaro?"

Again, Alfaro's flat brown eyes took in the detectives, then looked back to her cards.

Meredith felt Deb's tension. Deb carried a cultural defensiveness about the criminal Hispanics she dealt with on the job. She resented the low-lifes who betrayed their race through addictions and crime. Meredith thought she was harder on them than on whites. It occurred to her that Deb's defensiveness could hinder rather than help the investigation. Meredith geared up to take the lead in the interview. Then, in a soft voice that surprised Meredith, Deb introduced themselves.

Still nothing from Alfaro.

"Teresa, we're here because of your daughter…"

Suddenly Alfaro straightened and eyed Deb. "Is Esme okay?"

"That's why we're here." Deb pulled out a chair and sat. "We don't know where she is."

Eyes that had been dull only seconds ago sparked with anxiety. "Whaddya mean? She's with her auntie in Rohnert Park."

Meredith sat opposite Deb. "She left school on Friday without her phone or backpack. She hasn't been home."

"Home." Alfaro stared at the cards, then swept them off the table with a vicious swipe. "She doesn't have a home. She's sleeping on a fuckin' couch."

Deb nodded, her eyes soft with sympathy. "It's not the best circumstances, for sure. But being with family is better than being on the streets."

Alfaro glared at Deb. "You think I don't know that?"

"We're looking for her," Meredith put in. Maybe she could thaw Alfaro's anger. "Her cousin said Esme was going to meet a man who would find her work. She wants to save enough money to get an apartment so you can be together."

With a sigh, Alfaro dropped her head into her hands. "Jesus Christ, what has she done."

"Do you know who she planned to meet?" Deb's voice softened even more. The television volume had lowered. The two women on the sofa strained to listen without being too obvious.

"No clue." Alfaro shook her head. "She hasn't been in touch for a couple of days. I thought she was busy with a boy or something." Meredith cringed at the implications.

Deb's eyes narrowed. "She's only thirteen."

"She's very mature for her age...tall and well...developed." Alfaro shrugged. "She's already got guys sniffing around her. Even the old guys like her."

Jesus, Meredith thought. Meredith noticed a tic above Deb's eyebrow. What's Alfaro got her own kid into? She's not protecting her child at all. Child Protective Services did the right thing by removing Esme from her care.

"Does she have any other relatives around here," Meredith asked. "We know about Raul. He's a non-starter."

Alfaro's eyes widened as she looked at Meredith. "Shit, you're the cop he saved from that maniac judge." Her upper lip curled. "I always thought you were sleeping with the guy."

How could she recognize me? It had been years since the pictures from the news were out. She'd have interest in the matter since her brother-in-law saved her from being murdered. Meredith chose to ignore her comment. "We know about the aunt and her family. Anyone else?"

Alfaro shook her head slowly. Meredith got the feeling she was thinking but had no intention of sharing information. "Who were her friends at school?"

"How the fuck am I supposed to know?" She shook her head in disbelief that she was expected to know these things about her daughter.

"Who did she spend time with?" Meredith pushed Alfaro, wondering why Deb wasn't more assertive with her questioning.

Alfaro squinted at Meredith, finally seeming to get the idea that the detective wasn't going to go away with nothing. "She had a buddy, an older girl who lived next door to us in the apartments on Yulupa."

"What's the address on Yulupa?"

"1310. We were in apartment fourteen. They were in fifteen."

"Their names?"

Alfaro flung her arms out like a petulant teenager. Meredith thought the emotional intelligence of this woman was about the same. "I don't remember."

"C'mon, Teresa." Meredith reached across the table to the

woman's hand. A gentle appeal to the shred of maternal instinct was in order. "We need your help to find your daughter."

Alfaro held Meredith's gaze for a second, then pulled her hand away. "The kid was Sofia, and the dad's name was Michael. That's all I remember."

"Does Esme have access to cash?" Deb asked.

Alfaro pursed her lips with a sarcastic smile and left that as her answer.

"Call us if you hear from her, no matter what time." Meredith laid her business card on the table. Deb did the same.

The detectives stood. As they left, Meredith took a last glance at Alfaro. The woman kicked over the chair Deb had sat in.

IN THE CAR behind the wheel, Deb sat for a minute. "What do you think?"

Meredith was silent for a moment, pondering over the weighty probabilities. "My mother was a mess, but this one's a real piece of work."

"Do you believe her?"

"Not a syllable."

"Do you think Esme's been in touch?"

"I don't know how she would. Burner phone maybe." Meredith thought a moment and added, "I get the feeling the mom's pissed because Esme's out on her own, or with someone other than her."

"I got the same vibe."

"What next?" Meredith had an idea, but this was Deb's investigation.

"I'm thinking." Deb rubbed her temples.

"Do you think Alfaro's going to blow this sober-living BS and try to find her kid?"

"With a week left on probation? She'd screw up her whole sentence and get slapped back into jail. You saw how forgiving Eberling is. She's not that stupid." Deb sighed and looked out the window. "Is she?"

"That's the problem. Regardless of how smart she is, she's a drug addict, therefore sneaky and manipulating for their own gain." Meredith thought. "Does she have a car?"

Deb pulled the mobile data computer up, tapped the keyboard, and waited. "Nothing registered to her."

Meredith pointed across the street from the Aurora House. "There's a bus stop right there."

"We don't have the staff to watch this place and trail her." Deb frowned.

People wanted crimes against them solved but didn't want to pay for it, nor did they want to see the cops doing the dirty parts of the job. The department had suffered an unusual exodus of experienced officers moving to larger agencies or out of law enforcement altogether. It was a tough time to be in law enforcement. Being short-handed meant fewer open cases were solved.

Meredith offered an idea. "You want me to call Santa Rosa PD and see if they can put an extra patrol on this place? Maybe we'll get lucky, and one of the patrol guys will see her leave."

"Yeah. Do that, will ya?" Deb rubbed the bridge of her nose.

Meredith made the call. When she disconnected from Santa Rosa PD, she waited a beat. The next step was basic police work. Why didn't Deb think of it? "How about we go over to Yulupa and see if Sofia or her dad know anything about Esme's whereabouts?"

Deb looked away and twisted the key in the ignition. Meredith thought she might be embarrassed to not have figured they'd need to follow that lead.

Chapter Seventeen

Wednesday, March 7, 10:30 AM

1310 YULUPA AVENUE WAS A TIRED TWO-STORY MULTI-UNIT apartment complex of 1960 vintage situated off a main thoroughfare. Across the street was a busy strip mall surrounded by homes built in the same era.

Apartment 15 was upstairs. There was no answer to Deb's knock. Meredith looked through the window but couldn't see past the dirty vertical shades. The detectives walked the complex until they found the manager's office.

A lanky, 60-ish man with a long mane of poorly dyed brown hair answered Meredith's knock. Wearing jeans and a faded blue Grateful Dead sweatshirt, Meredith noted the piercings in his ears, nose, and forehead. Tattoos decorated the backs of his hands, and an ink vine crawled up the side of his neck. He wasn't going to be helpful to the police.

"Are you the manager?" Deb pulled out her ID at the same time as Meredith.

"Yeah." He glanced at the ID, then focused on something over Deb's shoulder.

"Your name, sir? I like to know who I'm talking to."

Through a smirk, he looked at her. "Dennis Crane." He leaned against the door jamb. He wasn't going to invite the detectives in for tea.

"I'm Deb Lang from Rohnert Park Police. This is Meredith Ryan from Sonoma County Sheriff. We're trying to contact the resident of apartment fifteen, Michael. Does he still live here?"

"Michael? Naw, he bailed last month. Left without paying the last two months' rent." Crane straightened, ready to turn back into his apartment. "You find him, let me know. I'll take the back rent out of his slimy hide."

"What is his last name?"

"Fedorov." Crane shrugged. "Yeah, something like that."

There was an edge to Deb's tone. "Is it Fedorov or something else?"

"Fedorov." He thought for a moment, then met her gaze. "Russian, I think. He spoke like an American, mostly, until he got hot. Then his accent came out. Fedorov."

"Can we see the application he filled out for the apartment?"

He paused. "Uh, no. It's gone. I sent it off to corporate when he split. They oversee all the civil stuff."

Meredith tried a question, raising her phone to show him Esme's school photo. "Can you tell me if you've seen this girl recently? Until six months ago, she was a resident in apartment 14. We want to know if she's come back to visit her friend, Michael's daughter, Sofia."

"I remember her. A real cutie. The cops carted off her mother for drugs. Didn't get rent from her, either."

"Have you seen the girl recently, especially in the past few days?"

He shook his head. "Nope."

"We've been told she was friends with Michael's daughter, Sofia. We thought she might show up here to visit."

"Nope." He shook his head, with his long hair falling over his eyes. He brushed them away and eyed Meredith. "Haven't seen her.

But I'll tell you one thing. Sofia ain't Michael's daughter." He squinted as if to see if Meredith understood what he'd said.

She had. "Thanks for the information."

Chapter Eighteen

TERESA ALFARO BLEW OUT OF AURORA HOUSE WITH LITTLE EFFORT. She'd planned it in advance, knowing there would come a time she had to get out. The little-used basement afforded just the avenue for her escape. In the early days of its existence, the building used a coal-generated furnace for heat. It was delivered by a truck whose driver dumped their appropriate load down a coal chute in the rear of the building. A door from the basement to the parking lot sat three feet away. Both the coal chute and the door were locked. After the county bought the building and updated the heating system, the chute door was welded shut.

Teresa didn't care when the updating was done. She only needed to be able to get out of the building through the door.

The county used the basement for storage of extra office and facility furniture. It was unusual for a resident to go downstairs, but it happened every now and then. Everyone knew where the key to the basement door hung.

She'd crept through the discarded desks, lamps, and sofas to the exterior door. It was locked, but she was prepared for that. A sharpened dinner knife did the trick.

Outside, she breathed her first free air in almost six months. The exhilaration that overcame her suddenly dropped like a trapdoor under a dancer on stage. Where would she go? And how would she get there? She had to find Esme. Michael had shown interest in her daughter when they'd been neighbors before she went to jail. He'd even approached her once. But she'd refused, unwilling to compromise her daughter in that way. Things would have to get really bad for her to sell Esme.

Teresa had put together what the two cops said about Esme missing. She suspected Michael or Sofia had reached out to Esme, promising her work and a regular salary. With Esme missing, Teresa supposed her daughter would take them up on their offer. She knew there was more to them than it appeared. She didn't like what she saw.

She remembered hearing rumors that Michael had a house in Rohnert Park. Somewhere in B section. Mimi might know where.

Locked up in the Aurora House vault, Teresa wouldn't see her phone until her release. That counted on the successful completion of her probation. Without it, she would have to reach out to someone for a ride. She'd thought this out weeks ago when she figured she might have to bail. Her friend Mimi lived with her brother four blocks away. She couldn't remember the house number but recalled it was on Sonoma Avenue, a major thoroughfare. Also, it was three blocks from the Santa Rosa Police Station. She'd have to be smart about getting there.

Chapter Nineteen

Wednesday, March 7, 11:30 AM

"Mimi!"

"Teetee!" Standing at the front door of her brother's house, Mimi's chubby midriff vibrated as she howled at the inside joke over the silliness of their names. Teetee for Teresa. "Come in, come in." She squinted over her shoulder and said, "My brother's not here, but he's due any minute from work. His bitch wife is in the kitchen. Let's go in my room."

The sound of pots clanging came from the kitchen. Mimi shouted as they walked down the hall, "I'll be in my room."

Sitting on her twin bed, Mimi caught Teresa up on the travails of living in another woman's house. "My brother's okay, but the witch he married is something else. I'd give anything to get out and have my own place."

Teresa couldn't believe her ears. This could play right into her hands. "I have an idea that might put you and me together again as roommates."

Mimi's eyes closed with a look of supreme satisfaction. Her

sparse brunette hair didn't move when she swiveled her head with delight. When she opened her eyes, it was with a laser focus. "I knew something would come along. I just had to wait."

Teresa grabbed her friend's hand. Her voice lowered to show how serious she was. "Here's the deal. My little girl, Esme...you remember Esme, right?" At Mimi's nod, Teresa continued, "She's out looking for work to earn enough money to get an apartment for us. She's at a house with Michael in Rohnert Park. You remember where that house is?"

Mimi squeezed her eyes closed, thinking. "Burton Avenue just down from Bonnie. It's a gray house with white trim. I can't remember the number. 734, maybe? I'm not sure." She opened her eyes, looking surprised at what she'd recalled.

That was closer than she'd been before. Teresa hugged her friend. "When Esme gets the money, you can move in with us."

Mimi flashed a forlorn smile. "I don't have a job. I got no way to make rent." She rubbed her temples; the pressure getting to her.

Teresa saw her hopes fading. "No way, Mimi. We won't abandon you. All you have to do is get a job flipping burgers or stocking shelves."

Mimi shook her head slowly. "I don't know."

Her friend's whine was threatening Teresa's plan. "You can do it, Mimi. I've worked with you at the jail. You were really good in the kitchen."

"You think?"

She looked so hopeful, and Teresa didn't dare dash her hope. "Yeah, you were." Teresa remembered why Mimi was such a challenge for her. Her neediness was overwhelming. She couldn't do anything without a rooting section.

She glanced around the room. "My brother will be glad to get rid of me. So will his bitch wife." The pots banging in the kitchen testified to her statement.

Teresa had a thought that might serve more than one purpose. "You said he'll be home soon?" Maybe she could get a ride from her brother to the Burton Avenue house in Rohnert Park. On the way, she'd sell him on the idea of Mimi moving in with her. The woman would be a trial, but it would be easier to share the rent than relying only on Esme's wages.

Mimi pulled out her phone from a pocket. "Yeah, any time now."

"Well, listen, I've got an idea."

Chapter Twenty

Wednesday, March 7, 12:30 AM

THE CALL CAME SOONER THAN EITHER DETECTIVE EXPECTED, BARELY an hour after calling SRPD. Deb and Meredith were heading south on Highway 101 and had just taken the off-ramp north of the DPS station when Deb answered. Her face lit up as the Santa Rosa police officer introduced himself, Officer Roger Goudy. "Are you Detective Lang?"

"Yep, is this about the extra patrol I requested?"

"Yes, ma'am." Deb winced at the *ma'am.* "I had just gotten into position to watch for the subject you're interested in, Teresa Alfaro."

"Go on."

"I hadn't even turned off the ignition when she ran out of the Aurora House. At least, a woman fitting her description."

Deb rotated her hand to encourage the officer to speed up the information. "I'll have my partner send you a mug shot if you have any doubt."

Meredith tapped her phone, glancing at Deb's phone to get Goudy's number. The mugshot was on its way.

"Okay, that would be good." Santa Rosa Police were known for their adherence to rules. Goudy would want to be sure about the identity of the person he was following if he had the means. Meredith heard the tone indicating Goudy's phone had just received a text.

"Describe her."

"Hispanic female in her late thirties, skinny, long dark hair in a ponytail, medium height, wearing a blue sweatshirt and jeans."

"That's her." Deb pulled over to the shoulder, waiting for Goudy's report. She positioned the sedan to get back on the highway northbound. "I just saw her less than two hours ago. The clothing matches. Are you in a marked unit? Do you have a visual on her?" Deb pulled onto Highway 101, northbound.

"Yes, to both. She was on foot for a while. I followed her to a house on Sonoma Avenue. She was there for twenty minutes or so, and then she caught a ride. I'm following at a distance on Summerfield Road."

Meredith had a thought. "Coming back to Rohnert Park on the back roads?"

Deb identified Meredith for the officer. "That's Deputy Meredith Ryan of the Sheriff's Office. We're partnered up for this."

"Yes, ma'am."

"Teresa's in a vehicle, then?" Deb rolled her eyes at Meredith.

"Yep, a gold Saturn, older. Can't see much of the driver, but he appears to be a dark-complected male."

Deb repeated the description so Meredith could note it with the license plate. "Where is she now? Still moving or stationary?"

"On Summerfield Road, they're turning onto Yulupa. You may be right about their destination. Can you pick them up at the city limits on Bennett Valley Road?"

"Yeah, I'm less than ten minutes out. Let me know when you get to the city limits."

"Sure thing."

Off the phone, Deb stomped the accelerator. Pulling in front of a box van, she veered onto Golf Course Drive, under the overpass, then pushed the department sedan up the Highway 101 onramp. She stayed in the Santa Rosa Avenue exit lane.

"Do you want the lights," Meredith shouted to Deb. Adrenalin, coupled with the urgency to intercept the Saturn, made her want to be certain Deb heard her. This run didn't qualify as an emergency authorizing them to use lights and the siren. But Deb was driving fast, over the speed limit, although still cautious. Deb shook her head, then rolled up the car windows to minimize the noise.

Meredith would keep an eye out for the Saturn. "Do you have a plan for Teresa when we stop her?"

"Not at the moment."

Meredith considered her idea and then offered it up. "What if we don't stop her?"

Deb's foot hesitated on the accelerator. "And do what? Nothing?"

"We're really looking for Esme, not Teresa. Even though we could pop her for violation of probation for leaving Aurora House, the mother's a means to an end. What if we follow her? She might lead us to Esme."

Deb rolled through the offramp light, up Santa Rosa Avenue, a mile to Mountain View Avenue. The street was a rough, two-lane, country road that T-boned another rural artery, Snyder Lane. A jog to the left teed at Petaluma Hill Road. Then a right onto Petaluma Hill Road. Meredith knew Deb was headed for Crane Canyon Road. With luck, they'd pick up the Saturn somewhere on Crane Canyon or Grange Road. That is, if she was right about their destination being Rohnert Park.

They took a left at the signaled intersection of Crane Canyon at Petaluma Hill Road. This was county jurisdiction, an area Meredith hadn't spent a great deal of time in. But she'd always admired the green, gently rolling hills dotted with manicured horse farms. The much-improved roadway lay like an asphalt ribbon bordered with stone hedges and eucalyptus, pine, and cypress trees.

Traffic was sparse on this country road, so when the Saturn popped over a rise a half mile distant, it was easy to spot. Goudy's marked unit followed a half mile back. Meredith sent him a quick text saying they'd pick up the follow.

"Gotcha," Deb whispered, pulling into an almost unnoticeable driveway. Gravel crunched beneath the tires as Deb steered the Ford behind a mound of blackberry brambles. Meredith had a clear view of the roadway out her side window. Tense seconds passed as the Ford idled.

"There," Meredith barked. The gold Saturn whizzed by.

Deb eased the Ford toward the asphalt and then stopped.

Meredith jumped out and eyed the taillights. Then, back in the car, she snapped her seat belt on. "They picked up speed when the cop car broke off."

"Time to go." Deb pulled out gingerly, scouting for anything irregular, like the Saturn pulling off the road.

Following at a distance of more than a half mile, Meredith felt sure they hadn't been made. She got a good read on the license plate and ran it for 'stolen, warrants, and registration.' It was clear all and registered to a couple who lived on Sonoma Avenue. There was no local history on either of the registered owners.

"You were right," Deb smiled, as she turned the Ford back onto Petaluma Hill Road. This time, they headed south toward Rohnert Park. The afternoon was advancing toward dusk. It would be dark in a half-hour. But coming into town, they'd have streetlights to help keep the Saturn in view.

Ten minutes later, the gold Saturn rolled onto East Cotati Avenue, headed to Rohnert Park. They drove past the modern Sonoma State Campus, and for a little over a mile, apartments lined the street. A right turn on Adrian Drive put them into a single-family neighborhood. Homes built in the mid-1960s, some enduring better than others, but all aging. They took a right turn into the 700 block of Burton. The Saturn slowed. At 734, it pulled in front of the driveway of a run-down gray home that had a neglected front yard. It wasn't the worst house on the block and wasn't the best.

Deb kept the Ford moving past the house as the male driver got out. In her passenger mirror, Meredith saw Teresa Alfaro charge out of the passenger seat and run up the sidewalk to the house, hunched over in a fury. Even half a block away, she heard the front door slam. The Saturn drove off.

Parking at the corner of Bonnie and Burton Avenue, Meredith had a visual on the house. Deb tapped on the keyboard, adding notes to her report. After a moment, she sat back.

"I messaged Eberling. He said he'd be down in an hour." Deb pulled her phone out, studying the screen. She spoke without meeting Meredith's gaze. "It's the best way to get into the house. We could arrest her ourselves, but it looks better in court if we get the probation department's cooperation." At the very least, they'd find nothing, and Alfaro would have to appear before a magistrate to answer for her violation. At the most, Meredith suspected the detectives would find a home for trafficked women, a porn studio, or something similar.

"You're sure you want to risk the delay?" Meredith held her breath. Why hold off? The property owner or resident would need to give permission for them to enter, but it was a fifty-fifty proposition. Either they could get in with resident consent, or they had to wait for the probation authorization. They had the power to arrest Teresa Alfaro, but being inside the house complicated things. Their luck seemed to be fading. They were hoping Teresa would lead them to Esme.

"There's something else." Deb finally met Meredith's gaze. "Your sergeant is pulling you back to VCI. Says he needs you to help out with an investigation."

Meredith sighed with frustration. "Now?"

Deb nodded with a rueful smile. "We didn't get too far with this, did we?"

Why did she accept this so easily? The Deb she knew would've fumed, and stormed to her sergeant to enlist his help to keep Meredith in Rohnert Park. "No, we didn't." Meredith had to untangle herself from this case. It wasn't hers, and she'd done her best to find Esme. She'd be pushing, if not crossing jurisdictional lines, to investigate any further. The case wasn't hers to work.

Deb had called for a beat unit to meet her at the intersection three doors down from 734 Burton. When he arrived, she got out of the car and briefed him. He would continue to watch the house while Deb took Meredith back to pick up her car parked at the DPS Station.

Meredith thought it odd that Deb didn't have the patrol unit take her back to her car while she kept the Burton house under surveillance.

Chapter Twenty-One

Wednesday, March 7, 3:30 PM

ESME WOKE UP SLOWLY THAT AFTERNOON. SHE'D SLEPT DEEPLY AND better than she had in a long time. It took a few moments to orient herself. The surroundings were foreign. Lifting herself on an elbow to look around, she found that she was on a mattress on the floor in a bedroom. Oh yes. Sofia's room.

A wave of comfort washed over Esme as she got her bearings. She basked in the glow of safety for the first time in days. Suddenly energized, she got up to go pee.

It was quiet on the way to the bathroom; none of the girls were around. Now she had a chance to glance around. The house had the bare minimum of furniture, no pictures, and nothing to suggest a home. A 55-inch TV, two couches in the living room, a dining table near the kitchen, and beds in the bedrooms was the entire furniture inventory. The interior had been painted recently. The walls breathed temporariness.

Esme heard muffled snoring through closed doors as she walked back to the bedroom. She pushed open the bedroom door. Sofia stood in front of a mirror folding the collar of a tailored shirt around her neck. She seemed lost in thought. Looking up, she smiled broadly at Esme. "Hey, girl. You ready to hear what's in store for you?"

Esme ran to her and looped her arms around her friend. "Yes, I am. And thank you for everything." She inhaled her fragrance, *Bombshell*, a popular Victoria's Secret scent that Esme found a bit overpowering. But this was her friend, and she loved her.

"We'll get some food and find you some clothes." Sofia held Esme away from her. "I'm sure one of the girls has something you can borrow until we get to a store."

Delighted with the prospect of new clothes but put off by the idea of borrowing someone else's, Esme followed Sofia to the kitchen and said, "Don't bother yourself with that."

"No way. You can't go around outside the house in sweats and a T-shirt." Sofia pulled open a cabinet and fished out a box of cereal and two bowls. Milk from the refrigerator and spoons made the meal almost ready.

"Go around?" Esme glanced toward the empty living room. "Where is everyone?"

"Some of the girls are out working, and some are sleeping."

Esme looked at the stove clock. Four-thirty PM. "They should be home soon, no?"

"Some of them." A sharp nod from Sofia. "There are a few girls that will be getting up soon for a job all night. My uncle's cleaning business employs them—and you. Mostly they work nights—off hours at office buildings—and sometimes daytime jobs, weekends, and holidays."

"It looked like more than a dozen girls here earlier."

"Some rooms can have more than four. But right now, all I have is twelve girls. They sleep at various times. Occasionally there are visitors who only stay one or two nights."

Something in Esme warned her not to ask, but she did anyway. "What about you? Why are you the only one in your bedroom?"

Sofia's delicate features sharpened, her mouth set in a thin line, and her eyes narrowed. "Me?" Then her face softened again to the Sofia that Esme knew and cared for. "I'm like a house mother. That's why I get my own space." She pushed a bowl of cereal across the counter to Esme. "These girls are young, not quite as young as you. Most of them are away from home for the first time. But they're here to work; to make money to send home to their families."

Esme's heart swelled with this information, despite Sofia's initial prickliness over her question. "Perfect. This is exactly what I want. I need to make money…" She was certain she'd said that she wanted to find a way to support her mother in their own apartment. Had Sofia forgotten?

"You will. But we'll get to that later. Right now, we eat, then, before the stores close, we go buy you some clothes."

Esme pushed her soggy Special K flakes around the bowl. "I don't have any money."

Sofia put her hand over Esme's. "Don't worry. We'll take it out of your salary."

Encouraged by this idea and not wanting to be a burden, Esme said, "I don't need much."

"Of course, you'll need a uniform." Sofia shrugged as she picked up the breakfast bowls and put them in the sink. "We'll get this all sorted out when Michael gets here."

"Michael?"

Sofia cocked her head, and her eyes seemed to twinkle. "Have you forgotten my daddy?"

Esme hesitated. She hadn't forgotten. She'd hoped he'd gone somewhere else. But there wasn't a choice. He and Sofia were her tickets to a new life with her mother. Besides, she knew how much Sofia loved her father. "No, I haven't forgotten."

"He'll be here by tomorrow."

"Do you have an extra toothbrush?"

"In the hall closet. There's toothpaste in the bathroom." Sofia busied herself with her phone.

Esme dreaded dealing with Michael, but that was hours away. She resolved to enjoy the afternoon with her friend, shopping for clothes. And tonight, she would go to work and start earning cash to pay for an apartment.

Chapter Twenty-Two

SOFIA'S IDEA OF A SHOPPING TRIP DISAPPOINTED ESME JUST A LITTLE. A quick trip to a Ross Dress For Less ten minutes away resulted in the purchase of two pairs of jeans, two sweater tops, and a sweatshirt jacket. She replaced the flip-flops with tennis shoes.

As Sofia pulled into the driveway at 734 Burton Avenue, Esme noticed a black Dodge parked in the open garage. It was shiny and slick looking, not the kind of car any of the girls from inside could afford. Michael. Sofia told her he'd be here to talk with her. But he was supposed to arrive tomorrow. She also noticed that nasty Bernardo's pickup parked down the street.

Esme's gut was clenched before they got inside. An eager Sofia swung the front door open and shouted for Michael.

"I'm here in the kitchen, honey."

"We'll be right there." Sofia nodded to Esme to drop their shopping bags in the bedroom. Esme noticed two bedroom doors open and all quiet from inside. The girls must be working. If they were sleeping, the doors would be closed. Esme thought it odd that Sofia followed her from the bedroom to where Michael waited for them.

When they entered the kitchen, Michael smiled like a proud father. He embraced Sofia tenderly and kissed her lips in a surprisingly unfatherly way. Esme had to look away as her stomach turned.

Sofia stepped back and put a hand on Esme's shoulder. She addressed Michael while looking at Esme. "Here she is. Our newest team-member."

Michael held his hand out for an embrace. "Esme. I'm so glad you've come to us."

Esme side-stepped Michael's arms and bent down to re-tie a loose shoelace. When she stood, her back was straight, and her face expressionless. "Sofia said you had work for me."

Michael smiled, but his dark eyes narrowed. He reminded Esme of a snake. "Yes, I may have something for you. Do you have a work permit? You're thirteen, right?"

Esme looked at her shoes. Her stomach fell with disappointment. "Yes. I'll be fourteen in eleven months. But no work permit yet."

Michael cocked his head like a teacher setting a student straight. "You know you can't get one in California until you're fourteen."

She knew that. "Yes, sir."

He huffed, dismissing the rules, and looked around the room. It was empty but for the three of them. "We can work around that." He refocused on Esme. "We just have to adjust some dates."

Esme didn't like fudging the truth. Both her mother and father had lived and died, showing her the reasons not to lie. But to get what she needed, she would do this. "Will I be cleaning like the other girls?"

He nodded, his golden curls unmoving. "Yes, for now. I may have something different for you in a week or so."

Esme acknowledged the news with a nod. Her gut tightened.

"You won't have time to go to school. I hope that won't be a problem for you."

Esme shrugged, trying to act nonchalant. She liked school. Especially the new school she attended in Rohnert Park. She liked the kids and the teachers. Her history teacher especially challenged her mind. She sighed inwardly. "No. And I left my backpack and phone there like you told me to."

"Good. I'm glad you can follow directions."

Sofia had left and returned with a gray cotton jumpsuit. She handed it to Esme. "This is your uniform. I'll have a spare for you tomorrow. You can wear this tonight."

"Tonight?" So soon?

Sofia glanced at her phone. "Yes. You'll be working all night. You'll leave at nine PM and get back when the job's done. You'll go with Yevgeny. He takes the others to this job, too."

"What kind of cleaning is it?" Esme wondered what she was in for.

"Industrial buildings for now," Sofia said. "The girls will tell you what to do and how to do it. Yevgeny will stay with you."

Michael picked at a fingernail. "Esme, you should get some sleep."

Sofia added, "Yes, and I'm going to my room. You nap on the couch out here. It will be quiet."

Esme walked past Sofia to the bedroom and gathered her blankets. The new clothes sat on the mattress in bags. She'd wear them some other day. She grabbed the folded uniform she'd been given earlier and walked out of the room.

Esme settled in on the living room couch. She couldn't help but notice that Michael followed Sofia into her bedroom. The door closed behind them. Esme thought she heard Sofia giggling. *Ewww.*

Chapter Twenty-Three

Wednesday, March 7, 5:00 PM

BANGING ON THE FRONT DOOR ROUSED ESME FROM HER BRIEF NAP ON the couch. An angry voice yelled for Michael. The tendrils of sleep fell away as she recognized the voice. A woman's voice. Her mother, Teresa.

Esme stood, shrugging off her blanket, and walked toward the front entry.

Michael flung the bedroom door open. Wearing only shorts, Esme halted with a glance at him. She looked away quickly.

"Get the fuck out of my way." Michael pushed her aside. "Sofia, get Esme into the bedroom now." He didn't wait for an answer as he walked down the hall to the front of the house. He flung open the door with a fury that Esme didn't understand. "What the hell do you want?"

Sofia tugged at Esme's elbow, pulling her into the bedroom. Michael wanted her out of the way. The room smelled musky and stuffy. Yuck.

"You asshole," her mother hissed.

Esme pulled away from Sofia and peeked around the door jamb. Sofia tugged at her, but Esme stood riveted.

Teresa's face was red. "You know who I want. Where is she?" Teresa lifted an arm to push Michael aside. He grabbed her wrist and twisted it.

He pushed her off the front step. "She's not your concern anymore. Get out of here."

Teresa's face twisted into a mask like a gargoyle Esme had seen in a book. "What're you going to do? Call the police?" Her laugh was a snarl. Esme had seen her like this before but not often. There was a familiarity in how they spoke to each other. This argument wasn't new. They knew each other.

Michael puffed up his chest and pointed outside. "Go."

"Not without my girl."

Michael re-grouped, seeming to realize this was getting him nowhere. "Teresa." His tone was cajoling. "She's my girl now. You know that's the way it works."

Her mother's face turned to granite, particularly her jawline. Her voice got really low. "You just want her because she's a virgin."

"Mom!" Oh, my Lord, Esme's inner voice yelled. How could she say that to Michael? Of all people? He'd always given her the creeps. Now that he knew something so personal, she could only wonder what it meant.

Michael's voice softened. "You don't say."

Sofia zipped up a sweatshirt over her sweatpants as she ran out of her room. Esme stood in the hallway. Sofia looked at Michael like he would tell her what to do. Then she trotted back to the hall, standing between Michael and Esme.

Teresa howled, "No way you're going to..." She burst past Michael, who stepped back, wide-eyed.

Esme croaked, "Mom..." as Teresa pushed Sofia back and out of the way.

Michael grabbed Teresa's hair, jerking her to a stop. He whirled her around and shoved her out the front door. Momentum pushed her forward but off balance. Then Michael kicked her on the butt, truly humiliating her. Then he picked her up by the nape of her shirt and pushed her to the sidewalk. Leaning over, he said something to her. They were far enough away that Esme couldn't hear. Whatever he said made Teresa turn and walk away.

At the front door, Esme was so surprised, her jaw dropped.

Chapter Twenty-Four

Wednesday, March 7, 5:00 PM

SETTLING IN BEHIND HER DESK, MEREDITH SCANNED THE COMPUTER monitor to check the status of her sergeant. He was listed as 'busy in Administration'. The rest of the VCI detectives were either in court, off duty, or at a detail on Llano Road in Santa Rosa. Sergeant Bennett had called her back to the office, after all. It grated on her nerves that she sat here with nothing to do until he contacted her. She could be searching for Esme.

With time on her hands, she pulled up the department call log and included Rohnert Park in the search parameters. Odd. No surveillance detail on the Burton house was listed. Deb had told her she would have a unit watch the house. But there wasn't one. Why Deb would cancel the stakeout mystified her.

A half-hour later, Sergeant Bennett strolled into the empty office. "I need you to help Terry over on Llano Road. He's got a ton of stolen property and a lot of guns he's seized, and it needs to be logged into evidence. You'll be doing that."

She memorized the house number on Llano Road and found a

cross street. She logged out of the records program and grabbed her backpack. "Okay. On my way."

In the hallway, she did some calculating. Nick would probably still be sleeping, so she texted Tina, asking her to keep Davy until she could get home. Tina would. Meredith didn't bother texting Nick as she didn't want to disturb him.

THE VCI UNIT worked through dinnertime into the evening. It was well past dark when the team rolled back into the office. The evidence sergeant had procured a van to haul the stolen items and guns back for booking into the property vault. But it had all been logged in while in the field so that the team wouldn't have to work too late tonight. Except Terry Dean, who was in the property room. He still had a report to write and needed Meredith's help. As she walked down the hall to her office, she thought about the words she would use to begin the account.

Meredith turned the corner and entered the VCI office.

Nick sat with one hip perched on Meredith's desk in the empty Violent Crimes Investigations office. As always, the first thing Meredith saw was his brilliant smile. Then, his wavy brown hair that she loved to run her fingers through, and his shoulders, broad from hours spent at the gym. She loved how he looked; imposing—tall at six-foot-three—yet approachable.

Surprise turned into delight. He was in uniform already, unusual for this time of day. He normally worked as the graveyard patrol sergeant. She glanced at the wall clock. Seven-thirty.

"Hey, you." His warm smile melted her heart. She loved him so completely that a difference of opinion over a case seemed trivial. She was happy to see him.

"Hey yourself." She dropped into her chair and smiled at an incredibly silly feeling of pride that she was married to this man. "You get called in early?"

Nick grimaced. "Joe's out for the week with gallstones ."

"You're acting lieutenant on patrol?" It was a real tribute to his leadership skills that Admin had assigned him the acting position.

Nick smirked, shaking his finger at her. "And don't you forget it."

Meredith chuckled. "Is Davy with Tina?"

"Yeah. He'll be busy as long as the puppy is awake."

"Does this mean we're going to get a dog?" Meredith smiled at the idea.

"We should talk about it." He nodded with approval. "I like the thought of having a pooch around."

Meredith's smile evaporated. "I got called off the missing juvenile in Rohnert Park. Craig wants me to help with another case."

"I know. I volunteered to bring you up to speed. He needs you to stay and help with the property report."

Meredith shrugged. "I planned on it."

"Of course, he could've done this himself." Nick smiled as if she were the only person in the world, and he'd been starved for her presence. "I just wanted to see you."

Meredith looked away, a little embarrassed at her ill temper last night. "I owe you an apology."

"None needed."

He reached for her hand. His touch still made her tingle inside. She covered his hand with hers. "There's something about that missing case that gives me the creeps. But..." She decided to forgo the explanation and why Deb's manner had her mystified. There was an open Sheriff's case here that needed her attention. "But it's Deb's problem now. I'd better get started."

After glancing around the room, Nick leaned over and kissed her deeply. "See you later."

Her heart thumped in her ears, recalling memories of their beginnings together. How she loved this man. How she longed to be alone with him with no interruptions.

But they had a job to do. Terry Dean needed her help, and Nick had a patrol unit to run. She stood, kissed him on the cheek, and turned to her monitor.

Chapter Twenty-Five

Wednesday, March 7, 7:30 PM

"ESME, YOU HAVE TO WAIT HERE. BERNARDO WILL BE HERE SOON." Sofia tugged on a camel hair coat and threw a woolen Burberry scarf around her neck. "Michael and I have to go run an errand. We'll be gone for a while. No work tonight. Yevgeny won't pick you up."

Esme was glad she didn't have to work but dreaded seeing Bernardo. He'd been so cruel when he transported her here. Esme said goodbye as the door shut behind the couple. She pulled off the uniform and dressed in a pair of her new jeans and shirt. She poured a tall glass of tea from the fridge, wrapped a blanket around her shoulders, and settled on the couch with the TV remote.

It had only been ten minutes since Michael and Sofia left when Bernardo flung open the front door. He pushed into the room, glaring at Esme. "You do what I tell you, and we'll get along. You don't, and I'll beat the shit out of you."

Esme shrunk into her blanket, wishing she had her phone or a tablet or something. She didn't reply to his orders. They were implicit, and she was clear enough on the picture to know he wasn't kidding. She worried about what he would tell her to do.

Bernardo went to the fridge and rummaged around for a beer. He twisted the cap off a dark lager and took a long pull. All the time, he eyed Esme.

Esme heard a noise from another room, either the dining or the family room. Odd, no one else should be here. She couldn't tell where it came from because both rooms were opposite where she sat. But it sounded like a slider. The family room then, someone coming inside from the back yard. It wouldn't be Michael or Sofia.

Bernardo hadn't heard the noise. Esme held her breath. Who would...

Teresa.

Her mother tiptoed around the corner, holding a large screwdriver in her hand. She held it high, like she was ready to strike.

Bernardo hadn't seen or heard her yet. He took another swig of his beer and slammed it on the tile counter as he stared at Esme. His attention was laser focused. "Now, let's get down to business." He reached down to unzip his jeans.

Esme noticed two men coming into the house. They stood at the open door, mouths agape. One of them was Isaac from Aston Avenue. She shivered and ducked behind a wall, barely able to see her mother fight for her.

Teresa was four feet away from Bernardo. She screeched his name, swinging the screwdriver wildly from side to side.

Bernardo turned. He batted her hand away, sending the screwdriver clattering to the floor. They wrestled a moment until Teresa kneed him in the groin.

Bernardo folded over, and Teresa kicked him in the jaw. He fell sideways, tripped over his foot, and fell backward. His head hit a corner of the hearth. As he slid down the edge of the brick, the side of his scalp split open. The room filled with a mushy sound like a smashed melon.

Esme had stood poised around the corner, ready to jump on Bernardo if he overpowered her mother. Though it didn't happen, the shock bolted her in place. She watched Bernardo slump to the linoleum. A sigh escaped his lips, and Esme wondered if he was dead.

"Momma."

The surprise on his face was unnerving. Teresa watched the man take his last breath. Then she turned to her daughter and said, "We gotta get out of here."

She barely recalled hearing the two men yelling at them as they ran out the slider.

Chapter Twenty-Six

Wednesday, March 7, 7:45 PM

TERESA GRABBED HER DAUGHTER'S WRIST AND TUGGED. "C'MON, let's go."

"But Mom. I got a job. I'm going to work so we can afford an apartment."

Teresa heard men's voices. Ignacio talking to another man. Not Michael, probably his pal, Gustavo. With alarm shooting through her body, she didn't hesitate. "You don't want to work for Michael." She shoved Esme out the door.

The two ran, but slowly. Esme had left her tennis shoes at the house and was in flip-flops. They ran five blocks, and Teresa was satisfied that no one was following them. Teresa stopped at Benicia Park to breathe. Esme sat on a metal bench, her feet freezing cold.

"Momma," Esme panted. "Where do we go now?" She began to shiver and hugged herself to stay warm in the late winter cold.

Teresa's body vibrated with the adrenaline rush. She paced in front of her daughter. Clad in the sweatshirt and jeans in which she left Aurora House, the dropping temperature seemed not to have an effect on her.

"Mom—"

"Wait a minute, Esme." Teresa ran her fingers through her tangled hair. "I have to think about this."

"But where—"

"Shut the fuck up for a minute." Teresa's voice carried. The pair of teens sitting and sharing a cigarette on a nearby bench stared at them. Esme felt like crawling into a hole.

Her mother was like that sometimes. Mostly she was fun and liked to laugh. She had her days when she was down and wouldn't get out of bed. And sometimes, when she felt pressure, she was short-tempered. That's when she snapped at Esme, sometimes even hitting her.

"We can't go to Mimi's." Teresa was talking to herself. "What about...no, he's in jail."

"Mom, why can't we go back to Tía Almita's?"

"No!"

The kids picked up their backpacks and left. Whether they were out past their curfew or just messing around, Teresa's outburst had put them off. Esme wanted to crawl into a hole.

"I'm cold." Esme rubbed her toes, trying to warm them. "My feet are freezing."

Teresa wiped her runny nose and sat down beside her daughter. "I don't want to go back to Tía Almita's. She'll turn me in again. This time, no rehab. They'll send me to jail, Esme." She searched her daughter's face. "Do you want that?"

"No." That was the quick answer. And the right one. She couldn't bear the thought of her mom in an institution of any kind. It would mean they would be apart. She hated the idea. Her mom had her problems, for sure, but she was all the family Esme had left. She didn't count Tía Almita because they hadn't been close while she was growing up. Esme and Teresa had lived in California's Central Valley town of Gonzalez, the nearest residential area to Soledad Prison. Even though Teresa had moved there to be close to Arturo while he was incarcerated, Esme never saw him.

During this time, her mother's health began to deteriorate. When Esme got a bit older, she was able to see that her mother's health problem was an addiction. When her dad died several years ago, his sister, Almita, offered her place for them to live while they found something more permanent. They didn't take her up on the offer until Gonzalez became a problem for her a year ago. Child Protective Services were threatening to take Esme away, and Teresa had been in and out of county jail. She never told Esme what for, just that the damn cops had it out for her.

"Mom. I'm freezing. Please, let's go to Tía Almita's."

Teresa's shoulders sagged. "Maybe just for the night."

Chapter Twenty-Seven

Wednesday, March 7, 8:00 PM

Esme wasn't surprised when she twisted the doorknob at Tía Almita's apartment and found the door unlocked. Her auntie rarely locked it, not out of any sense of security she had about living in Rohnert Park. It was more because she often forgot where she'd left her key. Esme had never even gotten a key when she and Teresa moved in.

The place smelled of spices simmering in tomato sauce, although the stove was empty. Tía Almita was a terrific cook. Esme's mouth began to water at the thought of a warm meal. It was warm inside, too. It surprised her how much she missed her auntie and her home. The home was warm and comfortable but crowded.

Teresa elbowed her. It was the pre-arranged signal for Esme to call to Almita. Teresa thought she'd be more open to Esme than to her.

"Tía Almita?"

A door closed in a back room, and she heard movement. Almita wasn't a big woman, and this noise was from someone who carried some weight. A dark-complected, barrel-chested man sauntered into the living room. "Tío Ulises, I'm glad to see you." Esme hoped being cordial would help welcome them back to this safe place.

He nodded, his face blank, his eyes sliding from Esme to her mother. "Teresa, Esme."

"Is Tía Almita here?"

"She's sleeping."

Esme cleared her throat, irritated that the questions should fall to her. Her mother wasn't acting like an adult. "We'd like to come back and stay here." Before he could react, Esme rushed across the room and grabbed his calloused hand. "Tío, I promise…we promise to follow the rules that you and Tía Almita set down. I promise." She glanced at her mother, standing in the open doorway, her face sagging. "We promise."

"I don't know…" he grunted.

"Please. We need this security. It's dangerous out there on the streets. We don't have any other place to go." This was true, although Esme had only the tiniest suspicion of the danger she'd been in.

"Please, Ulises." Teresa finally spoke up, the plea in her voice so stirring that Esme kicked herself for agreeing to ask. Her mother should have. Why couldn't she?

"Okay. I'll talk to Almita in the morning." He sauntered to the front door and closed it behind Teresa. "You can stay tonight. Anything more will be up to her. She's the one who has to cook and clean for everyone."

Chapter Twenty-Eight

Thursday, March 8, 7:30 AM

ALMITA STOOD, HER SPINE STRAIGHT. IN THE MORNING, SHE'D listened to Esme's and Teresa's pleas, but Esme was afraid her auntie would turn them out anyway. The lines and creases in her middle-aged face, usually so soft, looked sharp and hard. Esme's hands clenched into fists, ready to fall to her knees and beg her auntie for shelter.

Esme and Teresa needed a safe place to hide. Esme still wanted to find work with or without a work permit. She'd have to wait until she was fourteen for a legal one if she wanted to follow the law. Work permits were issued through the school. But she couldn't wait more months. Her mom needed help now. The goal was to get an apartment for her and her mother, but they needed a plan. Teresa had suggested taking the grocery money that Almita kept in the freezer, but Esme talked her out of it. That money fed the entire family. She couldn't live with the knowledge that she'd stolen food from her family's mouths.

Almita shook her head. "I hope I'm not sorry to do this, but if you both promise to keep my rules, you can stay."

"What are the rules? Anything new from last time?" Teresa's voice oozed with skepticism. Esme hoped Tía Almita hadn't noticed, or at least that it didn't change her mind.

Tía Almita raised her fist, then counted off the rules. "They're the same. Number one: carry your load, meaning pick up after yourself. You'll be responsible for one meal every two weeks. I'll tell you when. Number two: respect others' property. No borrowing, stealing, or pranking with other people's things. Number three: no lying. This is Tío Ulises' rule. He hates liars."

Esme felt guilty. They were already breaking rule number three. It occurred to her that her mom might break rule number two. She had little respect for other peoples' property, especially if it was something she wanted. Like cash.

Then something changed in her. Esme was tired of remembering the lies she and her mother had told. Keeping track of them was more work than telling the truth. She loved her mother, but Tía Almita's constant generosity and support had been her safety net. She knew her auntie would care for her. Not so much her mother. She loved her mom, but she acted more like a friend than a parent. An out-of-control friend. But Esme couldn't lie anymore.

"We'll obey your rules, Tía Almita." Esme felt her mother's gaze on her. "We'll do what you say. I'll go to school and study and help around the house."

Tía Almita's face softened as she looked at Esme. When she turned to Teresa, her eyes narrowed. "And you? Will you live by our rules?"

Teresa looked at Ulises, who had just entered the room. "Of course. I knew what I had to do when I asked to come back."

Esme recognized the faint nasal quality of her mother's lie. Thinking back on the times she'd lied in the past, she recognized the tell. Esme decided she'd work on her mom. She'd convince her that all she could want was right here. A family, a roof over their heads, and plenty of food. Her own bad behavior was killing her. The drugs and drinking were eating at her soul—and her body. The men— Teresa didn't know that Esme knew about them—wouldn't satisfy a need in her that Mama couldn't even define.

Esme changed the direction of the conversation. "Will someone call the police to let them know I'm home?"

Tío Ulises snorted. "They don't care."

Almita pushed Teresa aside to pick up the phone on a coffee table. "Don't be silly, Ulie. Esme needs her phone and backpack."

He nodded with understanding and flopped into a recliner.

Chapter Twenty-Nine

Thursday, March 8, 9:30 AM

THE CLERK AT THE ROHNERT PARK DEPARTMENT OF PUBLIC SAFETY front counter shoved the phone and backpack through a glass-enclosed pass-through. Then slipped through a form with a pen. "Sign here that you received these items, please."

Deb leaned on the counter and watched Esme as she and her auntie took possession of the property. "I don't mind telling you that we looked all over for you. We were sure something awful had happened."

Esme noted the detective's narrowed eyes and arms folded across her chest. She didn't look pleased that Esme was home.

"What about your mother? Is she with you?"

Esme shook her head. "She talked to her Probation Officer, and he said he'd be out to pick her up on Monday. She had to go back to Aurora House to complete her sentence, but he said they were too busy to mess with filing on her. She only had a little time left, anyway." This was the truth. Her mother had made a call.

Deb's lip curled into a grimace. Esme could tell she'd wanted her mother taken to jail. The detective straightened and stretched out a hand. "You give me a call if you need me in the future." To Almita, "You still have my card?"

"Yes, ma'am." Almita had ripped it up but still had Meredith's. Almita fished around in her pocket, pulled out the sheriff's office card, and handed it to Esme. "Here."

OUTSIDE IN THE COOL SUNLIGHT, Esme looked at the card. Tía Almita stopped beside her. Her aunt's sinewy fingers covered Esme's. "Keep this card. This detective wasn't so…"

"…bossy?"

They looked at each other's eyes, searching for reactions in the other. Then they broke out laughing. Tía Almita looped an arm around Esme's shoulders. "Yes, bossy. This one listens. More like someone you could talk to."

Esme folded the card and tucked it into the front pocket of her backpack. She'd keep the card in case she needed it in the future.

Chapter Thirty

Thursday, March 8, All Day

LAST NIGHT, MEREDITH CUT TERRY DEAN'S WORK TIME IN HALF. They made it back to the office from the property room in two hours and left for the night before midnight. Today, Thursday, March 8th, was the usual report writing at the VCI office. Both detectives were tired but used to catching little sleep when work dictated. Meredith helped Terry to polish his narrative and typed out the master property list that would be attached to the report. At noon, just when the VCI detectives were returning for lunch, Meredith heard a call over the VCI radio scanner that caught her interest. A possible dead body in a field off the west side of Highway 12 near Sebastopol.

Bennett heard it, too. "Hardy, you're up," he yelled from his desk across the room. Vic Hardy was next up on the major crimes call rotation. Vic would respond with his partner, Janeen Sondergaard. The beat unit would arrive first and check the validity of the report. If it were a body, the deputy would secure the scene, and detectives would already be on the way.

MEREDITH WAS sure that she and Jerry were next to be called for extra help. The sergeant on scene had called for a physical search of the area. The department's two K-9s were occupied on a search out at the coast, so it was up to the detectives to do door-to-door.

Later, Meredith swore she'd banged on a hundred doors that afternoon and into the early evening. She and her partner, Jerry Peters, searched homes and outbuildings looking for a suspect. Law-abiding white-collar residents were only too happy to have the deputy sheriffs check their property for a murderer. Homes were tough enough to search, but rural outbuildings were a challenge, especially with a flashlight in one hand. They combed through decades-old sheds with surplus furniture, sprinkler equipment, and black widows. In the end, they had nothing to show for it but splinters.

The Ver-Ni Road neighborhood held seventeen homes, each on an acre in the flat Santa Rosa flood plain off a dead-end road. The only access was by Duer Road from Highway 12 to the south or on foot across the flat expanse behind the homes. That no one saw or heard anything was atypical for this neighborhood. The mid-century gentleman farmer acreages were occupied by office-types who commuted during the week and cultivated roses or snap peas on the weekend. They were neighbors engaged with their own lives but not too busy to recognize something unusual. These were responsible, steadfast citizens who called in incidents out of the ordinary.

The homicide occurred in a strawberry field south of Ver-Ni, west of Duer Road. Farmworkers had found the body of a dayworker in a farm shack, beaten to death. One worker whispered that there had been rumors of a card game in the shack the night before, but none of the employees confirmed it. Sergeant Bennett wanted the field searched. To ensure the safety of the neighborhood, he instructed the detectives to check the residences bordering the property on Ver-Ni Road.

Meredith and Jerry were finally released when the sun had almost set. "It's about damn time. There wasn't anything out here anyway. A gross waste of time and resources," Peters grumbled.

The responsible party had been apprehended at his home in

Graton. On their private radio channel, they heard the suspect was the victim's brother-in-law. The suspect's sister had asked him to put a stop to her husband's gambling. He did. But she didn't expect him to kill her husband, so she turned him in.

Sergeant Bennett released Meredith and Peters to go home at eight o'clock. They were expected to be in the office the next morning. Bennett said nothing about Meredith returning to Rohnert Park, and she was too tired to ask.

Grateful for the break from Peters, she hopped in her car, heading east on Highway 12 to Highway 101, south and home to Petaluma. She used her work phone for an update on Esme Alfaro. The call went straight to Deb's voicemail. She usually answered Meredith's calls, so Deb must be busy.

Her next call was to her daycare provider. She tapped her icon on the dash-mounted phone—her personal phone. "Hey there, Tina. It's Meredith." Tina was a neighbor and friend. They were the same age and had sons in pre-school together. Their friendship had included adding alley gates to their backyards so they could access each other's homes more easily. The backs of their homes were situated across a utility alley. If they chose to use city sidewalks to get to the other's home, it would be a full block. They used back gates exclusively.

"I know it's you. The phone tells me."

Meredith pictured a weary Tina with a bead of sweat on her brow from chasing toddlers. Tina carried a bit of excess weight, and some of it was upper body muscle from carrying kids. She was a dedicated child-minder whose father had been a police chief. She'd been raised, like Meredith, around a cop-dad's erratic life.

"I'll be home in twenty minutes or so, depending on traffic."

"'Kay, Davy will be ready."

"Thanks so much for watching him late today. Everything go okay?" This was no idle question for Meredith. She wanted to be sure Davy was all right. Eight years before, Nick's infant daughter from his first marriage had died from SIDS. Her husband still fought the paranoia that parents who have lost a child carry around for their lifetimes. Meredith had absorbed Nick's worry.

"No problems." Tina huffed, and Meredith visualized her shifting a toddler from one hip to the other as she so often did. "He kept the puppy busy all morning. He ate lunch and took his nap. He was a bit reluctant to go down, but the puppy was sleeping, so he thought it was a good idea to do the same. I just fed him a little dinner."

Meredith smiled. Kids squealed in the background, along with the high-pitched bark of the red terrier Chihuahua-cross puppy. "You're a Godsend, Tina. That'll help me tonight."

"Glad to help." Tina chuckled. "You can pay me later."

A nice bottle of Pinot Gris was in order. They'd share it together soon. "I'll let you go. See you in a bit."

Her last call was to her husband. "On my way home now."

"Yeah, I saw it on the computer." The mobile digital terminal, or MDT, in department cars, showed the status of each unit, all of patrol, most of the detectives, and even some administrators. Meredith had checked Nick's status before she left Duer Road and noted he was in the office.

"I called Tina. She said Davy's having fun with the puppy."

She heard the smile in her husband's voice. "Someday, when we get time, we should decide about getting a dog."

"Deal."

Chapter Thirty-One

Thursday, March 8, 8:30 PM

AFTER THEY DISCONNECTED, MEREDITH THOUGHT ABOUT HOW difficult it had become to find time alone. Before they were married, it seemed like they spent all their time together. She first met Nick when he was her patrol training officer, then later, they'd partnered up in VCI. Their personalities meshed from the beginning. He appreciated her smart, pragmatic compassion in the field. She respected his experience and wisdom. It made for a dynamic partnership with a remarkably high case clearance and conviction rate. After Nick's divorce, Meredith was widowed. It came as no surprise to anyone who knew them that they'd become a couple.

They had just begun to talk about marriage. Then came Davy's surprise arrival. With a romance in full bloom, the addition of a son added another powerful dimension. The responsibility was enormous, yet they savored each new page of their family life. Meredith wanted to make her son's childhood as healthy and happy as possible. Life got even better with the baby. The richness of their lives together was something neither took for granted. When Davy was born, things changed inevitably. Life got more complicated.

But when her family leave was up, and Meredith returned to work, their precious family time evaporated. These days they often left each other Post-its on the refrigerator. They were both professionals committed to their careers, not only for themselves but for the good they could do. They believed in their service, and that by being there every day, they would make a positive difference in someone's life. Some days it was less than they hoped, while a few days, it was more.

The irritating ring of her work phone jarred Meredith out of her ruminations. The phone display read, "Sonoma County Sheriff." She took the nearby exit and pulled over to the shoulder.

"Ryan."

"Bennett here. I need you to come back to work. This homicide we have going may get more involved, and you're next up on the case rotation."

Dang. The rotation didn't start until midnight, but the on-call guys were already busy. This was how the job went. "Sure. I'll be right in."

Bennett didn't need to know she was blocks from Tina's house. Meredith would have to beg for her to keep Davy all night. At least she'd get to see her little man, even if it was for a minute.

TINA OPENED HER FRONT DOOR, and Davy charged Meredith as fast as his three-year-old legs could carry him. Meredith swept him into her arms and breathed in the boy's smell. She longed to put him in her pocket and keep him with her all the time. The puppy slobbered wet kisses that dripped over her ankles. Tina grabbed the dog and closed the door behind Meredith.

"I just got called back to the office. I'm so sorry to put you out like this. Can you keep him tonight?"

"I'll be happy to. When the boys are together with the puppy, they get tired out really fast." Both women knew if Meredith got called in at eight-thirty PM, the likelihood that she'd be home before midnight was slim. They'd agreed early in their association that it was better to keep Davy at her house than to wake him up in the middle of the night.

Meredith laughed as Davy squirmed. As soon as she put him down, he trotted after the dog. "Have you named the pup yet?"

"Jury's still out. It's either Bandit or Willie."

Wishing she could tousle the fine dark waves of her son's hair once more before she left, Meredith sighed and said goodbye.

Chapter Thirty-Two

Thursday, March 8, 9:30 PM

BACK AT THE OFFICE, MEREDITH SHRUGGED OFF HER COAT AND backpack. Violent Crimes Investigations office lights were on, but no one was in the room. She walked down the hall to find the Records staff had gone home earlier, except the evening clerk, Noreen. She sat at a desk, entering data into a computer. The Records unit held all sheriffs' reports and county warrants, so it was staffed around the clock.

Meredith said, "Hey, Noreen. How'd you get so lucky to be working nights?"

Noreen looked up and flashed her pleasant smile. "My turn in the barrel. They call you out?"

Meredith nodded. "You know where Craig is?"

Noreen handed her a note.

Craig's on his way into the office. Meet him in the VCI office.

"You need a break before I go back there?"

With a grateful nod, the willowy blond stood and ran toward the restroom. As luck would have it, the phone rang. "Sheriff's Records."

"Noreen?" It was Craig Bennett, Meredith's sergeant.

"No, it's Meredith. Noreen's away from her desk for a moment."

"I called to talk to you, Meredith." Craig sighed. He was probably exhausted. He'd been on duty since eight AM, and it was almost eight-thirty PM now. Over twelve tough hours. "I want you to sit in on this interrogation. Meet me outside interview room B. This is Vic Hardy's case, so he's the lead. I'll watch through the mirror."

"Sure. The lieutenant said the suspect in the farmworker homicide has some info?"

"Yeah. He said he knows where a body is buried."

"Is this related to the murder we're questioning him on?"

"Uh, we don't know if they're connected. The Duer victim's name is Isaac Santiago. We stopped the interview when the suspect dropped the bomb on us. I want to do some checking on him first. I've called Nick in to do translation, although the guy speaks passable English. I want to be sure we cross our t's and dot our i's. We've got this guy for the Santiago homicide, and I don't want to jeopardize that case. If his info is good enough, we may consider a deal to take to the DA."

Meredith smiled as Noreen returned. "I'll be there in a minute. Is Peters coming in?"

"Naw." Bennett snorted. "I briefed him on the phone since he's also on call. But I told him to sit this one out. He doesn't have the patience for translation. His temper could flush this whole case down the crapper. I'd rather have you here. You're less likely to alienate the suspect."

"That's a weird compliment, but I'll take it. Nick just got here. We'll be there in a minute."

Chapter Thirty-Three

Thursday, March 8, 9:45 PM

Vɪᴄ Hᴀʀᴅʏ sᴇᴛᴛʟᴇᴅ ʜɪs ᴡɪᴅᴇ ʀᴇᴀʀ ᴇɴᴅ ɪɴᴛᴏ ᴛʜᴇ ᴄʜᴀɪʀ ᴏᴘᴘᴏsɪᴛᴇ murder suspect Gustavo Medina. The men were a study in opposites. Vic's exhausted demeanor accentuated his bad posture, ill-fitting jacket, and beer-belly. Medina was a field worker who didn't need gym time to stay in shape. He was young, trim, and alert. He had a recent haircut, and jeans and a leather jacket that fit him. His rough hands were the only testament to his manual labor.

Meredith had worked with Hardy before but never closely. When he first arrived in the unit six months ago, she'd been startled at the sharp mind that lay beneath the man's sloppy exterior. The stories that drifted her way about his successes in the field altered her first impression of his detective skills. She was glad he was the lead and hoped she could pick up a tip on technique from him.

After Hardy began the recording with the date, time, and case number, he named the people in the room. Nick introduced himself and explained his purpose to Medina in English and Spanish. He took up a position in a corner, leaning with his arms crossed over his chest.

Hardy leaned toward Medina. "Gustavo, in the last interview, you said you knew where a body was buried."

Medina's chin jutted toward the detective.

"Gustavo, for the recording, answer in words. Please."

"Yes. Yes, I know where the body of a man is. But I want a deal for this information. I don't want to spend the rest of my life in prison." Slumping in the chair, he looped his arms across his chest.

Hardy leaned toward Medina. "I've talked to my boss. He says we can't make a deal with you. That's up to the District Attorney. Here's how it works: we take the information you give us. We see if it's credible—real—information. Then we take all this to the DA with a recommendation. They decide. And it's not done immediately. It will take time to prove your claim." Hardy nodded at Nick. "Do you need this translated to understand?"

Nick cut across Medina's answer. "I'll translate. We don't want any misunderstandings that could compromise the deal, do we?" He spent the next minute translating the explanation into Spanish.

Medina pursed his lips as he considered Hardy's words. He sank into a sulk, and Meredith was worried they'd lose his cooperation. She spoke for the first time. "Gustavo, this is for your protection. The DA will look at all the information before he can decide about a deal. As far as the translation: this isn't an insult. We have to be sure you know what's going on." Any defense attorney worth his fee would be sure the translation into the interviewee's native language was provided. There were too many words in the English language that had innuendo or dual meanings. With many ways to misunderstand a question or direction, VCI detectives erred on the side of caution to be sure the interviewee understood.

Without looking at her, he nodded, then glared at Hardy. "Okay. I understand."

"Good," Hardy nodded with approval. "Now. Tell me where this body is."

"Off the top of Alta Monte Drive. There's a narrow road at the end with a...how do you say? *Un acantilado grande?*"

Nick supplied the help. "A cliff, a big ditch."

"That's a vague location, Gustavo. Can you narrow it down?"

"You have a map?"

Meredith walked to her desk in VCI and retrieved a tablet. Once back in the interview room, she pulled up Google and a map of Crane Canyon and Alta Monte Drive. She situated the screen so Medina and Hardy could both see it. After a full minute of tracing the roadway among the tree-studded Sonoma hills, Gustavo pointed to the screen. Past the last house on Alta Monte, the road narrowed to a gravel passage beside a drop-off. The camera couldn't take a picture of the ditch, but the dark splotch indicated something like a ditch could be there.

"Okay, Gustavo. Now we know where. Tell us who was murdered."

"I only know his first name, Bernardo."

"Why was he killed?"

"My brother-in-law was partners with Bernardo. Isaac and Bernardo were turning out young girls."

"Turning them out?" Hardy glanced at the one-way mirror behind Medina.

"Yeah, like giving them to men who pay for, you know..." He rolled his hand in a motion that suggested they understand the inference.

"They were pimping them out?" Nick supplied the correct Spanish word, *chulo.*

Gustavo shrugged. "Yeah. I guess."

"Did you see Isaac Santiago and Bernardo doing this? Did you see the girls?"

He shrugged again, a guilty man dodging a smaller sin.

"Answer with words, Gustavo."

"I didn't know for sure. Isaac always had women around him."

"Women or girls?" Meredith wanted to narrow down the answer.

"Girls. My sister is a woman. She didn't care about the others, as long as he brought home money. She hated the gambling, and him losing their money." Meredith wondered at the woman who was okay with her husband handling prostitutes but not with gambling. But this was getting into the Santiago murder. Hardy would have more time to deal with that later. Meredith felt an urgency creep into her. Was it a leap to wonder if either Santiago or Bernardo was Teresa's contact? What if Esme was being groomed for Santiago's stable? Where did the Russian guy Michael fit in?

Hardy sat back, seeming to know Meredith had another direction to follow.

She asked, "How close were you to Bernardo and his girls?"

Gustavo's muscular shoulders shrugged again, his standard evasion. "Isaac and Bernardo were just a couple of guys trying to make a few bucks off the backs of teen queens."

"Answer the question, Gustavo." Meredith's voice had deepened with the order. She meant business and wanted the murderer to know it.

"I saw enough to know how Isaac could put my sister in a Mercedes. I don't think she ever thought about the women."

"Where did Bernardo live? Where did you meet him?"

Gustavo cocked his head in thought. "I don't know where he lived, somewhere in Roseland. But he had a house in Rohnert Park that he and another man ran the girls out of."

Isaac or Michael? Both? "Do you know what the other man's name was?"

"No."

"Okay, let's get back to Bernardo's house. Where in Rohnert Park?"

"One of the B's. I don't remember. All the houses look the same." Rohnert Park was a planned community divided into alphabetical areas where all the streets began with the same letter. One got an idea of where an address was by the street name. Some thought the houses *did* look the same.

"Can you show us if we take you there?" Meredith thought as long as they would have Medina in a car on Monte Vista, they might as well check out the Rohnert Park location.

Hardy glanced at Meredith but stayed silent.

Gustavo answered. "Maybe."

"We'll do that later. Right now, I want to know what you know about Bernardo's death. When did this happen?"

"Last night."

"Did you see what happened?"

Gustavo harrumphed, clearly weighing how much trouble he'd get into by telling the truth. He took the dive into honesty. "I got there just after it happened. I was supposed to meet Isaac. He just got there, and I was going to pick him up after I got off work. We were going to party." His gaze drifted away from the detectives to a spot over the mirrored window. "Bernardo got a new girl and was setting her up with Sofia, the housemother. The girl's real mother showed up, and they got into a fight."

"'They?' Who got into a fight?"

"The woman was screaming at Bernardo, 'Where's my girl?' when Isaac and I came in. The woman said she heard it through a friend of a friend. I thought she was going to punch Bernardo. She was so mad, I don't think she even saw us. But she pushed Bernardo. He fell over and hit his head on the fireplace bricks. He was bleeding like a cut pig. Then the woman grabbed a girl, and the two ran out the back door. I think they ran out the side gate because I didn't see them after that. And Bernardo, he died." He paused, rubbing his eyes with his fingers.

Meredith knew that no amount of rubbing would erase the vision of a person bleeding out in front of him. Her voice softened. "What happened next, Gustavo?"

"Isaac said no police." His reasoning was obvious. Even if Isaac had no part in the death, the activity in the home would have been apparent to even a novice cop.

"Then what happened?"

Gustavo took a deep breath. He looked from Meredith to Hardy and back again. "Isaac and I took Bernardo's body and dumped it in the hills." He shrugged like it was a daily event. "Then he went to a card game today and lost all his money. I killed him."

"Can you remember how to get to the place where you dumped the body?"

He gave a solemn nod.

"Answer in words, Gustavo."

"Yes. I drove Isaac's car."

"We'll need you to show us."

He nodded, then remembering, said, "Okay."

"One more thing, Gustavo." Meredith mentally crossed her fingers. "Do you know the name of the woman or the girl?"

He shook his head. Then, he started and sat upright. "Isaac told the woman to fuck off. He called her Teresa. I don't know the girl's name."

Chapter Thirty-Four

Thursday, March 8, 10:30 PM

THEY HELD MEDINA IN THE INTERVIEW ROOM WHILE HARDY, Bennett, Nick, and Meredith met in an office two doors down.

Bennett opened the meeting with some terse words. "We're looking at two homicides that are indirectly related. Hardy's got the Santiago case, and Ryan, you'll take the Bernardo murder." He looked at Meredith. "See if you can pin down the two locations he referred to. First, the body dump, then the house in B section, Rohnert Park."

Nick cleared his throat. "Before we get any further, Meredith has something that has a bearing on these cases."

Meredith was grateful for the neat segue to her part of the story. She launched into it for Hardy and Bennett, men who needed to understand the connection to Rohnert Park's case. "Sergeant, you remember the missing juvenile case I worked on with Rohnert Park DPS a few days ago?"

At his curious nod, she started at the beginning addressing the room. "This thirteen-year-old girl, Esme Vela Alfaro, took off from school last Friday without her phone or backpack. She had been placed with her aunt in Rohnert Park because Child Protective Services took her away from her mother, Teresa Alfaro. Mom lost custody of her due to drug convictions and the inability to care for her. Esme told a cousin who lives with her that some guy promised her work. She wanted to make money to pay for an apartment so she and her mother could be together. From a different source, I received information that Esme was either coerced or conned into leaving school and her aunt's home by some type of predator.

"Since Rohnert Park Police took a runaway report, I got hold of Deb Lang. She and I talked to the mom's PO, then made contact with her at Aurora House. We thought she might know where Esme would go. But after we left, the mom left there, violating her probation. We alerted SRPD to watch the rehab house while we went over to her previous residence at an apartment on Yulupa in Santa Rosa. That was a dead end, although we did find out that Esme was close to a neighbor girl named Sofia. Sofia lived there with a man thought to be her father—but maybe not—a man named Michael Fedorov. Santa Rosa PD sighted Teresa in the Yulupa area shortly after we left. Deb and I intercepted her and the driver on Crane Canyon Road, and we followed them.

"We got as far as a house on Burton Avenue in RP before I was called off. The probation officer was going to come and arrest Teresa, but it sounds like Teresa left before he arrived. I haven't yet confirmed that. Deb said she arranged to keep the house under surveillance—but that didn't happen." She selected her words carefully so as not to cast doubts about Deb. "She also told me that she'd been talking to Rohnert Park's Officer Rogers, who is attached to the DA's Drug Interdiction Unit. I haven't been able to connect with her to see what's going on there. But I believe that's the house where Bernardo was killed, and Isaac, maybe Michael Fedorov, too, kept his girls."

"Holy shit, Ryan. Way to tie up a case." Hardy's eyes bugged out in admiration.

"There's more. Esme's mother, Teresa Alfaro, is in the wind. We'll get a warrant for the homicide. If she turns up before the warrant is signed, her PO, Eberling, will arrest her. At least we'll have her behind bars."

Hardy asked, "How come you and Lang didn't do a knock and talk at the house on Burton Avenue?"

It was Meredith's turn to shrug. "Deb seemed strangely reluctant to do that. It was like she knew something she wasn't telling me, so I didn't press it." Meredith tucked her hands in her pockets. "Anyway, that's when I got called back to our office. But I suspect that the Bernardo homicide occurred while it was under observation."

"That will make DPS look ineffective." Bennett shook his head, knowing how fast the media and the public were to jump on any law enforcement error.

Meredith considered how much she should say to this group. "It's possible that the Drug Task Force had that house as a point of interest. But again, I can't confirm that. I haven't been able to get in touch with Deb. I got the feeling there was a hands-off order. Could be from someone at the Task Force." She shrugged, a bit guilty about not coming clean about her concerns about Deb. "One other thing. I ran the Alfaro girl through Missing Persons this morning, and she wasn't there. The case has been cleared." Why didn't Deb let her know Esme was home? She decided to talk it over later with Nick. Her husband had a good perspective and made a terrific sounding board.

"Thanks for the information, Meredith." Bennett rose, checking his phone. "It would be good to clear two homicides at the same time. For now, you and Hardy take Medina to where he dumped Bernardo." He checked his phone again. "It's dark now, but give it a try. The house on Burton will be easier. But I want specific locations as soon as you can get them."

Nick spoke up. "The Alta Monte Drive location will be tough to pin down. There aren't any streetlights up there. He says the body is off a cliff, so it could be tough to access."

Bennett acknowledged Nick's concerns with a nod, then looked at Meredith and Hardy. "Give it a try anyway. It'd be a bitch to have predators chewing on our evidence because we had to wait to find him in the daylight."

The detectives dispersed, heading for their assignments. After a discussion with Medina, Bennett decided not to ask Nick to accompany them to the dump site.

Meredith pulled Nick aside in the hallway and whispered, "I want to talk to you about something on this case."

"Is it directly related? I mean, maybe you should be talking to Bennett."

"No, it's more of a hunch than a fact."

Hardy dangled car keys at her. He'd pulled the handcuffed Gustavo Medina beside him. To Nick, she said, "We'll talk later."

Chapter Thirty-Five

Thursday, March 8, 11:30 PM

IT WAS DEAD DARK ON THE TOP OF ALTA MONTE DRIVE WHEN Gustavo Medina grunted. They had arrived. With the nearest street-light two miles back, the few homes were either shrouded in oak trees or below the road. The asphalt gave way to gravel, and Hardy pulled the plainclothes car to a stop in the middle of what had shrunk into a one-lane road. With no shoulder on which to park, he put on the hazard lights and got out. He flicked on his flashlight and went to the back door of the sedan.

Meredith zipped up her jacket and clicked her flashlight on to meet Hardy and Medina. She didn't like being out here at night on such a questionable mission. Searching in the dark for a body off a cliff seemed pointless.

They walked until Hardy called a halt. "We've walked a mile at least, Medina. Are you sure this is the road?"

Medina's head swiveled toward his surroundings. Meredith couldn't believe he could see anything beyond the flashlight beam.

Gustavo moaned. "I'm not sure. I cannot tell one tree from the other."

Meredith's concern had been well founded. If it had been daylight, Gustavo would've seen her glare. "You're not even sure this is the right road?"

Hardy's posture straightened. "All right. I'm calling this. We come back tomorrow."

Meredith was relieved, but there was still something they could do. "How about we drive by Burton Avenue before we take Mister Medina back to jail? We can get the house number and look over the neighborhood."

FIFTEEN MINUTES LATER, the department Taurus slowed to cruise by 734 Burton Avenue. A streetlight two houses away illuminated a 1960s-era house that hadn't seen paint in decades. It had been white but was now dotted with black mold along the stucco walls. Two windows in front had lights on inside. They faced the street, and Meredith figured, from the size, they were bedrooms. To the right of the house, a garage sat back off a cracked concrete driveway bordered by overgrown yucca. The front yard was covered with bark and nothing else. A utility pole to the right carried wired service to the house. The nearest streetlight was one door east. Meredith noted the old unstained wood fencing on both sides. She wondered how Teresa and Esme had made it out of the backyard. There…a side gate to the east.

"Gustavo, is this the house?"

From the back seat, Gustavo answered. "Yes."

"Okay." Meredith recorded the address on her phone. She texted Bennett to get someone started on a search warrant for that address. "734 Burton Avenue. We'll get a search warrant and go in tomorrow early AM. By the way, this is the same place Teresa came to. Keep your eyes open. We might find a cop keeping an eye on the place nearby."

Hardy craned his neck, glancing in each direction. "There. The dark-colored Chevy parked three doors down."

Hardy pulled up to the Chevy—driver window to driver window

—and rolled his down. He flipped open his flat badge. When the police officer behind the wheel opened his window, Hardy introduced himself. "I'm Vic Hardy from the Sheriff's Office."

"Larry Killeen, SRPD, attached to the DA Drug Task Force. What's up?" The middle-aged, blond-haired cop offered a world-weary glare.

"We're looking at 734 Burton as the scene of a homicide. We're on our way to get the search warrant. Anything of interest?"

"Plenty. What are you looking for specifically?"

"Evidence a murder took place inside the home."

"No shit." Killeen's gaze suddenly showed interest. "Suspect? Anyone in custody?"

"Not yet." Hardy shook his head. "We're thinking this is a place where pimps house girls and women used for sex."

"Duh."

Hardy paused. "You're here for drugs?"

Killeen nodded. "We got intel that there's some low-level drug activity going through the house. I'm here to see if there's enough for a search warrant."

"Anything?"

"*Nada,* so far." Killeen nodded his head wearily. "But I've never seen so many women in one house. I will be referring this address to Rohnert Park for possible prostitution or human trafficking."

"We're getting a search warrant for the homicide signed now. We plan to execute it tomorrow morning before dawn. We have information that a pimp was killed inside last night by a woman seeking to find her daughter."

One of Killeen's eyebrows rose. "That could be why the women inside have been kind of restless."

"Restless?"

"Yeah, walking outside in pairs, then running back inside. Almost always on the phone. They may even know I'm here." He shifted in the seat. Hours in one position took its toll on a body. "Why don't you try a knock and talk?"

"Sarge wants it done with a warrant. Can I get your phone number in case we need to holler?"

"Sure. I'll be here until midnight. Then someone else takes over." They exchanged phone numbers. Killeen promised his relief would text Hardy his number.

"It's going to be a long night," Meredith said, as they drove off. Anticipating the execution of a warrant, Nick had trained her to do her homework first. That continued to be the prevalent philosophy in VCI. Meredith anticipated hours poring over maps of the neighborhood, Google Earth, as well as city and power company utility billing. Nick had taught her the trick of checking for people with warrants who live nearby. For deputies' safety, they'd want to know if the guy next door had a weapons warrant.

Chapter Thirty-Six

Friday, March 9, All Day

THEY DIDN'T FINISH THE WARRANT AND PREPARATION UNTIL ALMOST three AM. Hardy got a judge to sign it at four AM. Meredith was so tired she debated driving home, trying to sleep for two hours, then returning to the office at five AM for the operational briefing. The warrant was servable at six AM. In the end, she washed her face in the restroom and fell onto the lunchroom couch for a nap.

Nick woke her at 4:45, the aroma of coffee wafting from a heavy paper cup nearby. "Wakey, wakey." He kissed her cheek.

Meredith had been in a deep sleep. Her voice was husky when she said, "What a great way to wake up." He smiled at her smile.

She sat up and wrapped her fingers around the cardboard cup. Breathing in the coffee aroma, she glanced at the wall clock. She had mere minutes to wake up and be present at the briefing. She polished off the hot coffee and stood. "I'm going to go wash my face and try to wake up."

"You said you had something to talk to me about?"

She had mere minutes to spare. Did she really want to get into this now? Yes, it was eating at her.

"So, Deb's been really weird about this whole Esme Alfaro thing."

"In what way?"

"At first, she didn't want to pursue the missing case at all. She assumed what everyone else did—that Esme ran away of her own accord."

"Making assumptions is the worst thing a cop can do, but we do it all the time. How is that weird?"

"She's been avoiding my calls. I'm not sure she's doing any follow-up. And, she never said a word about Esme coming home."

"That's not your job, Mere. You can't monitor another agency's case."

Stung by his criticism, she ducked. "I know, but a kid's life could be at stake."

Nick thought for a moment. "And what do you think is going on?"

"I don't know. I just see that she's not doing her job the way she should."

His lips curled in a sardonic grin. "So, do you think she's lazy or on the take?"

Hearing the phrases that defined some of a cop's worst behaviors, Meredith stopped. "No. No, I don't think that…"

"But something's going on, right?"

"Yes." The words felt insufficient to convey her dismay. She couldn't describe all the innuendo that went into her doubt. "But the more I talk about it, the less I believe it's true. Forget I said anything."

"You're sure? Based on what you've told me, there's not enough to look into her activity."

"Activity? Like internal affairs?" Holy crap. What had she done? "No. Forget it, Nick. And for God's sake, don't repeat anything I've said."

He looked into her eyes. "I'll see you in the squad room."

BENNETT LED the briefing while Meredith provided the team with needed background information. As liaison for Rohnert Park DPS and the DA's office, Officer Rogers from the Task Force stood and gave a brief outline of his team's interest in the property. There had been an anonymous tip of drug activity. Surveillance didn't reveal anything, although he repeated what Killeen had said about forwarding the address to Rohnert Park DPS investigations for possible human trafficking or prostitution. He provided vehicle information and all the intel he'd accumulated.

The overall warrant goal was to find the murder site, close it off and obtain evidence that could lead to a suspect. Of primary importance was the safety of the women inside. They hoped to get information about who might be behind Isaac Santiago and Bernardo's enterprise in view of Medina's impression of a third man in charge. The hope was that a ringleader might have a motive to off two of his employees, and they were not sure they were getting the full story from Gustavo. Bennett had called in two uniforms as well as another pair of VCI detectives. He had decided against using the Special Operations Unit. With a house full of young women, Bennett didn't believe he needed that kind of help. The two pimps in charge were both dead, so he didn't expect much resistance.

Each deputy had a specific job; Meredith and Hardy as the entry team, Bennett and Sondergaard covered the gated exterior of the fenced yard with two uniformed deputies in position at the rear to head off any who tried to flee. Bennett assigned a team of deputies and detectives for detentions. The sergeant's opinion was the women weren't the suspects but had to be detained for questioning. Rohnert Park's watch commander had been apprised and would be in the area. Almost as a postscript, Bennett added that Jerry Peters, Meredith's partner, and another detective from the property crimes unit would be searching for Bernardo on Alta Monte Drive with Gustavo Medina at daylight.

After thirty minutes, the sergeant brought the briefing to a close.

Nick stood in the back of the office during the briefing. He'd be going home at his usual off-duty time of seven AM because he'd already logged more on-duty hours than the department allowed. He waited for Meredith as the sheriffs' personnel filed out.

She faced him with a rueful smile. "You must be tired."

"Yep." He exhaled. "Look at you, running on two hours of sleep."

She grasped his hand. "Get some rest. Call me when you get up."

Nick shook his head. "No. You call me when you're done. I don't care what time. I want to know you're all right."

"Deal." She squeezed his hand and left.

Chapter Thirty-Seven

Saturday, March 10, Early Morning

AT SIX-OH-ONE AM, DARK STILL SHROUDED ROHNERT PARK'S B section. It would be another hour before the first glimmerings of daylight shone over Sonoma's Mayacamas Mountains. With the deputies all in place, Detective Vic Hardy pounded on the front door of 734 Burton Avenue. With his gun drawn, he shouted, "Sonoma County Sheriff. Open up. We have a search warrant."

Meredith heard some kind of movement inside and women's voices sounding frantic. Clenching her Glock, she shouted, "Sheriff's Office. Open the door, or we'll force entry. We have a search warrant." Repeating the commands had become a necessity in Bennett's world. He didn't like his detectives' cases thrown out of court on a technicality that could've been avoided by a simple sentence. He wanted the person served with the search warrant to know exactly who was at the door.

One of the units on the outer perimeter rasped over Meredith's radio earpiece. "Curtains moving in east front room."

Both Hardy and Meredith heard the unmistakable snick of an

unlocking deadbolt. Then a woman's screech from inside, "No. No, don't!"

Meredith twisted the handle, and the door swung open. With her Glock poised in front, there was movement before her. Three young women scurried from the living room to the hallway, away from the door. All appeared unarmed and dressed in sweatpants, T-shirts, and barefoot. They huddled against a closed door at the end of the hall.

A woman's voice in the back of the house shouted with insistence, "Go. Go."

A back door slammed. Hardy charged inside, pushing Meredith away. Her adrenaline kicked in. She was on his tail.

Hardy shouted at her. "Someone bailed out back."

"One of the women?"

"I couldn't see. Just a shadow."

Meredith followed and alerted the troops on the radio. "Unknown subject just left out the back door. David One, copy?" Bennett was in position covering the exterior back. She had to warn him that someone was coming his way.

Hardy ran toward the slamming door past two confused-looking females clutching each other. One of them stuck her foot out and tripped him. Hardy fell hard, his breath whooshing out of him. Meredith paused to check on him.

Hardy grunted. "I'm okay. Get him."

Meredith moved quickly, wondering why Hardy assumed it was a man. With his 'okay,' she took up the chase, running after whoever was fleeing.

The laundry room door had bounced open against the jamb. Meredith sprinted through. She heard shouting; Bennett's voice. From the porch steps, she saw the figure of a man, two strides, then hopping over the back fence. Short curly hair, thin build.

Bennett yelled. "Hardy, where the fuck are you?"

At the top of the fence, the man hesitated after swinging a leg over. He turned, gun in hand, pointing it toward Bennett's voice.

One of the uniforms shouted, 'Gun!' Nearby, the rustle of metal brushing against leather as Hardy's handgun cleared his holster, anticipating trouble. Meredith raised her Glock, aimed at the figure in motion atop the fence, and fired three rounds.

She couldn't tell if she'd hit him. He'd rolled off the top of the fence and dropped into the next yard. The shots shattered the quiet neighborhood. Deafened by the blast, she heard a muffled voice over the radio, "Shots fired, shots fired."

She called out to Bennett. "Sarge, you okay?"

"Yeah," he replied breathlessly. Meredith's pre-emptive shot had stopped the man from taking out Bennett. He hadn't fired.

She lowered her weapon, took a deep breath, and checked her surroundings. She waited after Bennett answered her, holding her position. A moment later, Bennett rushed through a side gate into the yard. "Meredith, what the hell?"

He hadn't seen the man with the gun.

Her ears were still messed up from the gun blast, but she took a chance she'd understood her sergeant's question. "I fired my weapon. The guy was on top of the fence, there." She pointed, taking a breath to slow her heart rate. "He'd pulled a gun and was pointing it toward where you were. I had to shoot."

"Jesus Christ. Did you get him?" Bennett's attention automatically went to where she'd indicated.

"I don't know. He fell to the other side of the fence. I couldn't tell if I hit him."

"Get someone over to that yard, now," Bennett spoke the command into his mic. "Get a description out ASAP for the nearby units." He walked across the scrubby yard with his flashlight on to where Meredith had pointed.

Meredith pressed the 'push-to-talk transmit' button on her bone conduction microphone, known as a 'bone mic'. Her ears were clearing up, and she gambled on the radio being clear. This was important. The troops needed to know who to look for. "Units in the area of Burton Avenue, there's an armed suspect at large. He's a male, unknown race, curly blond hair, slender build, wearing dark clothing. He had a handgun, unknown if it's still with him. Direction of travel would be south from 734 Burton, not necessarily on the street. He may be hopping fences. He is possibly injured from a gunshot wound. No further."

Hardy yelled from the back door holstering his gun. He reached up to hold the side of his head. "Ryan, you okay?"

"Yep. You?"

"A little humiliated," Hardy huffed. "But I'll live."

Meredith holstered her weapon and waited as Bennett's flashlight beam lit up the weeds. "Nothing here, Ryan." The beam ambled up the wooden fence boards and then stopped. "Uh, no. Got blood here."

"Crap." Meredith slumped, knowing what this meant. She'd been down this road before. She should be happy that she hit her target and Bennett was spared. But dread gripped her. Had she killed someone? She was sure she'd seen a gun.

And there were the procedures. With department-ordered counseling, she'd be on administrative leave until the department fully investigated the incident. She knew she'd be exonerated, but it could take weeks for the investigation. The waiting gnawed at her. Knowing what was on the road ahead, she felt like she wanted to throw up.

Bennett's light continued its search. One of the fence boards was warped, and he shined the beam through. "Gun," he shouted, unable to contain his excitement. "Got a visual on the gun."

Meredith sighed with relief as Bennett told Sondergaard to retrieve it. Finding the gun would give validity to her use of force. She watched her co-workers scramble to retrieve the weapon.

Bennett handed Sondergaard an evidence bag which she tucked into a pocket. She'd slipped on nitrile gloves while a uniform helped Hardy move a rickety picnic table to the fence. Sondergaard hopped onto the table and slipped gracefully over the fence. A moment later, she handed the bagged gun—slide open—to the waiting deputy. He gave it to Hardy, then helped Sondergaard back over the fence. Her voice was firm when she told Bennett, "I took a picture before I picked it up, Sarge."

He nodded. Now, they needed access to the neighbor's yard. Bennett busied himself with a tablet. He brought up Google Earth to get the address, then sent someone to knock on the resident's door. They'd take pictures of the drop site and collect any other evidence the suspect may have left.

TEN MINUTES LATER, in the department Taurus, Meredith sat with Hardy beside her. Bennett stood on the sidewalk next to the Taurus on the radio, coordinating the search for the suspect. Sondergaard trotted over to them. She pulled the bagged magazine in an evidence bag out of her jacket pocket.

"Gotcha," she said simply.

Chapter Thirty-Eight

Saturday, March 10, Early Morning

MICHAEL WAS MAD. NO WOMAN WAS GOING TO GET THE BETTER OF him. His hand hurt like a motherfucker. The knuckle on his middle finger had barely slowed down the round. It was bleeding, the skin broken. But the shock was enough to knock him down for a few seconds. Clutching his hand, he'd dropped into the yard on the other side of 734 Burton Avenue. The gun had flown out of his hand with the impact of the bullet and was somewhere in the knee-deep weeds. He didn't take the time to look for it.

Blood dampened his hand and dripped onto his pants. When he saw a towel hanging near a hot tub, he grabbed it and wrapped his hand. From the house on another side, a dog barked at the ruckus in the Burton backyard. Finding a weed-covered stone path, Michael crept to one side of the house. Without a sound, he opened the gate latch and scouted the street for movement. Nothing. He made his way around two blocks to Bonnie Drive. He estimated access to the house he wanted was off Bernice Court, just ahead. He dodged a nasty dachshund in one yard and climbed a Bernice Court fence to the back of a Burton Avenue house with power lines crossing over the roof to the seven-hundred block of Burton.

He'd judged it correctly. He scrambled from yard to yard until he was in position to see the activity at 734. The house across from 734 was dark, with no cars in the driveway. Hiding behind a lilac tree, Michael watched cops and deputies coming and going. The neighborhood was still quiet, although it wouldn't be for long. Police radios squawked and hissed. Rotating emergency lights shined into dark windows.

He saw the Crime Scene Unit arrive. He scoffed as they put on their outrageous white suits. A short guy who wore his authority like a crown walked out of the house with a woman. There she was. The bitch who shot him. He memorized her appearance and scrolled through his contacts. There was a correctional officer at the jail who gave him information from time to time. He'd reach out and see if he could provide this bitch's information.

As he watched, it struck him that he'd seen her before. She was with the Rohnert Park detective who went to Esme's aunt's place. Maybe she had a connection with the girl. That would bear looking into. He could kill two birds with one stone—catch Esme and rough up the bitch who shot him.

The short boss put the woman in a sedan. Soon teams of deputies surrounded him, and it was clear they were getting orders.

One good thing—Teo was gone. He'd spent more time in Sonoma than Michael wanted, but at least he was gone now, unable to complicate his life any further. After making a few changes, his brother seemed satisfied with the setup.

But now, it was time for Michael to blow. He was slick enough that they'd never find him, but he wanted to get the wound treated and start his plan to find the girl and the woman.

Chapter Thirty-Nine

Saturday, March 10, Afternoon

IT WAS WELL PAST LUNCH BEFORE MEREDITH GOT CUT LOOSE BY THE Internal Affairs guys. She didn't dare count the hours she'd been awake. It would make her crash, for sure. Sequestered at the department, a union representative sat with her. Her service weapon had already been logged into evidence. A Glock 22 was issued to her from the armory. Internal Affairs detectives had separated Hardy, Bennett, and her, and had each tell their side of the story. Bennett returned to Burton Avenue to assist Rohnert Park detectives with their investigation, independent of the sheriff's office. Since there wasn't a body, they were limited in what they could do for Meredith's shooting. However, the homicide site was another matter. Rohnert Park had jurisdiction, but the Sheriff's Office would collaborate as there was an existing case related to Bernardo's death.

Then, Meredith typed out her report as Bennett had directed. A separate case number was issued for each homicide. Even related, there were enough specifics to each death to warrant a separate but cross-referenced investigation.

She had two reports to complete. The first was her account of the shooting, and the second was her supplemental information for the homicide report.

The women taken from inside the home had been detained for their welfare. None of them had any money or identification, leading Hardy and Meredith to believe this was a human trafficking situation. She suspected none of the women would cooperate with the investigation.

The Crime Scene Unit had fingerprinted what they could and collected evidence throughout the house. Using luminol, they'd found the spot where Bernardo had fallen into the fireplace hearth and bled out. Even though someone had tried to clean it up, they'd found a large amount of blood on the brick and carpet. Bennett had told Meredith that the Medical Examiner was currently matching up the wound pattern with the impression of the hearth. The detectives had interviewed all the women but weren't surprised that none admitted to seeing anything.

But Meredith's job was done for today. She felt a shiver of satisfaction that the paperwork was completed when she pushed the "submit" button.

TWO HOURS of sleep in the last thirty-six had taken its toll. Driving home in her faithful and somewhat vintage Subaru, she had to open the windows to keep her awake. She pulled into the driveway of their modest bungalow on the west side of Petaluma at two-thirty PM. Their century-old Cottage-style home sat in the middle of an established westside neighborhood. Most of the homes were of the same vintage, but some had been modernized. The Reyes-Ryan family loved their gray shingled one-story home. Its sloping roof and sizable front porch offered a distinctive view of the Petaluma Valley from the curb. Inside, the open floor plan was short on storage but offered a welcoming feel to visitors.

Too tired to open the garage door, Meredith left the car in the driveway instead of the garage. She walked through the back gate and over to Tina's house to get her son. She'd texted the childcare neighbor before leaving the office.

She missed her son. It had been too long since she held him in her arms. Tired or not, she had to have him nearby. This was the toughest part of being a working mother. The guilt over leaving him was a close second. Raised by a miserable Irishwoman, Meredith had gotten a significant dose of guilt whether or not she'd done anything wrong.

Davy was ready when Meredith arrived. She hugged Tina, grabbed her little man's backpack, and scooped him up in her arms. On the way out the door, she stopped. "Hey, I'm on leave for a week or so. I'll be home. We can trade kids if you want. I'll be glad to watch Henry for you." Outside, a puppy barked.

"Deal. What about Bandit?"

"Not a chance. You settled on a name for him, then?"

She shrugged. "Yeah, for today." She flashed a goofy grin. "Who knows what it'll be tomorrow."

"See ya."

Chapter Forty

Saturday, March 10, 3:00 PM

NICK WAS SOUNDLY ASLEEP WHEN MEREDITH AND DAVY GOT HOME. Meredith held her index finger in front of her lips with a "Ssshhh" for her son. "Daddy's sleeping."

But Davy wasn't a quiet kid. Full of energy, and he liked to share it with everyone. In spite of Meredith's warning, he barreled down the hall, shoes slapping on the new hardwood floor. "Daddy, Daddy."

Meredith scooped him up as his little body slammed against the door. "Davy, sssshhh."

Inside the room, Meredith heard Nick rustling in the covers.

She turned the doorknob quietly, in case, against all odds, Nick was still sleeping.

The door swung open. Even with room-darkening shades, the room didn't stay completely dark. In the shadows, she saw her husband on his back in his usual sleeping attire, boxers, and a T-shirt. With the covers pushed off, his chest moved slowly up and down. At the doorway, Meredith held her son back, concerned that he'd wake his father. Backing out with one arm around her little human tornado, she reached for the doorknob.

A loud snore escaped from Nick.

She felt Davy's body vibrating. His poorly suppressed giggle elevated into a full-throated three-year-old's laugh. Meredith couldn't stop him. In truth, her son's exuberant laugh was so delightful that she didn't want to.

Suddenly wide awake, Nick sat upright, swinging his feet to the floor. "Is that my boy?"

Davy shrugged out of Meredith's loose embrace and ran to his father. Nick scooped him up and dropped him on the bed with loud belly laughs from both. Leaning over his son, he began a tickle routine that always melted Meredith's heart. Seeing and hearing her son's and husband's horseplay filled every crevice of her soul with joy. She loved these two. She'd give her life for them.

After a few minutes of hilarity, Nick's head popped up. "Mere?" His white teeth shone in a striking smile, a contrast to the semi-darkness of the room.

Meredith fell into her bed. She grabbed Davy, hugged him to her chest, and rolled to her side. She nuzzled the soft space below his ear. When she puckered and made kissing noises, lips brushing his neck, he shied at the tickle. He rolled out of her arms and back to Nick, where he dove under the covers and lay breathing hard.

Seeing their son's moment of rest, Nick reached out to Meredith's cheek. "Glad to see you're in one piece. You were supposed to call."

"Yeah." Meredith blew out a breath of irony. "We got busy…"

He tensed and sat up. "What happened?"

She leaned her head on her hand. "I'm on admin leave because I shot someone."

"What?" Nick picked up his son, holding him against his chest. Davy was tired enough to sit still for it. Again, Nick asked, "What happened?"

"It's not as bad as it sounds." She tried to avoid his gaze but couldn't help herself. He'd always been the quickest to see her distress and pick up her pieces. Nick didn't do pity, but his empathy button was stuck in overdrive when it came to her involvement in critical incidents. His eyes sagged with sadness.

"Tell me everything."

She gathered herself and re-told the story she'd gone through so many times this morning. But this was for Nick, not just anyone. Certainly, he wouldn't dissect every move. "I was on the entry team. Someone unlocked the front door, so we didn't have to break it down. There were eight girls and young women inside. Hardy heard one of them telling someone to go, so he ran after him. One of the women tripped Hardy, and he hit the deck. I ran after the guy running out the laundry room door. He went into the backyard and climbed the fence. He stopped at the top rail and pulled a gun. It looked like he was aiming at Bennett. I fired and must have hit him. He dropped off the fence and ran off. Bennett found blood on the fence board. But the shooter is in the wind."

"Did Bennett see this?"

"Some of it. But as luck would have it, Hardy witnessed it all from the back porch. The two uniforms saw the rest. Bennett pieced the scenario together from all the statements."

"Did they find the gun?"

Meredith nodded, suddenly very tired. "He dropped it in the bordering yard. Sondergaard found it." She paused. "It was a right-eous shoot."

"Damn straight," Nick whispered, as he caressed his son's hair. Davy was dozing off. Nick met her gaze. "And you? How are you doing?"

She shrugged. She didn't know how she felt yet. She shot some-one. Even if he deserved it, it wasn't easy to deal with. She'd gotten into this business to help people, not shoot them. She wasn't looking forward to the next week, but it was by no means an unknown.

"The emotions haven't yet kicked in."

Nick leaned over and took her hand in his. His grip was so soft, it was like an angel had touched her. "So, you're off for a week?"

"Seven to ten days." She shrugged. "However long it takes for the investigation."

"Who's taking over the second homicide?"

"Peters. He knows the most about it besides Hardy. I think Hardy may wind up with the whole deal, but Bennett put Peters in charge of Bernardo's homicide."

"It could be worse. Peters is an annoying little shit, but he's meticulous, methodical, and sensible. He'll find the killer."

She nodded with a smile. "In the meantime, I'm home. I'll text Tina and let her know she'll have to help me with dinners."

She felt his eyes searching her face. "Are you okay?"

They both knew her mood could change from moment to moment. One of the things they did for each other was what he called 'status checks.' At work, dispatch inquiries about a deputy's safety a few minutes after arriving at a call. He or she would radio back, 'code four,' which meant the situation was under control, and no further patrol units needed. Or if not, 'code three, backup.' She was code four. "Yeah. There wasn't a choice. I couldn't let him shoot Bennett."

He was ready for whatever answer she gave. Right now, she wanted to hear what his supervisor impressions were. He said, "It sounds like the suspect was mobile enough to flee the area."

"That's something, I suppose." She shrugged again. "It was the only thing I could do." She'd been around cops her entire life, beginning with her father and uncle. She'd used her weapon both on duty and off. But she wasn't a robot, and she wasn't built without feelings. Sometimes she struggled to understand the world. The department would conclude the shooting was "justified." Meredith would see a department-mandated counselor, and they'd all pat each other on the back at the conclusion of their successful paperwork. But she'd shot a man, even if it was a graze, even if Nick figured she could handle the stress. This wasn't Davy's 'cops and robbers' playtime. *She'd shot a man*, and tough as Meredith was, the fear of the thing, the adrenaline blowback, was the unfair burden she had to carry. She'd never meant for any of this—to be put in such a position, and painted into a corner, where the only way out was to use a gun.

"How about Hardy? Is he okay?"

"He'll be sporting a shiner for a few days, and his dignity is crushed, but he's fine."

He leaned over and kissed her forehead. "I'm glad you're okay."

"Thanks." She yawned. "Me, too."

Nick laid Davy out on the bed between them. "Want to take a nap?"

"Honestly? Yes. What about you?"

"Not sure I can get back to sleep, but I'll try." He flashed a soft, loving smile. "All three of us can snuggle right here."

Chapter Forty-One

Saturday, March 10, 5:30 PM

IT WAS LATE AFTERNOON, AND NICK HAD LEFT EARLY FOR WORK. Meredith zipped Davy's puffy jacket and pulled a bottle of Coppola Pinot Grigio out of the fridge. With wine in one hand and Davy's in the other, she hurried across the alley through the back gates to Tina's house, chilled by the late winter breeze.

Once over the threshold into Tina's laundry room, Davy ran for Bandit and Henry. An ear-piercing shriek announced the two boys' reunion. An urgent bark from the puppy meant he was also involved. Meredith handed Tina the wine and peered around the corner into the playroom. Alphabet blocks and build-it toys in John Deere Tractor shapes littered the floor. Puppy Kong dog toys were scattered among the playthings. Bandit had a small red ball in his mouth and shook it furiously. It would be in shreds soon.

"The puppy is cute." He looked to be about two months old. Meredith swore his eyes saw into her heart. *Awww.* It struck her how much she wanted one of these little guys for the family. "Is his name still Bandit?"

Tina pulled the cork out and poured wine into two stemless glasses. "It's either that or butthead. I haven't decided yet."

While Davy pulled tractor parts into his lap and smacked his lips with delight, Meredith returned to the kitchen.

"So, you're home for a while." Tina sat at the kitchen table across from Meredith. "All you had to do is shoot somebody."

Meredith frowned, then lifted her glass to meet Tina's in a mock toast. Feeling a little touchy at her friend's observation, she wondered if she was being too sensitive. "That's not what I had in mind."

Tina waved the thought away as she put the glass on the table. "You know what I mean." Tina's been raised with the weird sense of cop humor. She thought she was being funny.

Meredith shrugged off the irritation at her own response. "Yeah, you're a real card."

"What are you going to do with your time?"

"Well, first, I have to be available for the investigation. If they call me, I go in and answer questions. And the mandatory counseling session. I feel bad about dropping the homicide investigation in my partner's lap. He's up to the task, but he doesn't know all the nuances of the missing girl."

"You should call and fill him in."

Meredith turned the glass with one hand. "Yeah. That's a good idea." She thought over the vacancy of her days. When she was at work, she wanted to be home. This was an opportunity to do that. She wanted to watch Davy grow. Knowing her career wouldn't allow for much of this precious time, she felt like she needed to grab it. "Beyond that, I want to spend some time with my son. Maybe take Davy up to Cav's for an overnighter. Nick's working graveyards. He sleeps all day and works all night. He won't have time to miss us."

Tina nodded with approval. "How about some playground time? I was planning on taking Henry to McNear Park tomorrow. Want to join us?"

Meredith smiled. "Why yes, I'd love to." The chance to be a normal mom was too tantalizing to resist.

Chapter Forty-Two

Sunday, March 11, Morning

THE NEXT MORNING PROMISED A CHILLY, OVERCAST PLAY DATE WITH Tina and Henry. The almost three-acre McNear Park encompassed two softball fields, a large playground, tennis courts, picnic tables, group barbeque areas, and public bathrooms. Eucalyptus, redwood, and sycamore trees shrouded the playground. Generously sized equipment was modern, and recently refurbished with primary colors on swings, slides, playground climbers, see-saws, merry-go-rounds, spring-riders, and tubes.

Henry and Davy were both bundled up like the Michelin Man. Meredith and Tina were also well-wrapped. Once on the park's shredded bark, the boys didn't feel the cold. The moms sucked on their coffees and chased the boys as needed. Meredith wanted to play with Davy, to push him on the swing and catch him on the slide. Tina was more content to watch Henry, and today, she stayed by Meredith, chattering her usual "mom" conversation. Meredith listened while enjoying time with her son and was glad to have a friend adding to the sense of normalcy she needed.

Being a cop was an exercise in extremes: boring hours with little activity. A heartbeat later, ninety miles per hour, racing to a burglary-in-progress call. Then, there were the times you had to make snap judgments over who's a good guy and who's a bad guy. When you're wrong, it could cost your life—or worse, someone else's. The list of extremes included time wasters, such as crime reports that would never be adjudicated like a petty vandalism with no leads, and the pointless tasks assigned by an administrator who left the streets long ago.

Meredith tried to stay away from judging Admin and concentrated on following orders, including on the go-nowhere reports. She stayed sharp during her shift, trying to be ready for anything. She exercised regularly at a local gym and ran daily—when it fit into her schedule. She watched what she ate. She tried to get enough sleep, although sometimes the challenge of caseload and parenting made it impossible.

Her friend, Christy, had re-married and moved to Southern California. She didn't see her as often as she would have liked. Now, Tina had replaced her. She was as good a friend as she'd ever had—a straight shooter who didn't listen to excuses. She also had a wicked sense of humor. Sharp and intuitive, Tina found humor in the most unlikely places. The balance she struck between parenting and career was good for Meredith.

Tina and Meredith watched Henry launch himself from the top of a tube slide. Laughing all the way down, he landed in a heap in the sandy spot at the bottom. Seconds later, Davy piled on top of him. An elbow landed on a soft spot, and Henry howled in pain. Davy rolled off and stood wide-eyed at the drama he'd caused.

Tina walked over and righted her son. Checking for an injury, she found a red mark on Henry's cheek. "Oh, Henry. You'll be okay. You might even get a black eye from it." She picked him up, dusted off the sand, and stood him, pouting, in front of his buddy.

While Tina attended to the boys, Meredith's attention wandered. A chill ran down her spine. Something was wrong. Meredith knew it. She smelled it in the air. Felt it in the ground beneath her feet. At the start, it wasn't based on anything. Just instinct. But then instinct had saved her life a few times as a cop. Something was wrong.

Meredith turned a full circle to scope out her surroundings. A half-dozen other mothers had braved the cold to entertain their kids. And a father with two bundled-up little girls that looked like twins. They held her attention for a moment until movement behind them distracted her.

A thin, slump-shouldered man with blond curly hair stood leaning on a eucalyptus tree with his hands behind him. Twenty yards away, just past the tennis courts. He looked familiar. She straightened as she tried to recall where she'd seen him. In that second, he turned and left. A flash of something white wrapped on his right hand. A bandage. It was him, the guy she'd shot.

She watched him get into a newer black model Dodge muscle car. He fired up the engine, and the tailpipe blew out a white cloud of exhaust. The Dodge pulled onto G Street and turned left on Eleventh Street. With a roar of acceleration, he'd left only black exhaust. Too far to see the license plate.

He'd seen her glance and then left.

"Tina, did you see that guy?" She nodded in the direction.

Tina straightened and looked around. "What guy?"

He was gone. If Tina hadn't seen him, there was no point in pushing.

"Never mind." Meredith shook her head to clear out the heebee jeebees. "I guess the shooting freaked me out more than I thought," she said, as much to herself as to Tina.

Tina squinted at her, then turned and shouted at Henry. He was at the top of the slide getting into position to go down again. "Let Davy go first. You can land on him and give him a black eye." With a mischievous grin, she shrugged with false innocence.

Chapter Forty-Three

Sunday, March 11, Afternoon

THAT AFTERNOON, NICK GOT UP AT FIVE O'CLOCK. HE'D HAD A FULL day's sleep, a rarity. At the squeak of Nick's opening bedroom door, Davy ran down the hall. Meredith stirred the beef stew on the stove as the two Reyes men entered the kitchen.

"Smells good." Nick eyed the pot suspiciously.

"Don't get all wonky on me. Tina helped me make it."

Nick's smile broke through his reticence. "Well, that's okay, then." Meredith's cooking skills were legendary at the Sheriff's office, and not in a good way. Deputies' wives often made treats when someone on the staff got a promotion or had a baby. Meredith had given it up when she witnessed a K-9 walk away from one of her muffins. Nick did the cooking for the family.

"I decided now that I'm off and you're working; I'd try to learn some dishes I could make. Tina suggested this."

DINNER WENT WELL. Beef stew was a one-pot meal, not counting biscuits. Tina had written down the recipe as she put it together. Meredith was surprised at how easy it had been.

Nick pushed his chair away from the table and picked up his empty bowl. He shoved it under Meredith's nose and said, "You did a really good job on this, Mere. It was good."

Armed with a new enthusiasm, Meredith sat back to enjoy Davy stabbing cooked carrots and smushed potatoes. "I'll come up with something good tomorrow, too."

Still skeptical, Nick offered, "I'm working the next two nights, then off for three. I can still cook. We have enough for leftovers tomorrow, so you don't have to make anything."

"Okay. That will give me time to come up with a new idea for dinner."

Nick kissed the top of her head. "I'll do the dishes."

He gathered up all the plates while Meredith took Davy in for a bath. A half-hour later, their sweet-smelling toddler sat on Nick's lap in their living room while he read a story. Davy dropped off to sleep after ten minutes. Nick carried him to bed. Meredith followed and kissed her son's forehead. She made her way back to the living room and sank into the sofa. Nick followed with a yawn. "I'm going to take a shower."

"Before you go, I want to run something past you."

Nick stood, waiting.

She took a minute to collect her thoughts. "Today at the park, I thought I saw the shooter from Burton Avenue."

"What?"

"I know it sounds crazy. Blond curly hair, and he had the same build and height. He moved the same. On Burton, he was running. But today, he walked. It seemed the same stride."

"You can't ID this guy, can you?"

She shook her head. "He was a shadow. Then when he was on the fence, I only saw a profile. I couldn't even say what race he was."

He thought for a moment. "What's your gut tell you?"

"Same guy." She looked him in the eye. "He was definitely

watching me. When I made eye contact, he walked away. I think I saw a bandage around his right hand."

"I trust your hunches." Nick pulled up an ottoman and sat across from her. "Do you think it was a coincidence? An accident? Or something else?"

She took a long time to answer. "I don't buy into coincidences. That being said, it defies belief that he'd be at the same place I was, and at the same time."

"Yeah, what are the odds? Why would he be there?"

"I know. It's creepy, right?"

"What do you want to do?"

She sat back, slouching into the sofa. "First thing, I want to call Bennett and tell him. There's nothing he can do, but I want him to know." She pulled her work phone out of her pocket.

Nick nodded in approval. "And second?"

"I'd like to call Cav and see if he's free to entertain Davy and me for a night or two. I can always think so clearly up there." *Up there* were the hills west of Geyserville, an hour north of Petaluma. Raymond Cavanaugh owned a cattle ranch that sat in the vineyard-covered hills above the fog line. Their friend Cav had proven his dependability many times over. His family ranch had become a haven for Nick and Meredith.

Again, Nick nodded his approval. "I won't worry about you up there." He reached out and took her hand. "Don't sweat it. I won't starve while you're gone."

Stifling a smile, Meredith pulled out a pillow from behind and threw it at him.

Chapter Forty-Four

Monday, March 12, Morning

IT WAS NINE O'CLOCK ON MONDAY MORNING. THERE WAS LITTLE traffic to deal with driving north on Highway 101 the next day. Highway hypnosis threatened as Meredith replayed last night's phone conversation with Cav.

He'd been happy to hear from her, as always. "Sure, you can come up. You're just in time to help me stack hay."

"I'll be bringing Davy."

"Of course. Filomena will be here to watch him while you're working with me and Jake." Jake was Cav's grandson who was in the process of taking over the daily workings of the ranch. Cav was scheduled for knee-replacement surgery next month and was hustling to get ahead on the chores.

"That will work."

"Speaking of working, is Nick still on graveyards?"

"Yeah. For the next two nights."

"You're staying two nights, and he's working two nights." Cav's voice lowered. "What's going on, Meredith?"

"I was going to wait until I got up there and could tell you face-to-face." She sighed. "How about I give you a synopsis?"

"Uh-huh."

"During the execution of a warrant, I shot a man. I didn't kill him. He fled the scene." She took a deep breath. "I think I saw him yesterday when I took Davy to a local public park."

"You think? Or are you sure?"

She began to answer, but he spoke over her. "It doesn't matter. If you're worried, so am I. You're welcome to stay as long as you like."

Before saying goodbye, she promised to fill him in on all the details when she got there.

Glancing over her shoulder, she noted Davy's even breathing. He was still asleep in his car seat. He'd be a toddler tornado when they got to Cav's. Luckily, her friend had a couple of border collies, four barn cats at last count, a pair of milk goats, and a half-dozen chickens to keep Davy busy. He was too young to mess with the horses. That would come soon enough.

As per usual, Cav's cook and housekeeper, Filomena, would assume her son's care upon their arrival. At first, Meredith hadn't been sure about the woman. It didn't take long for the two to feel out their boundaries. They'd bonded over Davy in the way loving mothers do. Filomena had grown children of her own but no grand-babies yet. She loved kids, and Meredith appreciated how she cared for Davy.

In the first eighteen months since Filomena's arrival at the Cavanaugh Ranch, she'd proven herself quietly indispensable. She'd managed to mostly fill the empty role that Cav's wife, Shirley, had left when she succumbed to cancer three years before. Filomena did the chores and cooking, but kept Raymond Cavanaugh and his grandson, Jake, at a warmly professional distance.

Meredith was looking forward to seeing her friends again. Just after her arrival at the ranch, a hot cup of coffee at the kitchen table was the usual setting for her and Filomena to catch up. Fortified by Filomena's wonderful coffee and camaraderie, she'd seek out Cav and help with chores. Cav was usually in motion.

Basking in the warm anticipation of spending time at the Cavanaugh Ranch, she almost didn't see the black Dodge Charger in the rearview mirror.

Chapter Forty-Five

Monday, March 12, Morning

IT WAS TWO CARS BEHIND IN THE SAME LANE. HER FINGERS GRIPPED the steering wheel as she considered the possibilities. Was it the guy from McNear Park? How did he find her?

She had to find out if he was really following her. She tugged at her seat belt and scoffed at the thought of being chased by a modern muscle car. Her twelve-year-old Subaru was dependable but didn't have much in the way of speed. Mindful of her precious son in the back seat, she decided. She needed to know if the Dodge was following her.

On Highway 101, just past the Windsor town limits sign, she suddenly veered off to the Shiloh Road exit. The exit roadway was long and clear of trees, so she'd be able to tell if the Dodge trailed her.

The black sedan changed lanes and swerved onto the exit roadway.

Meredith slowed at the signal—an orange caution. She stood on the accelerator, blowing through the light that had just changed to red. At a left turn over the overpass, she recalled a grove of trees around a gas station a block or two down the road where she used to meet other deputies for information exchanges.

Traffic stopped the Dodge. She doubted a red light would make a difference to a man who'd try to shoot a cop. With her attention bouncing from the street before her to the street behind her, she found the gas station driveway. She swung in, inadvertently catching the curb with her rear tire.

Davy woke up at the jarring motion, protesting with grunts and fussing.

"Don't worry, sweetheart." Meredith drove to the rear of the station, hiding the Subaru so she could see if the Dodge drove past. "I'm just playing a little game. I'm sorry I woke you up."

He sneezed and wiped his nose with a sleeve, then settled back in the car seat.

Ten long seconds later, the Dodge drove the speed limit past the station, the driver's head on a swivel. Was it the guy she shot? Could be. She resisted the urge to catch up so she could be sure. Because she couldn't endanger Davy, she'd have to evade.

He continued westbound on the now one-lane Shiloh Road.

She decided to wait for a while to see if the Dodge had returned. Ten minutes later, it did. He wasn't driving the speed limit now. He headed eastbound to Highway 101, well over the speed limit. He drove up on the Volkswagen van's bumper in front of him, almost making contact. She heard a horn and couldn't swear to it but suspected it was the Dodge driver who was furious at losing her. The Dodge swerved into the southbound 101 onramp and sped up.

When he was out of sight, Meredith leaned back in the driver's seat and released the breath she hadn't known she was holding. The jerk was definitely following her. She unclenched her fist and stared at her hand. It was shaking. "Not today, fucker," she whispered.

She had to get back on the road. Cav's place was certainly the safest place for Davy and her, for now.

"Not today, fucker," Davy said.

Chapter Forty-Six

Monday, March 12, 10:00 AM

Traffic on Highway 101 slackened the farther north Meredith drove. After the last Healdsburg exit, there were fewer cars on the four-lane road. She was the only vehicle going in her direction. Still, she kept an eye on the rear-view mirror, just in case.

Davy slept like a baby. Meredith expected it. He was one of those kids who fell asleep in a car after pulling out of the driveway. She was grateful that he was such a terrific child. With deep brown eyes like his father's, he listened. Sometimes she wondered if he understood much more than his three-year-old vocabulary would allow him to articulate. He obeyed when she or Nick told him to do something. Or not to. He tried to get along with others but wasn't above a shove or punch when he felt wronged. She and Nick were working on a compromise that he could use without being a pushover.

She'd never believed being a parent was easy. She'd seen the hardships, no, lived the hardships that her mother went through after her father abandoned the family for another woman. She'd learned from the mistakes of her first marriage. She'd married Richard Taylor because of chemistry. She believed physical attraction would be enough to hold a relationship together. It hadn't been. Richard had grown resentful of Meredith's independence, her long hours on graveyard patrol, and an unpredictable schedule that interfered with his social plans. It hadn't taken long before he began to work late, and stay over in San Francisco, where he worked as an architect. It wasn't until after his murder that she found out how he had strayed. She had put off starting a family because of her career. Later, she'd considered that luck.

But she and Nick were another matter. Twice he'd been her mentor and work partner. Now he was her life partner. Though they didn't always agree, they could talk over their differences. Parenting with Nick was fulfilling.

She glanced over her shoulder at their son asleep in his car seat, a feeling of tenderness welling up inside her. Her son. The words still surprised her sometimes as much as the fact.

Behind him, in the rear window, a car approached at high speed.

It was the Dodge.

"Crap," she whispered. She'd almost let him sneak up on her. Any tenderness she'd felt evaporated and, in its place, grew a raging need to protect her son. Her whole professional life had prepared her for this, to stand and defend. Fighting the urge, she concluded that again, for now, evasion was the answer. She wouldn't stop and face down this guy. She wouldn't endanger Davy.

In the fast lane, Meredith stood on the accelerator of her little Subaru, wringing every bit of speed out of the engine. She began to look for highway exits to take. Dry Creek Road? No, too much traffic for her to maneuver effectively. And went into downtown Healdsburg. Farther on, Lytton Springs Road exit turned into Dry Creek Road, which to the north would lead to Lake Sonoma. If she turned south, wineries and tourists enjoying the area's bucolic charm littered the roads. No, she'd stay on 101. What about the next exit, Geyserville? The offramp and onramps were tricky, and she might be able to slip behind either Trione Winery or Francis Ford Coppola Winery. Both had substantial grounds where she could hide her car.

She heard the rumble of the Dodge's engine as it drove closer. It was difficult to gauge its distance and speed from her rear-view mirror, but he was gaining on her. Up ahead was Lytton Springs Road exit. She re-evaluated the decision not to take it but stayed in the fast lane.

These thoughts shot through her mind like lightning, faster than it takes to say: Maybe she could double back at the next exit and make it to Healdsburg Police Department. It was the only law enforcement office from here to Ukiah in Mendocino County, almost an hour away. She searched her memory for Healdsburg PD's location, then dismissed it. Too dangerous to go into town.

Seconds later, the Dodge closed the half-mile she'd gained. He was a car length behind the Subaru. He changed lanes and pulled to the right alongside them. She risked a sideways glance at the driver. He was a white male, with short-cropped curly blond hair, and she guessed, in his mid-forties. Dressed in a dark turtleneck, his thin lips gave neither frown nor smile at his success. A bandage covered his right hand. She was certain he was the guy she'd shot on Burton Avenue.

Suddenly, the Dodge slammed into the Subaru, and the sound of metal crushing metal shocked her even though she'd prepared herself for an aggressive move. The Dodge had hit the passenger side front. The Subaru swerved, and pushed into the center shoulder. Dropping speed, she wrestled the steering wheel back. Furious that he'd endanger her son, she slowed even more.

Davy sputtered, then wailed at his rude awakening.

"Hold on, Davy," she said, knowing it would reassure her more than her crying son.

The Dodge backed off, then pulled up again. Meredith knew what was coming this time. Without taking the time to look for traffic behind her, she dropped behind him and veered to the right and off the highway. Running over a mile marker, she steered the Subaru over the rugged sloping grass that separated 101 from Lytton Springs Road exit. The exit she'd just passed.

By the time the driver of the Dodge realized what she'd done, he was crossing on an overpass and parallel to a serious-looking guard rail. He couldn't follow.

To keep out of his sight, Meredith turned left under the underpass. From there, it was a short quarter mile up Lytton Springs Road to tree cover. She sped up the two-lane grade to the trees, only once daring a glance to see if the Dodge followed. It hadn't.

Seeing a turn-off for an industrial area, she pulled in and parked behind the first building she found, an aluminum storage shed. She took a deep breath and looked around. No one followed. Davy was whimpering in his car seat, upset by the jolting movement of the car. She got out, opened his door, and unhooked his seatbelts. She gathered him in her arms and in her best motherly voice, offered comforting words. She stroked his silky hair.

It didn't take long to calm him. She put him down and let him walk around the car with her while she inspected the damage to the Subaru. The wheel well and across both doors on the passenger side caved in to a depth of six inches. But it was still drivable.

Meredith secured Davy into his car seat again. Behind the wheel, she decided to continue up Lytton Springs and take the Dry Creek Road turn-off. It would mean a longer trip, but surely a safer one.

"See eehees?" Davy had morphed the word horse into the sound they make.

She smiled as she answered, "Yes, see eehees."

"Not today fucker." Davy's innocent voice repeated Meredith's premature celebration from Shiloh Road.

Chapter Forty-Seven

Monday, March 12, 11:00 AM

MEREDITH'S SUBARU PLODDED UP THE GRAVEL ROAD TO THE HEART
of the 700-acre property, the ranch house. Raymond Cavanaugh built
it in the early 1970s after his return from Vietnam for his wife,
Shirley, and their two children. Shirley passed away three years ago,
and their grandson, Jake, had come to live with Cav. The home was a
ranch-style favored in the suburbs and kept immaculately tidy. The
driveway forked at the house. The other branch wound around past
the cabin where Filomena lived, then on to the barn, corral, and a trio
of sheds.

TEN MINUTES AFTER HER ARRIVAL, Meredith had told her story to the
Cavanaughs and Filomena. Cav's gravelly voice cut through the
tension in the Cavanaugh kitchen. "You could've been killed!"
Filomena held Davy on her hip and listened, wide-eyed. Jake stood
like a statue. His knuckles whitened from their grip on the back of
his grandfather's chair.

Meredith lifted the coffee mug to her lips and took a sip. "Don't I know it."

Cav looked away in anger. Meredith knew he kept his opinion to himself because of Davy. The older man would normally use plenty of cussing to describe his reactions.

Jake took a step toward Davy and reached out for the baby's pudgy hand. "This guy was in danger, too." Davy grabbed onto Jake and said his name, "Jake, Jake, Jake." The freckled and red-haired young man reached out and took Davy from Filomena's grasp. He was tall and wiry like his grandfather and just as devoted to the three-year-old. Davy was a squirming armful after sleeping most of the way up to the ranch. But his sweet smile and easy disposition won over the Cavanaughs. Nick, Meredith, and Davy were family.

Jake splayed his work-hardened hand over Davy's shoulders and dropped him, catching him just before he would hit the floor. Davy squealed and yelled, "More." Jake did it again and again. The child's squeals filled the quiet as the adults stayed silent.

Finally, Jake asked Davy if he wanted to see the chickens. On the ground, Davy jumped, repeating, "Chickens, chickens, chickens." He led Jake outside.

Meredith covered her coffee mug when Filomena offered a refill. "I'm tense enough, thanks."

Cav stood, stretching. "I've got to move some hay into the shed." He needed time to digest this news. He eyed Meredith, squinting for emphasis. "Should give you time enough to fill Nick in."

Filomena said something about laundry, and suddenly Meredith found herself alone with her phone. She touched the icon for her husband's cell.

"Hey, you. You at Cav's?"

"Yeah."

"What? What happened."

He could tell from the tiniest inflection of her voice that something was wrong. Long ago, she abandoned any notion of protecting him from the truth. In some matters, he knew her better than she knew herself. They spoke a language unique to them, and had seen the other in the worst situations, and the best. They spoke cop-to-cop often, but the husband-wife relationship influenced all their conversations. "Some guy in a big Dodge sedan followed me and then sideswiped my car."

"Oh my God. Are you all right? Davy?"

"We're fine. Safe at Cav's."

Nick took a deep breath. "Do you know who it was?"

"I'm not 100 percent sure." She had to lay it out for him. No use lessening the import of the incident. "I believe it was the guy I shot on Burton. Same guy from McNear Park. He had a bandage around his hand. I can't ID the shooter for sure, but his build and profile are the same."

"Jesus," he sighed. "Is Davy freaked out?"

"When the other car hit us, he was shaken up. He's settling down now, thanks to Jake and Cav. Jake has him outside checking out the chickens." A note of normalcy might reassure him. "I inadvertently taught him a bad word."

"Jesus. That's the least of your problems. You must've been stressed." Meredith didn't usually cuss.

"I was worried about Davy."

Nick grunted. "You kept him safe, Mere."

"It took every ounce of energy I had not to chase him down."

"You did the right thing." Nick breathed into the phone betraying his own anxiety over the incident. "Did you get a police report yet?"

"No. I'll stop by the CHP office on my way home. I hate to make them send a unit all the way out here."

"Mere, don't minimize this. This is ADW." Assault with a Deadly Weapon was a felony. "Call CHP and meet the beat officer somewhere convenient, but don't wait for two days. Do it now."

"I'm going to call Bennett and tell him."

"Meredith. Do it, but he'll tell you the same thing. Meet an officer in Geyserville if you don't want to make him or her drive all the way up to the ranch. Your evidence is mobile."

She saw his reasoning. This would give the bad guy a two-day advantage. Anything could happen before she drove home. "Okay. I'll call CHP now, then Bennett."

"Good. I'm going to get someone to fill the next two shifts. I want to be with you and Davy."

"Great. I'm glad to hear it." She wouldn't have asked him to be with her. She knew she could manage whatever came up, but having Nick beside her would make it easier. "Let me know when you'll be up here."

"Will do. I love you. Hug my boy for me."

"I love you, too."

"And Mere. Take pictures of the damage before you leave."

Chapter Forty-Eight

Monday, March 12, 12:30 PM

"DID YOU FLIP HIM OFF OR DO ANYTHING THAT MIGHT PROVOKE him?" Sergeant Bennett wasn't so sure about Meredith's complaint. "It could've been a road rage deal, Meredith."

"It wasn't, sarge. I'm telling you. This guy followed me for miles. He singled me out. Then he pulled up alongside me and rammed into my car."

"You must've gotten a good look at him."

"The driver? Yes. I can ID him, but I can't say, for sure, that he was the guy who was going to shoot you on Burton."

Bennett paused. "Okay. I'll get back to you. Soon. I have to run this up the chain."

"Fine," Meredith replied. "But I called CHP now to get a collision report. I suspect they'll call it ADW and shoot the whole mess to you. It is a violent crime, after all." The sheriff held jurisdiction on Sonoma County highways for criminal matters. Traffic incidents fell to the California Highway Patrol. "But the why is what puzzles me."

"Good question, Meredith. Revenge for shooting him?"

"How could he find out I was the shooter? I mean, it just happened."

"No idea. But we'll handle this ourselves, after CHP takes a report." He cleared his throat. "The fingerprints on the gun your guy had belong to a career criminal from Russia, Mikhail Fedorov. He's not a big player but looks dangerous anyway. These guys don't use the same rulebook that we do."

"Russia? What could that mean? Is he a gangster?"

"Interpol hasn't associated him with an organized group or gang. He may be just an entrepreneur. Or a career criminal looking to build an empire here in the U.S."

"Why would a career criminal come after me? He must know how much trouble he could get in if he..." She couldn't finish the sentence, the thought too jarring. More for Davy's safety than hers.

"Like I said, they use a different playbook."

She asked again, "Revenge? For shooting him?" Her voice rose an octave with surprise. "I didn't even know if I hit him or not."

"Well, now we're pretty sure." He sounded disgusted. "But it's irrelevant, apparently."

She'd planned to stay two nights here with Nick, but this changed it. "I'll stay here overnight, then come back. How soon will they be done with the investigation?"

"The report's sitting on the sheriff's desk. He just has to sign off on their findings."

"Which are?"

"A righteous shoot, Meredith. One of the uniforms had his body cam on and filmed the whole shoot with you and the Russian. It couldn't be anything else."

"A body camera wouldn't have shown your position."

"All the supplemental reports from the deputies at that location verified my location in relation to you."

Meredith fought the rising blossom of irritation. "You're picking at details that are easily explained. All I had to do was tell them where I was. I used the overhead map and showed them the position of the three of us."

"Okay then." Her pulse quickened. "When can I come back to work?"

Bennett considered her question. "In view of what happened to you today, why don't you come in...in three days? That'll be Thursday."

"What will happen in those three days? Are you going to be looking for this Russian guy?" She hated waiting around for others to do the work she felt she should be doing. The department would prohibit her from participating in the ADW investigation because she was the victim. Even though it was probably related, it wouldn't change her standing in the homicide case once she got back to work.

"We've already got a BOL out on him for the attempted shooting. We just added a booking photo from some European country. Interpol sent it. We'll ramp up our search. I'll keep you posted."

"Send me the photo, and Nick, too. He'll be coming up here."

"Sure. Where will you be? At home or the ranch?" Anyone close to Nick and Meredith knew they spent time at the Cavanaugh Ranch.

"The ranch for now, overnight. I'll let you know when I'm back at home."

They disconnected, and Meredith sighed. The Cavanaugh's Ranch was the safest place for Davy and her. But there was work to do. Important work.

She rooted around in her backpack and found the work gloves she carried for her ranch trips. She'd help Cav move the hay into the shed. She could fill him in on what was going on while they worked.

Jake had handed Davy to Filomena. She was soon chasing him, running after chickens. Jake joined his grandfather, moving bales of hay. Meredith grabbed a pair of hay hooks and followed Cav's direction. After they stacked the bales, the three of them took a break before attending to the other chores. They sat on the hay bales while she filled them in. When she finished speaking, Jake spoke up, his eyes smiling. "Stay here as long as you need."

Chapter Forty-Nine

Monday, March 12, 12:30 PM

MICHAEL GLANCED AROUND THE INSIDE OF THE NEW HOUSE ON Curtis Drive in Penngrove, a rural hamlet between Petaluma and Rohnert Park. He'd picked the place for its seclusion. Two garages were a plus, especially now when he had to hide the Dodge. The property was a half-acre plot on a quiet country cul de sac with a vineyard on one side and the nearest neighbor half a block away. Keeping his inquiries low profile, he'd found just the right landlord to rent from. He paid over the market price, but the guy guaranteed privacy. No surprise visits. He might even pay rent on this place if it works out as well as he hoped. The house itself was a spacious three bedrooms and two baths, with a pair of outbuildings for storage—or, if needed, punishment. His women didn't often act up, though. Michael took pains to cultivate his intimidation factor.

Sofia and Yevgeny had taken the four girls who'd been working during the raid and moved them here. He had to admit that Sofia was accomplished at moving people and getting a home set up in record time. Starting over was a pricey venture, as he had to outfit the girls and the house. They got bare minimum furnishings as always. These weren't homes to live in; they were hostel-style accommodations. No one except Sofia would be there for any length of time. These women were transitory as they believed they were working to send their wages to their families. In reality, they were only there until Michael decided which path they should take—cleaning as they were doing or prostitution. Because there was so much money at stake, he moved carefully to ensure each woman saw how dangerous it was to leave him or report him to the authorities.

Efficient or not, Sofia was growing into a pest. After she got Esme corralled, he'd decide how to deal with her.

Chapter Fifty

Monday, March 12, 1:00 PM

"PLEASE STAY." SOFIA WHIMPERED, PAWING MICHAEL'S CHEST. She'd known him as Michael but had heard someone call him Mikhail on a phone call. She didn't care what they called him. She needed him. She wanted him. She was so glad he returned to her. He'd come into her life over a year ago when he'd found her at the airport. Her dirtbag companion had left her penniless and without a ticket to anywhere. She'd been sitting in the baggage terminal at San Francisco Airport, crying because she had nowhere to go. Michael had rescued her, charming her with money, a living space, and a job —of sorts.

He grabbed her forearms and shoved her away. "I need your car. Mine's too hot right now."

She went to the hall table, and her fingers swept a shallow plastic bowl. He heard the clink of the keys against the bowl. She held them out and leaned toward him. He reached for the keys, and she snatched them away. "Not until you promise to come back tonight. The girls will be gone. I'll be all alone." She swept the keys behind her back and pressed her body against his, shifting to avoid bumping against his sheathed pocketknife. "I get so lonely here at night."

Michael reached around her. He grabbed her wrist, pried her fingers apart, and took the keys. Even with an injured hand, he was strong. She hadn't believed the story that he'd cut himself.

"Ow." Sofia danced in pain, holding her wrist. "You hurt me."

His smile was the thin-lipped expression that he saved for when he tried to control his anger. "I don't have time for this. Is your car in the garage?"

Sofia nodded, holding her wrist.

"Go. Move it out so I can park mine in its place. I'm taking your car." He handed the keys back.

She took them, her cheeks burning with humiliation. Her emotions ran up and down around Michael, extreme need for a moment, and shame at how he chose to treat her. But he gave her things, not money, a credit card. Then he'd often buy her jewelry, especially after he'd hit her, and new clothes whenever she wanted. All the fine cosmetics she could use. He liked it when she dolled herself up for him.

"Keep the garage door closed when my car is in. I don't want anyone seeing the Dodge for now."

At the front door, she paused. She blinked, trying to look appealing. She straightened to her five-foot-three height. Her figure bordered on voluptuous, in Michael's words. Chubby in hers. "Will you come back tonight?"

"I don't know. I have business. Those idiots Bernardo and Isaac got themselves killed, so now I have double the work."

"Can't you hire someone?"

"No." He huffed his answer. "Bernardo and Isaac had special skills. They're not easily replaced."

"I can help." She put her hand on his chest again, rubbing her breasts up against him. "I have special skills, too."

"You foolish bitch." His Baltic accent revealed his anger.

She was sorry she'd brought him to this point, but she wanted him to stay. She stepped away, thinking the way to his heart was to make herself indispensable. "You think you can find this girl, Esme?

She could be anywhere." Esme was a child, nowhere near as enticing as she. Sofia tried again. "You don't need her. She's not even grown."

"That's exactly why I want her." His words cut into her heart. "She's a virgin. She'll bring a fortune at a sale."

Sofia's mood was also darkening. "If she's so important, I can help. She trusts me. I'll reach out to her. I can arrange to meet her somewhere, and you can take her."

"She's not the only mess I have to untangle. Wait for my word to do what you suggest. Until then, mind your own business."

Her voice was soft as she turned to face him. "You *are* my business."

Michael's face darkened with the look of thunder in his eyes. "Go," he shouted.

Chapter Fifty-One

Monday, March 12, 1:30 PM

MICHAEL SAT BEHIND THE WHEEL OF SOFIA'S COROLLA, THINKING about that bitch cop. He intended to do her like she had almost killed him, but he needed to figure out how. His small empire and grand schemes were at risk because of her. She'd almost killed him. Now she was snooping around Esme.

Finding the girl would be challenging, but she'd be worth it. She was a little too tall to give the illusion of a child yet a budding beauty, not yet in full flower. As a virgin, he could auction her off for a huge chunk of cash. She'd be worth all this hassle. Even if he decided to do an online auction like Sofia suggested, he'd have to fly her and an escort to wherever the buyer chose to meet her. He'd most likely do it himself. The cash outlay for transportation wouldn't put a dent in his profit.

He'd already put the word out on the street that he was looking for Esme. They'd check her home with the aunt in Rohnert Park and the school. No doubt her mother would be nearby. Teresa wasn't a fool about how beautiful her daughter was. Michael believed she planned to sell Esme herself to fuel her drug addiction. But Teresa was a minor problem, and he could manage her easily with whatever street drug she favored. That was the trick, making a death look accidental. Everyone would accept Teresa's overdose.

The cop was another matter.

No doubt she'd already reported the collision attempt in Healdsburg, so repeating that method was out. The next attempt would have to appear accidental. If he ambushed her, every cop in California would be looking for him. He couldn't have that.

Figuring out how to deal with the cop would take some imagination. His brothers had told him creativity was not one of his strengths. He'd have to find her and come up with something to suit the situation. Like, if he found her hiking, he'd push her off a cliff. No one would know it wasn't some crazy accident.

But how to arrange such a thing? He thought of some variations, like if he found her at the park as he had earlier, or at home. Maybe coming home from work, a good distance from the sheriff's office. Walking to her car in a supermarket parking lot. All this takes time. He was confident there would be an opportunity. He just had to be ready to take advantage of it.

Chapter Fifty-Two

Monday, March 12, 2:30 PM

NICK ARRIVED AT THE CAVANAUGH RANCH SHORTLY AFTER Meredith returned from meeting the CHP officer in Geyserville. The officer took a report and, as Meredith had told Bennett, promised his office would forward it to the sheriff's office.

She parked in the side driveway, and Nick drove in behind her. They got out of their cars and met in a tight embrace. Nick pulled away first and looked at her. "Are you sure you're all right?"

"Yeah. I'm good. Really."

He turned to inspect the damage to the Subaru. "Holy shit, Meredith." Eyes wide, he looked at his wife. "That's worse than I imagined. Jesus. You could've been hurt."

She grabbed her backpack from the passenger seat and straightened. "But I wasn't. It was only through superior driving skills that I managed to avoid a catastrophe." She flashed a cockeyed grin that told him she was okay. Davy was okay.

Nick shook his head at her resilience and glanced around. "Where's my boy?"

"He's probably rounding up sheep or chickens with the other cowboys."

"He'll sleep well tonight." Nick grabbed a gym bag from his car.

"For sure," she said, as they walked to the house.

"I'll send pictures to you," Meredith said. "You'll be doing the insurance claim, anyway, won't you?"

He shrugged as they announced themselves at the front door.

Filomena met them with an eager smile. "Welcome, Mister Nick. The boys are in the big barn giving Davy roping lessons."

"Roping lessons?" Nick lifted an eyebrow.

Filomena shrugged. "Davy-sized."

After Nick tossed his bag in the guest bedroom, he and Meredith walked hand-in-hand to the corral attached to the big barn. The barn was an acre away, far enough that flies from the livestock wouldn't make it to the house.

Cav and his grandson had set up a hay bale with a dummy steer head in the middle of the dusty corral. Squatting to his level, Jake had a grip on Davy's fist. He swung a rope over their heads while the lasso took the shape of a flat circle. Jake pushed the boy's arm in a loop and said, "Let go." The rope flew ten feet and fell onto one horn of the plastic steer's head.

Cav and Jake exclaimed simultaneously, "Way to go, Davy."

Davy jumped and clapped. "Way to go."

Meredith's heart swelled at the scene. All the men she loved in the world were right here. They were doing what they most wanted to do—spend time with each other. Jake picked up Davy by the arms and swung him like a lariat. Cav and Nick laughed along with Davy's exuberant squeals. This was a dream she could never have imagined, but it was real.

"Are you all ready for an early dinner?" Filomena stood leaning on the corral gate. "Jake said he wanted to take you on an evening ride. The weather should be perfect. No wind tonight."

"Davy and I are in," Meredith shouted. Cav grunted his assent, but Nick's grin twisted into a grimace, not so sure.

Nick wasn't an equestrian, but he could stay in the saddle,

relying on his impeccable balance. Meredith was confident that he'd join in because he wanted to be with them. He'd go to be with the family, embarrassed to be a city slicker.

Chapter Fifty-Three

Tuesday, March 13, 10:00 AM

"I TOLD YOU, NO DRUGS." IT ONLY TOOK FIVE DAYS FOR THE TWO women to face off in the living room of the Pacheco home.

"It's methadone, Almita." Teresa's hand shook as she reached for the pill bottle. She had to have them. But Almita held it in a fist out of reach.

"I know what it is. It's the road to your ruin."

Teresa fought the urge to grab the medication and run. She would have except there was Esme to consider. "The doctor prescribed it for me."

"You're better off without them." Almita dropped the bottle into a pocket in her apron and sniffed. "So is your daughter."

Teresa's spine straightened as she scrutinized the older woman. "Almita. I need those pills."

Almita turned toward the kitchen, the discussion over. Teresa dived toward her, reaching for the pocket. She grabbed the pill bottle. Scrambling to avoid hurting Almita, she slipped and fell against the wall. Her elbow hurt, but she'd manage.

"You promised, Teresa." The sadness in Almita's eyes almost stopped her. "For your daughter."

"This *is* for my girl." Her nervous system twitched her mouth and hands. Tears popped out. "I must keep straight. This stuff helps me."

Almita's eyes narrowed. Where once Teresa saw sadness, now she saw anger. "You have your own agenda. I can see it. You still act like an addict. This isn't about your daughter's welfare. It's something else." Teresa saw the gears grinding behind her sister-in-law's eyes, trying to fathom Teresa's plan. Almita would never figure it out, and she wouldn't tell her.

"How are you going to live? You won't work. You have nothing to sell." Almita squinted as a new reality dawned on her. "*Mentirosa.*" Almita's body went rigid with rage. *Liar.* "You want Esme for what you can get out of her. How far must you fall for this to be your answer? You're going to sell your daughter to men, aren't you? To get money for drugs."

Stunned that she'd guessed correctly, Teresa righted herself and gripped the pill bottle. "I don't need you. Esme doesn't need you, either. I'll get her to come to me."

As she fled the apartment, Teresa heard Almita sob.

Chapter Fifty-Four

Tuesday, March 13, 10:30 AM

MEREDITH WAS ALWAYS A LITTLE SAD WHEN SHE DROVE AWAY FROM the Cavanaugh Ranch. It was where she found the peace that she sought for so many years. She mulled over yesterday's evening ride —an easy one, walking only, because of Nick and Davy. The late afternoon sun hung on a little longer these days. Spring equinox was a week away, but Meredith already felt the season changing.

Buckeye trees budded out and would soon bloom spiky white flowers. Oaks were gaining a deep green color from more daylight hours. Wild mustard sprung up in the meadows where sheep hadn't grazed. Conversation was as easy as the trail. Jake kept it graded for stock feedings. At Jack Rabbit point, they paused in silence and watched the sun lowering toward the hills. Even Davy was still for the moment. Meredith marveled that she could be out on the land and far away from trouble. She wanted to stay here forever.

They turned back, making the last of the trip in the dusk. Back at the barn, Filomena took Davy for a bath while Meredith helped Jake and Cav groom the horses. Nick put the tack away, and by nightfall, they all were ready for the adult beverage of their choice. Beer for the men and a glass of red wine for Meredith. Filomena passed. She was exhausted from bathing Davy. This was an early-to-bed crew because the Cavanaughs rose before dawn to feed and water their stock.

RIGHT NOW, as she made her way down to the Dry Creek Valley floor, her car was empty, devoid of toddler fusses and snores. Nick took their son in his truck to spend time with him. Meredith snorted at the joke: Davy always fell asleep once the car was in motion.

Once on Canyon Road, headed to Highway 101, she decided to try cell service. At Cav's, it was spotty at best. She pulled onto the shoulder of the road and powered on her phone. She'd installed a dash holder so she could see it without fumbling around. She scrolled through a half dozen unimportant texts and emails and found Bennett had sent the photo of Michael Fedorov. She suppressed a shiver as she viewed it. Then she went to voicemails.

Almita Esparza Pacheco left a message an hour ago. With a growing dread, Meredith played the message. In her fractured English, Almita said, "Teresa very mad and leave. She will sell her daughter for drugs."

Meredith's first thought was to have Nick call Almita to get more information. Then she realized this was still Deb's case.

So, the right thing to do was to have Nick call her to explain she should call Deb Lang. Meredith couldn't help. She touched the icon for Nick's phone.

"Hey. Meet me at the red barn at the Highway 128 offramp at Geyserville. I need your translation skills."

THREE MINUTES LATER, both vehicles parked on the gravel lot in front of the barn. They stood outside, leaning on the hood of his Chevrolet truck, where they both kept an eye on their sleeping son. Meredith gave Nick a synopsis of Almita's message. Meredith called Almita and put the call on speaker phone.

The woman sounded relieved at hearing Meredith's voice. She launched into a Spanish tirade that Meredith had to stop. "*Espera, señora. Espera.*" Her Spanish was terrible but it would do for an introduction. "*Aqui esta mí esposo*, Nick. *El habla español* and *puede explicar…*" *This is my husband, Nick. He speaks Spanish and can explain…*what? How do I tell her I can't help?

Luckily, Nick had a solid grasp of the situation. Meredith followed along.

Almita: "*I found drugs on Teresa. I got angry, and we argued. She's going to take Esme and…I suspect she plans to sell her to men for drug money. Oh my God. What can I do?*"

Nick: "*You need to call Deb Lang at the police department…*"

Almita: "*I tried already. She's not there today. But I really think she didn't want my phone calls. Esme doesn't trust her. Neither do I.*"

Nick: "*Did you ask for another detective?*"

Almita: "*I only left a voicemail, and I don't know if they understand my English. It's not so good. What can I do?*"

Nick: "*Where is Esme now?*"

Almita: "*She's at school. I called the office and told them to hold her there until I could pick her up. I told them not to let her go with her mother.*"

Nick: "*What do you want Meredith to do?*"

Almita: "*I don't know. I don't believe she's safe here.*"

Meredith saw the mounting outrage in Nick's posture. His final translation went like this: "*Call the school back. Tell them to release Esme to Meredith. She will show them credentials. We will contact Child Protective Services and find a safe place for Esme until we find Teresa. We can send Teresa back to jail when we catch her.*" He tapped the phone to end the connection. To Meredith, he said, "Let's get on the road before something bad happens."

Chapter Fifty-Five

Tuesday, March 13, 11:30 AM

ALMITA HAD INSISTED THEY STOP AT HER APARTMENT TO PICK UP A bag with Esme's clothes. Meredith pulled up on the street in front of the apartment house with Nick behind her. Nick carried Davy up the three flights of stairs. There was no alternative to bringing him with them. Meredith would've preferred to come alone so as not to intimidate Almita. But Nick had become invested in this case now. The conversation translated over the hood of his truck was now more than just language. It was backstory, what was really going on behind what would've been a simple runaway report. Nick finally saw the holes in this story. How it was so much more than the original case appeared. Nick's Spanish would make certain that the law was observed and not misunderstood. She needed his help with Almita.

Almita answered the door in her standard outfit, a wrinkled housedress covered by an apron. A smile was absent in her greeting, her face lined with tension. She waved a hand for them to come in. Her face softened when she saw Davy in Nick's arms. She touched his cheek with the back of her index finger when Nick introduced them. Then she pulled her hand to her chest and with sad eyes, waited for their questions.

Meredith stood beside Nick after introductions. In Spanish, Nick asked the question that Meredith needed answers to. "Why do you think Esme is in danger? Is it only from Teresa, or is there someone else, too?"

Almita motioned for them to follow her. At a window, she pulled the vertical blinds aside an inch. "You see?"

Meredith looked first. Several cars were parked on the street around the corner from theirs. "I see four, no, five cars."

Almita spoke so fast that Meredith couldn't keep up. Nick moved to stand beside the woman and followed her finger, pointing out the window. "She says the light blue Toyota, which looks like a Corolla, has been there for hours. When she took the garbage down to the dumpster, she saw a man inside. She thinks he's waiting for Esme to come home from school."

"He could be waiting for someone else. How long has he been there?"

Almita answered Nick's question. "All morning. He got out one time and walked around the car. I think he's still behind the wheel."

"Can you describe him?" Nick was doing what he does, running with the investigation. Meredith was happy to have him with her now. Davy was quiet, watching the adults talking, and she suspected, feeling their tension.

Almita pinched her chin in a thoughtful gesture as she recalled what she'd seen. "A white man, pasty-looking, with blond curly hair. He was thin, hunched shoulders." She slumped over to illustrate her account.

Nick glanced at Meredith, who watched Almita's pantomime and knew his wife was etching the man's features in her mind. They had always worked like two halves of a whole. They knew the other's thoughts. She pulled out her phone and scrolled to Michael Fedorov's photo.

Nick asked Almita, "Is this the man?"

Almita stepped back in surprise. "Yes, yes. That's the man."

"Fedorov," Meredith said to Nick.

They moved back into the living area of the apartment. Nick asked Almita, "Have you called the school?"

"Yes. They said the police officer must show her identification to take her."

Nick, still cradling his son, reached out to Almita's arm. "Meredith is very dependable. You can be sure that she will do everything she can to keep her safe. I will also."

Almita's gaze dropped to the floor. For a moment, Meredith thought she'd burst out crying. "She's had too much trouble in her young life. Everywhere she turns, someone's out to get her for their own purposes, even her own mother."

Chapter Fifty-Six

Tuesday, March 13, 12:00 PM

AT THEIR CARS, NICK STRAPPED DAVY INTO HIS CAR SEAT. Meredith leaned in and kissed her little boy on the cheek. He was busy making motor noises for a Hot Wheels Mustang coursing down the side of his car seat. Then, facing each other at her dented Subaru, Nick said, "I don't mind telling you that guy in the Toyota spooks me. I've got to wonder what he's doing there for hours on end."

Meredith had the same concern. "I'll get the license plate when I leave."

"No, don't drive past him. It's looking like he's the same guy who tried to run you off the road. He'd recognize the Subaru, and that could put you at risk. I'll do it. He won't recognize the truck."

"Good idea. Thanks." Relieved he'd volunteered, she said, "I'll go to the middle school for Esme. I hope the school has contacted CPS. If you can call DPS and let them know Fedorov is here, we might be able to cut Esme's risk factor in half. And you can get Davy home."

He nodded and leaned into her. His lips grazed hers in a delicate caress. From inside the truck, she could hear their son making motor noises. She pulled away and smiled, thinking how she'd gotten the best of everything at this point in her life. She felt for Esme, having all this adult crap dumped on her at such an early age. No kid should have to deal with the trauma that surrounded this young girl.

Her cell phone rang as Nick walked back to his truck. The display on her phone read, County of Sonoma. Meredith answered while Nick pulled away from the curb and drove past her, heading for the Toyota.

She answered. "Meredith Ryan."

"Miz Ryan? I'm Oscar Nelson from County Child Protective Services. I got your name and contact information from Almita Pacheco about Esme Vela Alfaro."

"Yes. I'm on my way to Lawrence Jones Middle School to pick her up."

"Good. My Spanish isn't as good as it could be. Do you know what the problem is?"

"In a nutshell, Esme has been caught between a neighbor who traffics women into prostitution or domestic service and her drug-addicted mother who is trying to sell her to the highest bidder."

Nelson didn't miss a beat. Meredith could imagine the horror stories he'd seen and heard. "Okay, I got most of it right. What is the imminent danger? The mother?"

"Both the mother *and* the neighbor. I just left the aunt's home, and there was a man in a car that the aunt swears is watching for Esme to come home from school. She's identified him as the neighbor, Michael Fedorov. We've ascertained he is a low-level Russian criminal. He seems to be waiting. I don't want to take any chances with the safety of a thirteen-year-old girl."

"Right."

Meredith decided against telling him about the jurisdiction tangle between the sheriff's office and Rohnert Park DPS. That news could wait. "Do you have a temporary place for her?"

"Here's the thing." He sighed, and her heart fell as she braced herself for bad news. "My normal emergency homes are already filled to their maximum. Is there another relative she could stay with safely?"

"No. Her father died in prison years ago, and her uncle is in San Quentin for life. There's no one."

"I'm not sure I can help. We have no place for the girl." He sucked his breath in through his teeth. "There's an outside chance we can put her in a home in the Sacramento area, but..."

Anger shot through Meredith at the ineffective system to protect children from harm. She'd heard it before—budget and staffing issues were problematic. Poor planning and gaps in the bureaucracy could profoundly affect the life of a child. "Let me pick her up, and I'll call you back. I want to get her under my protection before anything happens."

"Sure thing. In the meantime, maybe another county can take her. I've already placed siblings in Suisun today."

They disconnected, and she touched the icon for her husband. "Nick. CPS doesn't have room for Esme. At the very best scenario, they'll ship her out of the county."

"She needs to be protected." Nick huffed with frustration. "I ran that license plate. It returns to a female by the name of Sofia Toth. I did some checking, and Almita's hunch is right on. This Sofia woman has a rap for pandering. Nothing violent, but this is enough to raise a flag. She is probably associated with your Russian guy."

"Did you get hold of DPS?"

"They just called back. The Corolla is gone. I must've spooked him."

"What are we going to do with the girl?" Meredith had pulled up in front of the school, and she wanted a plan before she spoke to the principal. "Nick—"

"Wait. I know what you're going to suggest. I'll say it first. Bring her home. Bring her here, and we'll keep her safe until Teresa's picked up and the neighbor, well...I don't know how this will play out, but we'll keep her safe here, Meredith."

Neither Nick nor Meredith ever brought any of their 'cases' home. This was a first, complicated by the potential for endangering

Davy. But neither could they walk away from an endangered—from two sides—thirteen-year-old girl. Meredith knew of cops who adopted kids they'd rescued in the field, but they were infrequent enough that they made headlines in cop magazines.

She didn't plan on making headlines.

Chapter Fifty-Seven

Tuesday, March 13, 12:30 PM

ESME SAT IN A BUSTLING SCHOOL OFFICE, HER IRRITATION GROWING. Students retrieving confiscated items, teachers dropping off papers, and parents waiting to complain, kept the room noisy and hectic. A motherly-looking secretary keeping an eye on her amped the frustration level. Esme resented the attention. After all, she'd come back to school. Wasn't that what they cared about?

Watching the kids and adults interact made her realize she was only thirteen. These kids were her age, and they seemed silly and immature. The reality of her own limits dawned on her. She was just a kid.

The idea of getting a job had ebbed away. She couldn't do it without the school's permit. And she had seen her terrible mistake with Michael. She wouldn't make that error again. Her mother was too flighty to count on. She imagined leaving school and working all night just to have her mom go off on some drug binge. How silly she'd been.

She'd been deeply disappointed in her mother, but with Almita's help, a reality check had put Teresa's story in perspective. She couldn't help her mother. Teresa needed help, but it couldn't be her daughter who provided it. She knew that now. All she wanted to do was to go home. A tear snaked down her cheek. She wiped it away before anyone noticed.

She shifted her pack, debating whether to pull out her phone and start a game.

The door flew open, and a tall woman in jeans and a corduroy jacket hurried in. From the counter, she asked the secretary about Esme. Almita had texted her with a description of the woman who was to pick her up—Meredith Ryan. She'd told her this woman felt more trustworthy than the Rohnert Park cop. Almita was usually right about people. Schooled by her parents from a young age not to trust cops, Esme had learned that her auntie was a good judge of character. She'd go with the woman.

Esme stood as the secretary asked the woman for identification. The secretary leaned over the counter to scrutinize the ID. The flat badge lay open and clearly visible.

"I'm Esme. My auntie said you'd come to pick me up."

The woman turned and met her gaze. She seemed stunned for a moment, then smiled. "I'm Meredith Ryan from the Sheriff's Office. I'm your ride."

"How come my auntie couldn't come?"

The woman looked at the secretary. "Is there a room where we could talk privately?"

The secretary grabbed a set of keys from her desk and shouted something over her shoulder at another woman. Esme and Meredith followed her down a short hall and waited for her to unlock the door to a closet-sized room with a table and four plastic chairs. Metal bookshelves lined the walls and insulated them from the racket next door.

Esme slid her backpack onto a chair and sat down. The woman sat, too, opposite her. The woman's face held something Esme couldn't read. She laid her arms on the armrest and sat back.

Was she going to interrogate her? The other woman detective had tried to get information from her, but Esme didn't talk. She couldn't trust her. The information she held could hurt so many people. She disliked Michael but loved Sofia, despite her wobbling loyalty. She was sure Sofia depended on Michael for her survival and understood why the choice would be simple to go with him. But something was wrong with them. And there was her mother. Esme had been in the room when her mom pushed Bernardo, and he died. She didn't want to get her mom in any more trouble than she already was.

Finally, the woman spoke. "Esme, you're in a bad position here."

At this, Esme sat up with a protest on her lips.

Meredith raised her hand to stop her. "Wait. There are things going on that you don't know about."

"My mother…"

"Yes, your mother is part of the whole scenario. But not in the way you expect."

"What are you saying?" This didn't register in her brain. What was the lady cop talking about? She braced herself for bad news like she had so many times before in her life—like when her mom told her that her father was dead. And when Uncle Raul got caught and convicted, then sent to prison for life. Like her mom disappearing after an argument with Almita. No phone calls, no texts, nothing. Oh yeah. While Teresa said her phone was at Aurora House, Esme didn't believe for a moment that she wouldn't find a phone somewhere.

Meredith leaned forward, putting both her palms on the table. "I think Michael is out to get your mother. I believe he thinks he can get to her through you."

This didn't make any sense. At the Yulupa Apartments, they always got along. "Why does he want her? I don't understand."

The lady cop licked her lips. Here it comes…Esme thought…the bad news. "Michael is a criminal. He buys and sells human beings for work and other things. He believes your mother is getting in his way to do business."

"What? How?"

Meredith cocked her head. "We don't have all the information yet, but I believe that Michael is planning to make you do things that aren't right. Your mother is trying to stop that."

This is all wrong. Her voice cracked when she protested. "No, you have it all messed up. I went to Michael. I asked him for a job so

I could pay for an apartment where my mom and I could live." Esme felt she needed to explain about her mom. "She doesn't do real good at normal jobs." She shrugged, hoping the lady cop would connect the dots. She didn't want to explain any further. This was her mother's personal business.

Meredith nodded. "That's how it starts. He operates a scam that leads young girls like you into prostitution. You know what that is?"

"Sure." Esme didn't get it, but she let it go for now. She hated to appear as silly as her classmates. "So why are you here instead of Almita?"

The lady cop, Meredith, took a deep breath. "Here's the deal. I'm afraid you're in a bad position at your auntie's. If Michael comes looking for you there, he could hurt your family. I have a call into Child Protective Services…"

Esme pulled back, the shock almost overwhelming her. The idea of endangering her auntie and the family horrified her as much as Child Protective Services. She'd been in strangers' homes before. She hated it. The rules always changed, the kids there were punks, and the parents usually weren't much better. "No way…"

"Let me finish." Meredith waited for Esme to agree. "There aren't any local homes open at the moment. CPS is looking for a safe place for you out of the county. Until then, you're going to stay with me. You'll be at my house in Petaluma with my husband and son."

There it was. Another stranger's home. She began a protest but stopped. This time it didn't feel so bad. Still, Meredith was a cop. Another stranger, but maybe she'd be safe there. She wasn't sure how she felt about this, but she hated the idea of getting used to another home only to have it yanked out from under her. "What about school?" Maybe that would keep her at Almita's.

"I'll bring you up here every day as long as we feel it's safe."

"Who is 'we'?"

"My husband and me. He's also a deputy."

Esme's phone vibrated from within her pack. From a side pouch, she pulled it out and glanced at it. "It's a text. I don't know who it's from. It could be my mom." Her eyes widened. She held out the phone for Meredith to see.

She read, "'If Michael or Sofia get in touch, ignore them.'"

Meredith stood, pushing the chair out behind her to crash into the wall. Stunned, Esme looked confused and not sure what to do. Teresa had identified the bad actors for her.

Meredith knew what she had to do. She reached out and held up Esme's pack. "Let's go. Now."

Chapter Fifty-Eight

Tuesday, March 13, 1:00 PM

MEREDITH'S INSTINCTS TOLD HER TO MOVE. WITH ESME IN TOW, SHE blew past the school secretary with a brisk "thank you." When she got to the front door, she peered through the glass. Nothing looked out of the ordinary, but she couldn't see her car from this viewpoint. She pushed open the door and shifted to the edge of the building, using it for concealment, with Esme behind her.

There he was. Michael Fedorov, the jackass who forced her off the road. He stood at the front fender of her Subaru, inspecting the damage. He knew she was here. She'd led him to Esme. An overwhelming anger swept over her. She wouldn't let some two-bit pimp catch this girl. She'd keep her safe.

It didn't take any time for her to figure she—they—were on their own. Calling the cops wouldn't help right now. With the open layout of the school parking lot, Michael would see them coming. He'd get away or, worse, take aggressive action toward them at the school. From this distance, she thought he was the same guy, but she didn't see the Dodge in the lot. Doubt clouded her decision-making.

Calling Nick was out. It would take him twenty-five to thirty minutes, depending on traffic, to get here from Petaluma. And, he'd have to take Davy to Tina's—if she was available. That would take too long. She took a moment to text him. 'Call DPS to tell them Fedorov was at Lawrence Jones Middle School. No vehicle or weapons seen. They were safe on foot and making a strategic exit.'

If DPS could capture Michael Fedorov, that would eliminate an immediate threat.

Meredith silenced the phone and put it in her pocket.

With a hand across Esme's front, she peered around the corner. The garbage dumpster enclosure would hide them—if they could make it across the lot without being seen. Esme peeked around the corner at the man. "Michael," she whispered.

Meredith nodded, glad to have an additional ID on the guy. She looked at the dumpster enclosure again, gauging the distance and the cover they'd need to get there.

Esme caught her idea. She put a hand on Meredith's arm. "That's where all the kids go to smoke. They'll run if an adult shows up."

The girl was sharp, Meredith thought. She figured that Michael would know they were there if the kids scattered. She glanced from one side of the school to the other.

In the back, behind the gymnasium, were four asphalt basketball courts. Beyond that were two huge commercial shipping containers with doors open.

Esme pointed to where she looked. "Storage for sports equipment." Her face brightened. "I know how to get there without anyone seeing us. Mostly. We can go through the gym."

Meredith didn't hesitate. They needed to move. Michael was walking through the lot toward the office. "Okay, show the way."

Esme grinned. Meredith hoped the kid took this seriously, but her smile encouraged her with her resilience.

They walked into the gym, past a cheerleader practice, and into the *thankfully* empty boys' bathroom. Meredith was happy to see a door that led outside. "I'm not going to ask how you knew where this led."

Esme's grin told her she'd have to ask later.

Esme pushed open the door. In the farthest court, three boys ran after basketballs, then pitched them at the rim. They'd need more practice.

Meredith held Esme back until she'd given the layout a good viewing. No one around other than these boys. Meredith whispered, "Walk like you have all day."

The two sauntered across the asphalt toward the shipping containers. Meredith glanced inside, noting the general disarray, and decided against going inside. She led Esme around to the back of the structure. Feeling safe for the moment, she squeezed her waist holster for reassurance. She sank to her butt and waited for Esme to do the same.

Now she'd have to figure out what to do next.

Chapter Fifty-Nine

Tuesday, March 13, 1:30 PM

MEREDITH PULLED UP THE COLLAR OF HER JACKET AGAINST THE LATE winter wind. She took out her phone and reviewed her choices. Making a run for the Subaru was out of the question. Even if they got to it, there was no way it could outrun any car, even a Toyota Corolla. She thought about taking Michael down by herself. There were too many variables—the students and staff were only one consideration. With the student sports teams practicing outdoors, she worried about how provocative their presence would be. It wasn't that she didn't trust DPS. She'd feel the same about her own agency. What if he overpowered her and took Esme?

Nick had already exercised the option to call the police. A glance at her phone showed his reply to her text. 'DPS enroute.'

She couldn't wait for DPS to escort her to her car. She and Esme needed to get away now.

Nick was too far away but had already helped.

Deb lived nearby, a mere three or four blocks away on Santa Cruz Way. She wasn't on duty, but this was a simple request. Pick Esme and her up at the middle school and drive them to her home in

Petaluma. Leaving the Subaru at the school was a no-brainer. It might even serve as a distraction if Michael stakes the car out, waiting for Esme and her.

Deb was her best possibility. Meredith hoped she was home and that she picked up her phone this time.

Deb answered on the third ring. "Yeah, Mere. What's up?"

"I need your help. Esme and I are stuck at the middle school. Michael is hanging around, waiting for us to leave. Can you come pick us up?"

"Meredith, what the hell?"

"Deb, please."

"What have you got yourself into? And with Esme? Damn, Meredith."

Meredith was losing her last shred of patience. "I'll fill you in when you pick us up. And hurry."

"Wait, I haven't said I'd do it yet—"

"Deb. We need help."

Deb sighed. "Okay, I'll pick you up at the community gardens on Keiser Lane. You should be able to get there across the field behind the school."

"We'll be there." Meredith disconnected before Deb changed her mind.

Meredith studied Esme's profile. "You doing okay?"

She nodded, keeping her gaze straight ahead.

"You know where the community garden is?"

Esme nodded and then glared at her. "I knew there was a reason I didn't trust the other detective."

"She's acting weird. She's not normally like this." Meredith wondered what the hell was going on with her friend. She was grateful that Deb would help her but dismayed that she'd had to practically beg—with a dangerous criminal on their trail.

Esme led the way across the field, past the track, to the adjoining community garden. They climbed through an old barbed-wire fence that was older than either of them easily. They trotted alongside the chain link fence that marked the boundaries of the gardens from the pasture.

The only car in the gravel and dirt parking lot was a silver Porsche 911. The engine was running, and Meredith casually walked toward it to see if it was Deb.

It was. Nice car for a detective. *How could she afford this?*

Deb jumped out of the driver's seat and motioned for Esme to get in behind her. The back seats were small jump seats, but Esme was agile enough to fit. Meredith slid into the passenger seat and hooked the seatbelt. She glanced at Esme to be sure she'd buckled up, too.

Deb pushed in the clutch, shifting into first gear. The rear tires engaged and kicked up a rooster tail of dirt as they rolled onto Keiser Lane.

"We're trying not to attract attention, Deb." Meredith sounded like a mother cautioning her child. She regretted the comment as soon as it was out of her mouth.

Deb's lips tightened in a frown. "I know that." Slowing at the stop sign, she turned right onto Petaluma Hill Road. "Where are you going? To the auntie's? I assume you're not going to the office."

"No. Someone might be watching the auntie's apartment."

Deb flashed Meredith a wide-eyed look. "No shit." She thought this over for a moment. "Then where to?"

"My house."

"Petaluma? Jeez, Mere. You're full of surprises."

"It's the one place I can be sure she is safe."

Once on Petaluma Hill Road, Deb settled into third gear, then fourth with no theatrics. The women were silent. Then Meredith tried to break the chill between them. She was grateful Deb had come to their aid. "I hope you weren't in the middle of something important when I called."

Keeping her eyes on the road ahead, she answered. "I was. My ex was moving out."

"Oh, damn. I'm sorry." No wonder she was so stressed. Meredith realized that she didn't know her friend had been living with someone. It felt odd that Deb kept so much to herself when they'd been best friends all through the academy. They'd drifted apart through the years, but they'd always been able to pick up their friendship like no time had elapsed.

"I don't trust him not to take any of my stuff." Her jaw set like granite.

"You can drop us at Penngrove Firehouse if you want to get back. We'll catch an Uber from there."

In a sudden drop of her tension, Deb waved the thought away. "No. I'll take you home. If he pulls some shit, I'll just...deal with it later."

Chapter Sixty

Tuesday, March 13, 2:00 PM

AFTER DRIVING A CIRCUIT AROUND THE HOUSE ON MELVIN STREET, down Dana Street, and around to Wooddale Drive, they all felt there was no one watching the house. Deb dropped Meredith and Esme off at 503 Melvin Street and went on her way.

Nick had the door open before the pair even got to the front gate. He met them on the path to their home. Davy was in his arms as he hugged his wife, squishing their little boy. Davy giggled at the pressure.

Finally, he looked at Esme. "Esme? *Estoy encantado de conocerte.*"

"Nice to meet you, too." Esme replied in English, shifting her backpack to her other shoulder. Then tousling Davy's brown curls, she flashed a huge smile. "Is this little guy yours?"

"Yep. This is Davy." Nick put his son on the concrete sidewalk. "Tell Esme how old you are, Davy."

His big brown eyes settled on her. He wobbled a bit as he lifted his hand and stuck out three pudgy fingers. "Free. I'm free."

Esme giggled. "You're a big boy for a three-year-old."

Meredith stood back to watch her son charm this girl. To Nick, she whispered, "Her bag?"

"In the extra room." Nick took Davy's hand. "Hey, son. Let's show Esme where she's staying."

"Okay, Daddy." Meredith watched them walk into the house, feeling the gratitude of a woman who started with nothing but has gained everything. Her heart grew at Davy's little swagger as he marched down the hall, followed by Nick, then Esme.

Meredith followed them to observe the girl. Esme liked Davy without reserve but held back a bit from Nick. If Nick realized it, he ignored it and put on a charm offensive. Esme was getting the full house tour. "This is the living room, obviously. The kitchen is back here. Are you hungry? Have you eaten?"

"I'm not hungry."

"Good. Behind the kitchen is the back porch. It is also our laundry room that leads to the back stairs. Out there is the backyard, and below us is the garage." These old houses had been built small enough that some rooms must do double duty.

Esme craned her neck to look out the back porch.

Nick explained. "It's a little backyard, but we like it." She stepped forward and stood next to him, her posture stiff. "It's pretty quiet now, but we hope to have a puppy in the near future."

"Is that an alley?" Concern shone in the girl's eyes. Her awareness of her surroundings surprised Meredith.

Nick nodded. "It's for the garbage pickup. But we also use it to get to Davy's daycare. He stays with our neighbor, Tina. She lives over there." He pointed kitty-corner to the yard where Esme could see a back gate similar to the Reyes'."

Esme stood silent, but her gaze took in everything. Meredith thought she was memorizing the layout.

Nick asked, "Are you ready to see your room?"

She looked at Meredith to be sure it was okay. After Meredith's nod, Esme followed him down the hall. "We had new floors installed last week." Esme glanced at the floors then her gaze took in the doors in the hallway. "On the left is Davy's room." He opened the door so Esme could look in. Davy charged in and threw himself on his big boy bed, yelling, "Mine, mine." Esme blinked with surprise.

"Our room is the last one, there on the left. The bathroom is on the right." He pointed to the open door. Then he swung open the last door and stood back. Meredith recognized the pride in his voice when he told her that was her room. Esme stepped inside, out of Meredith's view, but she heard the "ohhh." The wonder in Esme's voice moved Meredith.

Meredith had spent time and money on the guest bedroom, wanting it to be as comfortable as possible for the guest away from home. Esme's scruffy gym bag sat on a walnut luggage rack at the bottom of the double bed that anchored the room. A blue and green chenille comforter provided a refreshing counterpoint to the ivory walls. A white wood end table sat beside the bed, with a small desk and dresser on opposite walls. A woven cane cave chair sat in the corner.

Esme trotted across the room to the chair and found it swiveled. She giggled when she turned it to face the bank of corner windows that looked out upon the front yard.

Meredith wondered why she felt such a surge of satisfaction at Esme's obvious delight with the room.

Chapter Sixty-One

Tuesday, March 13, 12:00 PM

TERESA FLOPPED ON MIMI'S BED AND TRIED TO ACT COOL. SHE wasn't—by any stretch. She was coming down from her last hit. She had already finished that damn methadone Almita had tried to confiscate. But smack would be better.

"Doesn't your sister-in-law have any pills?"

"Yeah, she does. She takes Ativan, but she counts them every day." Mimi looked away, her face reddening. "She doesn't trust me. She'll be doubly paranoid with you here."

"How rude." Teresa was already thinking about how to get her hands on them. Mimi's brother and sister-in-law weren't thrilled that Teresa returned. They'd be watching for her or Mimi going near their room. It was midday, and she was a few hours away from crashing. She was already restless, and her muscles ached. Her stomach roiled, and she felt nauseous.

Who did she know who could provide her with the heroin she needed? With Mimi's help, they listed the names of sellers who might be willing to deal with her. Bobby? No, he was in jail. Silverton? He moved to Mexico. Jaydee? Serving hard time last she heard.

"Jeez. I was in rehab for almost six months, and everybody moved away. What the hell?"

Mimi shrugged. She didn't have the sense to fathom the 'why' out. Dealers came and went, replaced by new ones. It was an unpleasant fact. Mimi wasn't a druggie but was nosy enough to keep track of the street players.

"Is there anyone new that I could reach out to?" Teresa knew about Mimi's snoopy nature.

Mimi perked up. She liked helping her friend. "There's a guy from Russia who's moving in a little dope. He mostly deals in people, but it looks like he's broadening his horizons. Last week, my buddy Luigi bought some meth from him. He said the guy was scary, but his dope was good."

Teresa's alarm bells went off at the mention of Russia, but she was past worrying. "Do you know how to get hold of him?"

Mimi pulled out her phone and tapped on the screen. "Just a minute." In a few seconds, the screen lit up. She had an answer. Teresa's heart thumped against her chest. She reached out to the phone. "Give it to me. What's the number."

"I don't know." Mimi's voice rose with indignation. "Pull up 'Michael'."

Teresa tapped the contact icon for 'Michael.' The phone rang, and Teresa suddenly grew cold. She couldn't talk to him. If it was the Michael she suspected, he'd end the call. She pushed the phone to Mimi. "You talk to him. I don't know him. He'll be suspicious."

A man's voice answered as Mimi's hand missed the phone and it fell onto her lap. "Hello."

Teresa lunged at Mimi, grabbed the phone, and held it up to her friend's ear. Teresa kicked Mimi's shin to jolt her into answering. "Yes, Michael?" She waited a heartbeat. "Michael, I have a friend who'd like to meet you. It would benefit both of you."

Teresa heard the man's voice but couldn't make out the words. Then Mimi spoke. "This is Mimi. I'm Luigi's friend...from Santa Rosa."

He seemed reassured, spoke some more. Then Mimi looked at

the time on her phone. "Yes, we can make that. And her name's Teresa."

He disconnected. Teresa heard the silence on the other end. He hadn't heard Mimi say, "Thanks, we'll see you there in an hour."

The women had a half hour to kill. A thirty-minute walking trip gave them time to talk things over. This would be the moment to ask Mimi for her additional need. "Aurora House took my phone. Do you have one I can use?"

Mimi's chubby cheeks flushed as she looked away. "Maybe." Her voice was tentative, almost reluctant.

"Mimi, either you have one, or you don't. I have to have a phone."

The other woman bunched her thin hair into a small ponytail. "I don't know…"

"Mimi, get me the phone." Teresa's voice fell just short of a yell.

Mimi slid off the bed and slipped out of the room. She returned in five minutes and handed Teresa an older iPhone. "This is my father's old phone from before he passed away."

Teresa snatched it from her friend. She dug out Mimi's charger and plugged the phone in. It should work in a half-hour.

"I'll need it back when you get your own back." Mimi's voice was soft, dreading when her sister-in-law would discover it missing.

Teresa nodded, finally feeling like something was going right.

Chapter Sixty-Two

Tuesday, March 13, 12:15 PM

MIMI AND TERESA WALKED TO THE MEETING PLACE AT SANTA Rosa's Howarth Park. A cool afternoon lunch hour, the parking lot on Summerfield Drive began to fill with hospital and office workers setting out at picnic tables. Few children populated the tree-covered playground as most had left for home. Mimi's house wasn't far away, but by the time they got there, the exhausted Teresa shook from the cold that seeped into her bones. Her time was running out. She needed a fix.

The women walked up the hill to the place where Michael had directed Mimi. Halfway up to the campgrounds, sheltered by the year around oak trees, was an old house, long unlived in. The small, tan, Craftsman-style structure with shiplap siding and a porch spanning the front of the house. It sat as a relic from the early 1930s, when this area was first developed as a park. Taken over by the city of Santa Rosa, it housed signs, campground gear, and playground equipment.

Mimi stopped at the sidewalk and glanced at the structure. She cocked her head at the house. "He said to meet him in the back of the place. I'll see you back home."

Teresa overcame her unease by the need to feed her addiction. In her jeans pocket, she fingered the cash she'd lifted from Mimi's brother. She hoped it was enough. No matter. She'd take what she could. She lit a cigarette and leaned against the building. In her other pocket, she had set her new cell phone on silent and thought over where she'd go. She didn't want to go back to Mimi's because she'd taken her brother's cash.

Mimi turned and left, her shoulders slumped, an uneasy wrinkle across her brow. Teresa groaned with relief at Mimi's departure. She was satisfied—she'd gotten a phone and would be getting a hit soon.

Thirty minutes later, she ground the cigarette butt into the dirt, figuring the guy stood her up. Trying to stay calm when all her senses were screaming for a hit, she rounded the corner.

What the hell?

A hand clamped over her mouth, and another clamped around her skinny body. She smelled something sour, like cabbage. Then in her ear, a hoarse whisper. "I thought it might be you. That's why I made special arrangements."

It was a familiar voice. Michael, her former neighbor. The asshole who enticed her daughter into a life of slavery and prostitution. She kicked at his shins, not making contact. Struggling to get free, she felt her limbs flailing, not hitting anything.

Finally, Michael freed a hand and slapped her head with such force that her vision blew like the fourth of July.

Chapter Sixty-Three

Tuesday, March 13, 12:45 PM

Teresa woke up to her face mashed into a stinking carpet. She'd puked in the car after Michael kidnapped her, and the smell lingered on her lips. She wasn't sure which was worse, the dirt and mold on the floor or her own mess. Shaking from the cold, she tried to roll over. In her jeans pocket, a cell phone stopped her. She laughed to herself that Michael hadn't searched her. The laughter soon turned to silent tears as she realized she had no idea where she was. And her ankles had been tied together. She couldn't walk out.

But she could warn Esme. She was sure Michael was after her little girl. She had to keep her safe. The phone.

She reached into her pocket and flexed her fingers around the phone. They were aching, the sickness moving into her body like a dark cloud. An index finger touched the screen, but she was shaking so hard, she couldn't hit the icon. She probably shouldn't call anyway. There was no telling where that big asshole was. He might be able to hear her warning.

No. A text would do the trick. Teresa struggled to recall Esme's phone number. She texted the number she remembered. "If Michael or Sofia get in touch, ignore them." She hit the send button.

She swiped to the left and punched the red "Delete" button. Sighing at her success, she held the phone against her chest.

Michael rounded the corner and marched up to her. His eyes bulged when he saw the phone in her hand. "What the fuck are you doing?" He grabbed the phone, twisting her wrist. She yelped in protest, and he kicked her in the ribs. "Shut the fuck up." He scrolled through the texts but saw nothing recent.

Teresa moaned, holding onto her injured wrist.

"Shut up, I said," Michael straightened, then kicked her again.

Chapter Sixty-Four

MICHAEL DIDN'T HAVE TIME FOR THIS TRAMP. SHE WAS A PATHETIC lump of skin and bones with no brains. Dried up inside and badly used, the woman wasn't worth a dime. He kicked her again, and the woman groaned. She wasn't even strong enough to try to get away. He'd bound her ankles but left her otherwise unrestrained. She'd never been to the Aston house so she wouldn't know where she was if she got loose. Not a chance.

But he wanted her daughter. In his mind, her only value was to lure her young daughter back into his plans. He'd had her once, but this bitch kidnapped her. When he got Esme in his stable, he'd take care of the mother permanently.

And the bitch had vomited in Sofia's car. He had to find someone to clean it up. A shot of irritation spiked through him as he thought about the loss of his two Mexicans. They'd been invaluable in helping him set up his business. He needed two more guys like them. Luigi might know of a pair of guys who could use the work. He already asked him to look into it.

He rolled Teresa over, and his gaze drilled into her. He wanted to intimidate her, crush her to his will. She'd do what he wanted, or he'd kill her. That easy.

His phone vibrated in his pocket. He walked out of the room and answered. "Luigi, my man."

"I got two guys who know the score. They're looking for work. Can I send them your way?"

"Yeah, I'll talk to them." Michael glanced around the room, a moldy carpet with beat-up vertical blinds. Stale pizza sitting on the table in a grease-laden box. He couldn't remember when it had been delivered. Yesterday? "I'll see if they're up to the job." No need to sugarcoat the terms of employment. They may as well know what they're in for. Their first job will be cleaning out the Corolla. If they make it past that, he'll put them on a trial basis.

Michael gave Luigi an address. "Send both over right away. I have a job for them and need it done now." He disconnected.

Hoping these new guys were capable of the tasks he needed performed, Michael sauntered back into the rear bedroom to check on the woman.

She'd come to and was staring at a phone in her hands. He stomped over to her and grabbed the phone from her fingers. He looked at the screen, but it was blank. Had he caught her before she could send a text? He sure as hell hoped so. Then his worry evaporated. She didn't know where she was. She couldn't send for help, could she?

But she'd given him a great idea. He'd keep her phone and send Esme a text to meet her. Then, he'd have her where he wanted her. He'd snag the little virgin and start building his empire. He almost drooled at the thought of the cash she'd bring in, even after the buyer deflowered her.

But it would have to be tomorrow. He had matters to deal with tonight.

Chapter Sixty-Five

Tuesday, March 13, 6:00 PM

BENNETT'S VOICE DRONED IN HER EAR AS MEREDITH BROWNED THE chicken breasts. She held the phone away from her for a moment while she re-read the recipe. This would be a good time to shut off the stove and focus on her boss' conversation.

"Yes, sir," she said with no conviction. She wasn't even sure what he was saying. She knew if she waited long enough, he'd repeat himself.

"The shooting investigation is done—finally. You're clear to come back to work tomorrow. I know I said Thursday, but we need you. You'll be helping Peters out with the Bernardo Nuñez homicide. He needs your assistance."

"Okay. I'll be there tomorrow morning."

With her quick agreement, Bennett stuttered a goodbye. Meredith disconnected while Esme measured out two cups of rice and stood by, waiting for the next order. As Meredith re-directed her thoughts from work back to dinner, she glanced at her houseguest. Esme seemed to blossom while helping with the meal. She'd only been at the Reyes-Ryan home for a few hours, but she seemed to be settling in without any problems.

The pot on the back burner was at a rolling boil. Meredith nodded toward it. "Dump the rice in, please."

Esme hesitated. "Don't you need a bit of butter and salt? My auntie always put them in."

Meredith reread the recipe. "Oh, you're right. It says, 'salted water with a pat of butter.' I missed that." She felt her cheeks redden as she faced the teen. "You must know how to cook."

"I like to experiment with different flavors. My auntie was helping me learn the basics."

"Your mom didn't cook?" Meredith regretted the question as soon as it escaped her lips. She'd fallen into the comfortable atmosphere in the kitchen and meant the question to be conversational. Expecting a negative reply, she wished she could take the words back.

Esme's mouth twisted with dismay as she shook her head. "She usually brought home fast food from wherever she worked."

Meredith looked around her kitchen in a grand gesture. "Well, I never cooked *either* until this winter. I have a friend and neighbor who's helping me learn."

Esme smiled. "The chicken smells good."

THIRTY MINUTES LATER, Nick arrived in uniform for his dinner break. His permanent assignment was graveyard sergeant, but as he was on the promotion list, he'd been hired as an acting lieutenant to backfill a vacant position—one he hoped someday to own permanently. As he walked in the front door, he shouted for Davy. "Where's my boy?"

Davy tore through the hall from his bedroom and into his father's arms. "Daddy, Daddy."

Meredith saw Esme leaning back to view the scene. A slow, almost reluctant smile spread across the girl's face.

Nick held Davy in one arm as he strolled into the kitchen. He glanced at the cook and her helper. "Wow, that smells really good, ladies."

As he washed up, Meredith set the food on the table. Rice mounded in a bowl, and a platter of chicken breasts with a boat of lemon and herbed chicken gravy sat at the center. A salad and steamed broccoli with parmesan cheese rounded out the menu. Esme had arranged table settings for three adults and one child.

Nick deposited his son in the highchair with a bib and pulled out a chair for Esme to sit. Meredith put water glasses on the table and sat. When everyone was seated and settled in, Nick took a moment to say grace. He folded his son's hands together in his.

Meredith watched Esme close her eyes, fold her hand, and suppress a smile. This was a scene that Meredith hadn't lived since she was a child. She doubted Esme ever had. With her father in prison and her mother struggling to feed them, she knew they hadn't experienced family dinners, much less grace.

"Thank you, Lord, for the blessings of this food, this family, and our guest Esme. Amen." He opened his eyes, looking at the table with a slow grin. "And I should've added a thanks to Tina for teaching Mom to cook." He finished with a sign of the cross and an, "Amen."

"Esme saved the rice," Meredith commented while cutting pieces of chicken breast into Davy-sized bites. She smushed it together with the rice and fed it to Davy. "She told me to put butter and salt in the boiling water. Otherwise, I would've just dumped it in. She said the salt and butter add flavor to the rice."

"I have to agree." Nick shoveled a forkful of rice into his mouth.

Esme shrugged to Nick but kept her gaze on the plate in front of her. "Meredith said you do most of the cooking."

He nodded, chewing. "When I was growing up, my parents owned a restaurant. Mexican food." He shoved a bite of chicken into the gravy on his plate. "But Meredith is learning. This is really good." He cocked his head in amazed appreciation.

Meredith warmed at the compliment. As diplomatic as Nick tried to be, he never sugar-coated his criticism of her cooking.

After she finished eating, Esme jumped to her feet. "I'll do the dishes."

Meredith straightened. "You don't have to—" she began.

Esme stopped her. "No, please. I'd like to help. I appreciate you letting me stay here."

Nick glanced at Meredith with a surprised snort. "It's our pleasure to have you, Esme."

Chapter Sixty-Six

Tuesday, March 13, 7:00 PM

DISHES CLATTERED IN THE KITCHEN WHILE ESME WASHED AND loaded the dishwasher. Nick and Meredith stood in the living room getting ready to say goodbye, Davy wobbling around Nick's leg.

Nick took the toothpick from his mouth and broke it in two. "She's a special little girl, isn't she?"

Meredith nodded.

"Too bad there's nothing we can do to help her out."

"I know. To make matters worse, Bennett called. I'm cleared to go back to work."

"How soon?"

"Tomorrow."

"What do you have planned for Esme?"

"I *was* going to take her to school and shadow her, but now..." She shrugged. "She'd be safer at Tina's with Davy. I texted Tina a minute ago. She's already agreed to Esme staying there, but I want to take her over to introduce her. Tomorrow, I'll call the school and get homework for her. I can stop by the office and pick it up on my way home."

"That won't work for a long-term plan."

"I know." Meredith sighed. "I'll call Deb and see what's going on with the search for Michael. And Bennett will fill me in on our case tomorrow."

"Do you think Deb will be straight with you?"

"I don't know what's going on with her." Meredith looked away. "If I didn't know any better, I'd say she was dropping the ball on this one. She doesn't seem to put any energy into this." She dropped into a chair and ran her fingers through her hair. "I wish I knew what to make of this—the expensive car, not pursuing the abduction case. She's put a distance between us that I've never felt before. It makes me wonder if she's into something dishonest."

"Do you think she's taking money from someone?"

Meredith felt wretched inside, her gut torn across her chest. "I can't speculate on that. I don't want to, anyway." She looked away.

Nick put a hand on her shoulder. "It's more likely that she's burned out and maybe spent more money than she earned. Got over-extended on her finances."

"Whatever is going on, I need to talk to her about it. When we get this case wrapped up, I'll ask her." Meredith took his hand and stood to face him. "We've got more important things to take care of now."

Nick's index finger caught under her chin. He turned her face toward his. "Maybe I can build a fire under Bennett on your hit-and-run case."

Hope and gratitude filled her smile. "Be careful not to tell him how to do his job."

He snorted a laugh and kissed her. She stood as Nick leaned down for a hug from his son. From the kitchen doorway, he told Esme, "Thanks for the help with dinner and the dishes. See you tomorrow."

———

AFTER THE DISHES had been put away, Meredith packed up Davy. Meredith handed Esme one of her jackets, denim lined with shearling wool. Esme's eyes lit up at the cropped denim coat. "This is a cool jacket." She tucked her hands in the pockets and snuggled into it.

Meredith smiled. "We're about the same size. You're almost as tall as me. You can keep this. The evenings can get cold around here."

Esme buttoned up and took the flashlight from Meredith. Davy climbed into his mother's arms, and they walked out the back porch door, through the yard to the alley.

Chapter Sixty-Seven

Tuesday, March 13, 7:30 PM

THREE MINUTES LATER, TINA STOOD AT HER BACK PORCH DOOR WITH Henry on her hip and a puppy yapping at her ankles. "Holy smokes. You two could be twins from a distance."

"Really?" Meredith doubted Tina's observations.

"Yeah, really. Same height, same hair color and length. Especially with that jacket. Wow." She turned Esme around. "You could be twins from the back, too."

Meredith laughed. "There's a small gap of fifteen, no, seventeen years."

"Never mind." Tina waved away the remark. "C'mon in. We've been waiting for you."

In the kitchen, Tina made introductions. Esme bent over to try to pet the little reddish dog, but he slid through her fingers. Henry and Davy chased the puppy in circles, while Esme's shy greeting to Tina and her husband Paul, who'd just come in, was drowned out by the kids.

"Don't worry about these two. They'll poop out after an hour of this." Tina motioned to the cyclone of activity. "And so will the puppy."

Meredith asked, "Have you decided on a name for the little guy?"

Tina laughed. "Bandit, because he's stolen our hearts."

Paul rolled his eyes and excused himself. Tina motioned to the chairs at the kitchen table.

With a glass of pinot gris in her hand, Meredith caught Tina's attention. "Here's what's going on. Esme's a victim in a case we're working on. CPS isn't available for her housing, so Nick and I took her in. No one is supposed to know she's here. School is not safe at the moment. We'll give you the girl's phone number. I want her to keep it because it's the best way to stay in touch while I'm at work. Nick will be sleeping during the day, so if there's any trouble, call me then him."

Tina nodded, then focused on Esme. "Mere tells me you know how to cook." She waited while Esme nodded in surprise. "Well then, we should be able to come up with some dishes to teach Meredith a thing or two."

Esme's broad smile left Meredith with no qualms about leaving them together.

Chapter Sixty-Eight

Wednesday, March 14, 8:00 AM

MEREDITH WENT INTO WORK EARLY THE NEXT DAY, AT EIGHT o'clock, figuring on catching up on the homicide. She read the report and Peters' notes. She sipped a mug of coffee, trying to put all the case puzzle pieces together but found her thoughts wandering to Esme and Tina and how they were managing together. When Peters arrived at nine o'clock, he sat across from her desk and dragged her attention back to the homicide case.

"Nuñez is the guy's last name. We just found out yesterday." At her puzzled look, he jumped to his own defense. "It took us all this time to recover the body. Gustavo Medina's memory isn't as good as he claimed. Plus, he was in a ravine, not a ditch. You have no idea how difficult it was to get the remains out of there intact. It wasn't like finding a body on the street." His lip rose in a snicker. "And the animals got to him. Made a mess out of him. It took us all day yesterday to get him out. There was enough left of him to get viable prints. That's how the ME identified him. He had an arrest last year for pimping." Peters glanced at his watch. "The coroner is doing the autopsy in an hour."

"You going, or you want me to?"

"You go," he grumbled. "No need for both of us to get bilious. Plus, I've got to chase up the forensics reports. They should be coming in soon."

"Did you notify the next of kin yet?"

"Yeah, by phone." His shoulder cocked in a defensive pose. "He has a mother in Mexico but no one here."

"So why did Medina pick up his body at the Burton house? 734, right?"

He nodded. "Medina says he had gone there to pick up his brother-in-law, Isaac, but when they got there, they saw Teresa push Bernardo. Isaac needed to get rid of the body, so Medina helped him out."

"And there was no other association with that address?"

Peters shrugged, looking away. He hadn't checked.

Meredith found her irritation level rising. He should've asked Medina about the house. So far, she'd observed some gaping holes in this investigation. "I ask because that house was under observation by the DA's Drug Trafficking Task Force. DTTF may have moved on to another lead, but that's where Bennett was almost shot. Do you remember? Where I shot at the guy taking aim at Bennett? The reason I've been off four days?" She sighed. The connections were there. All Peters had to do was to think beyond his nose. Most of this info was on the computer. "Who's the guy that called Medina? We should be talking to him."

"Medina only knew his first name—Michael. He said the guy didn't live there."

Her knuckles turned white as she gripped the armrests of her chair. "Did he say where?"

Peters' head swiveled. "Somewhere in Santa Rosa. That's all he knew."

"Michael is a common first name. But I suspect it's Michael Fedorov. Did Medina say anything about Michael having a bit of an accent? Maybe Russian or Eastern European?" She hadn't heard him speak, but the manager at the Yulupa Apartments said something about it.

Peters shook his head again. "Didn't ask. Why?"

Meredith took in a deep breath. "He was on Burton and fled the night we served the warrant. Bennett said the prints on the gun he had in the shooting returned to Fedorov, a criminal with a low-level record in Interpol's files. He lived in Santa Rosa and was a next-door neighbor to Esme and Teresa Alfaro. Remember them? Anyway, he went by Michael or Mikhail Fedorov. I'm sure he's the same jackass who tried to run me off the road in Geyserville."

Peters' eyes widened and his jaw dropped. "Whoa. Can you ID both players as the same guy?"

"No," she sighed. "Not with one hundred percent certainty. But the guy's build is the same. On Burton, it was dark, so all I saw was a profile. In Geyserville, he looked similar, but I was busy driving and had the baby in the car."

"Jesus Christ, Meredith. You're smack dab in the middle of this investigation."

"Back to the forensics. Did the crime scene unit come up with any usable prints at the house on Burton?"

Peters sat back in the chair. He had something to contribute to the investigation. "Yes, plenty, but Fedorov is the only one that helps us. A half-dozen others were distinct prints but not in any system. Although we did clear three missing girls cases from Southern California."

"I'm not surprised."

"Seems funny that the guy would be so lax with his own prints."

"Maybe the dude wasn't expecting to have his prints run through AFIS."

"Bennett told me Hardy had talked to the Burton Avenue land-lord. He said he had never talked to a male. All the rental business was made through Sofia Toth."

"Wait. Toth, Sofia?" She waited for his nod. "That's who the blue Corolla is registered to. The one outside Esme Alfaro's aunt's house. Only Nick and the aunt saw a male in the car. That's a solid connection between Michael and Esme. Did you talk to Toth?"

"She lawyered up during the interviews," Peters said. "But it was clear she's fronting for her pimp, Michael Fedorov."

Meredith had a sudden thought. "I'm going to call the manager at the Yulupa Apartments and confirm that Michael had an accent. You get hold of Medina and ask the same question. Then we might have something else to narrow the field down a bit." She couldn't get a conviction on that alone, but she'd know whether he was involved with Nuñez's murder. She could justify an Interpol warrant search for an offender outside the US. "And we'll try the name Michael or Mikhail Fedorov."

Deb had taken that name down to track down Esme. Meredith wondered if Deb had tried wants and warrants.

Chapter Sixty-Nine

Wednesday, March 14, 8:30 AM

IN THE MORNING, ON ASTON AVENUE, MICHAEL LOOKED OVER Sofia's Corolla. He knew the Charger was still too hot, so this was the best choice. The new guy cleaned up the vomit, and although the windows had been left down, a slightly foul smell remained. The stain was gone; a patch of drying upholstery the only visible reminder.

It would do. Luigi's guys might work out. They could do the grunt work, but Michael still had to test them to work around women. The men would not be permitted to bother any of them for sex. Their purpose was to keep the women in line, and transport them to and from business with no distractions. If they could do that, he'd put them on the payroll. He'd use them today for his adventures with the Alfaro women. He'd leave one to watch the Alfaro apartment in A section on the off chance the girl would return. The other would chauffeur him around—and watch his back.

If they didn't work out, he'd dump them. Neither of them would know enough to talk. He'd have another test for them soon.

But now it was time to text his young virgin, Esme. He leaned against the Corolla in the driveway and tapped his message, 'Hi honey meet me at Howarth Park in an hour.'

The reply came quickly. 'Can't. No way to get there.'

That bitch detective lives in Petaluma. Maybe Esme is with her. He'd checked where the investigator was by calling the Sheriff's Office just after eight this morning. He'd been transferred when he asked for Meredith Ryan. He hung up before they connected, but he was sure she was at the sheriffs' office in Santa Rosa.

He thought about the park in Petaluma where he watched her with her kid. What was the name? McNear Park. 'How about McNear Park?'

The reply didn't come quite as fast this time. 'Make it two hours —11:00.'

Michael wanted to get this rolling sooner. '10:30 would be better.'

He wondered how far he could push her without raising her suspicions. When she answered, 'OK', he knew he'd hit the mark.

It would take him a half hour to make it to Petaluma from Aston Avenue, Santa Rosa. He had a whole hour to kill. Maybe Sofia was at home.

Chapter Seventy

Wednesday, March 14, 9:00 AM

MEREDITH TOOK ESME'S CALL IN THE AUTOPSY ROOM. DOCTOR Blume had just made the incision in Bernardo Nuñez's shoulder, planning to make a Y incision running from shoulder to shoulder. The cuts would meet at mid-chest, and the tail of the Y would extend to the pubic region.

Meredith had seen a dozen autopsies, but nothing ever wore down the horror. Doctor Blume was exceedingly respectful of his patient, which made this a bit less difficult. But the smell always got to her. Even applying camphor ointment in her nostrils couldn't eliminate the antiseptic scent of the room and the raw smell of an exposed body's organs.

When her phone vibrated, she almost switched it to silent. But as Doctor Blume turned on the drill and hovered over the man's sternum, Meredith decided this would be a good moment to step out of the room.

"Esme? Is everything okay?"

The girl sounded breathless. "Actually, no. I just got a text from someone saying it was my mother on my mother's phone. She wants to meet me at McNear Park at 10:30."

"Okay." Meredith's mind switched gears and thought this out. Teresa had been in the wind. What did she want with Esme? How did she know McNear Park as she was a Santa Rosa girl? Why did Esme say, 'her mother's phone?' "You're upset about this. Tell me why."

"First, my mother never says, 'hi honey.' She just doesn't. Second, she's never spent any time in Petaluma. How did she know about McNear Park?"

"Do you think someone else sent the text?"

"Yes."

Meredith glanced at the wall clock. It would take her twenty-five minutes to get to the park in Petaluma. She'd have to set plans in motion first to let him know she'd be there. But she wouldn't, really. Plus, she'd have to go by Tina's house. "Okay, Esme. You did the right thing by calling me. I'll be down in less than a half-hour. We'll get to the bottom of this."

Esme blew out a relieved sigh. "Thank you."

Meredith poked her head in the autopsy room. "Doctor Blume, I've been called away. I'll be in touch this afternoon."

He gave an absent salute and went back to drilling.

Meredith tapped the phone icon for Bennett.

"Sergeant, this is Ryan. I'm at the coroner's office now, but I just got a call from Esme Alfaro. She got a text from her mother's phone that didn't sound like it was from Teresa. The text made arrangements to meet her at McNear Park at 10:30 this morning."

"Why do I care?"

"This could be the lead we've been waiting for to find Fedorov."

"You think he made the call?"

"Yes. I think Michael Fedorov is desperate to grab Esme to put her in his stable. Even if it *is* Teresa Alfaro, we need to question her for Nuñez's homicide."

"Yeah, we do." She heard his finger tap the desk. "Okay. Peters is in an interview, but I'm free. I'll meet you at the coroner's office, and we'll go down together."

"I'd rather have my own ride, Sarge. Hope you don't mind."

"Okay. I'll call Petaluma PD and clue them in." His voice

lowered with urgency. She was pleased that he took this so seriously. "Where do you want to meet?"

"Meet me at my house." She thought she should have a plan fully fleshed out by then.

Chapter Seventy-One

Wednesday, March 14, 9:30 AM

MICHAEL MULLED OVER THE IDEA OF PETALUMA. HE'D HEARD THE cop lived in the south part of the county. That would be Petaluma. Two birds with one stone? With luck, he could give the detective what she deserved at the same time he captured Esme. He wanted the girl, but this was growing into a major project.

Months ago, he weighed going into the drug business instead of trafficking people. He still moved a little bit of drugs. Some substances were good for keeping control over the women. He'd thought over both enterprises but finally decided to stick with people. He'd liked the fact that law enforcement found working with people so much more difficult to find than dealing drugs. And the laws hadn't yet caught up with the human trafficking penalties as a deterrent as they had with drugs. While he'd thought moving people would be easier work, it was now snowballing into a labor-intensive job.

No. He'd set this in motion, and his one goal was to set up an empire that would bring in more cash than his brothers' drug and prostitution domains. If he could just get the Ryan woman out of the way and get his hands on Esme Alfaro, he'd be set. Teresa wasn't of any concern. Once he dealt with her, he'd have one of the new guys dump her in the ocean. At a bit over thirty minutes to Bodega Bay, it was an easy drive with little or no law enforcement nearby. Disposing of Teresa's body in the ocean would remove any evidence. It was a no-brainer.

But doing in the detective would be complicated. He'd have to think about how to make it look like an accident so there wouldn't be any cops searching for him.

On his phone, he pulled up the number for one of Luigi's thugs.

Chapter Seventy-Two

Wednesday, March 14, 9:30 AM

MEREDITH WAITED FOR BENNETT IN FRONT OF HER HOUSE. NICK WAS still sleeping, and she didn't want to disturb him. On the way down, she'd called Deb and left a voicemail for her. She had to know what was going on. Some of this incident had involved her friend and her jurisdiction. Truthfully, she'd be glad for her help.

Meredith had gone to Tina's and traded jackets with the one she'd loaned to Esme. She was a half-inch taller than the girl but had the same length of brown hair. Their builds were similar. This might just work, she thought.

But Esme was frantic, worrying over her mother. "But Meredith, if it wasn't my mom, what if it was Michael? What happened to my mom? What if he wants me back in his house?"

Meredith clutched Esme's shoulders with a soft but firm grip. "I hope to get some answers for you, Esme. But you have to promise me you'll stay here with Tina and Davy."

Esme's face paled. She looked down at her hands, folding into fists and releasing.

Meredith had to have the girl's word. "Esme. Do you trust me?"

"Yes, Meredith." The teen met Meredith's gaze with serious brown eyes. "Yes, I do trust you."

"Then trust me to do my job and keep you safe." Meredith was ready to turn away and get to the park.

But Esme had one more question. "What about my mother?"

Meredith sighed, knowing she couldn't fix Teresa's problems now. They'd have to wait. "I'll do what I can to keep her safe. I promise."

While that seemed to satisfy the girl, Meredith had no idea how she'd find Teresa and get her out of trouble.

Chapter Seventy-Three

Wednesday, March 14, 10:15 AM

MEREDITH WALKED INTO THE PARK AT 10:15. SHE AND BENNETT HAD driven around the perimeter of the park and saw nothing that raised concern. Michael's Charger was nowhere in the area. A glance at the park occupants yielded nothing suspicious.

Bennett parked the county sedan in the Cavanaugh Recreation Center lot adjoining the park. An occupied Petaluma PD patrol unit sat at the opposite end. It was an easy walk to the playground, where Meredith found a bench to sit on. She slumped over her knees, appearing to be a teen engaged on her phone.

She'd bent over for twenty minutes. Her back was getting tired. Bennett's voice hissed in her earpiece. "Someone's coming your way from G Street. Could be our guy."

Meredith stretched, keeping her face away from the person's advance but didn't get a look. She slumped over the phone again, pretending to tap on it. Bennett said, "White male in his mid-forties, short light-colored hair, very curly, trim build, wearing jeans and a brown leather jacket."

"Might be him." Meredith kept her answer quiet. She felt the man approach. The air resonated with static. A chill ran up her spine, and she felt her waist for her Glock. Reassured, she steeled herself for what was to come.

His voice was gentle, not like she'd thought it would be. "Esme, dear girl." His hand touched her shoulder as she pocketed the phone.

Meredith stood, her hands free to twist him around and grab his arms. "Michael Fedorov. You're under arrest for pandering and pimping. You have the right to remain...oof."

"Ryan, you bitch," Michael spat. With a snarl, he turned away and grabbed Meredith's hand. Spiraling around, he slammed an elbow into her chin, knocking into her jaw. Meredith's head flew back, and she lost her balance, falling to the ground on a hip. Michael grabbed the lapels of her jacket and yanked her to her feet. She rose with a fist that swung into his cheekbone.

Bennett pulled Michael off Meredith swinging him around to face the sergeant. Bennett reached for an arm, and Michael swung a fist into his belly, knocking the wind out of him.

Meredith looped an arm around Michael's torso, but he flung her off like she was a bug. She fell to one knee beside Bennett, who'd dropped to the dirt struggling for air.

A stranger arrived—a long-haired, lanky young man wearing a hideously bright yellow knit cap—and shoved Meredith to the ground. He leaned over to pin her down when Deb came out of nowhere and tackled him.

The two sprawled on the ground. Meredith scrambled up and pinned the wiry man, and with Deb's help, turned him onto his chest. Deb had handcuffs out when Michael kicked her in the head. Deb fell over, stunned, and Michael grabbed the man's arm. He yanked him to his feet, and both men ran off toward G Street.

Meredith bent over Deb. The shoe print on the side of her face would turn into a black eye. Meredith held her upper arm steady as Deb rolled to her knees and slowly got to her feet. "Jesus. I feel like I've been hit by a truck." A glance at Bennett showed him getting to his feet.

Meredith worked to calm her breathing. "Yeah, well. Your timing was perfect. Thanks for the save."

Deb tilted a defiant chin in the direction the two men fled. "Fucker got away."

"Yeah, but we're alive to gripe about it," Meredith said.

Bennett pressed his mic button and spoke into the air. "Copy. Let me know the results." He looked over at Meredith, his face coloring pink. "Petaluma PD is following a possible suspect. There were two cars, and they split up. The PD picked a blue Corolla and will stay with it. They'll let me know if it's our guys. All he got on the other was a dark RAV4."

"Sarge, this is Deb Lang from Rohnert Park." Meredith nodded toward Deb. Then, to Bennett, "Are you okay?"

Bennett blew out a raspberry and shook his head. "He knocked the wind out of me. That's all. How about you two?"

Deb answered, "I'll have a hell of a bruise, but otherwise, I'm fine."

Meredith spoke up. "Let's go to my house. It's a few blocks away. I want to check on Esme."

Chapter Seventy-Four

Wednesday, March 14, 12:30 PM

"KEEP YOUR FUCKING MOUTH SHUT. I'M TALKING NOW." MICHAEL ran his fingers over the tight curls on his head. "I want to talk this through. Just sit there. Don't say a word."

Sofia sat on the couch in the Aston Avenue house. She was a distraction at the moment, and he had to puzzle through the ambush he'd just survived. Who knew the two women looked so much alike? He never doubted the girl in the park was Esme. Then there was the Petaluma cop who tried to follow him. Even in Sofia's gutless Corolla, Michael was able to evade him. Petaluma's pre-civil war streets and alleys made his getaway easier than he could have imagined. His adrenaline had slowed a little but was still pumping through his system.

Next, Michael was able to text Frank, who fled in the opposite direction. He'd told him to follow the woman to see where she lived. If she went back to the Sheriff's Office, he was to return to Aston Avenue.

But Michael appreciated Frank's ingenuity by escaping in the opposite direction. Splitting up the pursuit was a clever idea. He thought he might offer Frank a job.

Teresa was still in a bedroom, tied up. Seeing her pushed his temper to limits he didn't want to go to. He was on the brink of uncontrollable fury, the unavoidable consequence of things turning to shit for him. When he got like that, afterward, he seldom recalled what he'd done. It was like they said—he saw red. Nothing else.

Focus. Think about how to get Esme and prevent the cop's efforts to catch him. He stood at the kitchen window, unseeing, considering what he had at hand.

Earlier today, Frank had been recalled from watching Almita's apartment so he could keep an eye on Teresa. She had inadvertently offered a quicker, easier way to capture Esme than sitting in a car waiting for her to come home from school. Sofia had given Frank a break and sat with Teresa. She and Sofia had never gotten along, so Michael was confident of Sofia's loyalty.

He had to focus. "The priority has shifted," He said to himself. "Esme will wait. I must stop the Ryan bitch first. I have to get her out of the way. Then, I can take care of business." He paced across the grimy carpet. "The trick is how to do it without advertising that it's a hit. I don't want the entire county's cops on my ass. I just want her out of the way."

He strode into the kitchen and reached into the refrigerator for a beer. He twisted off the cap and swilled a long gulp. "How to do her in. Already tried running her off the road, and that didn't go well. Shooting her is a last resort. I can't get close enough to strangle her —that would be an obvious homicide anyway."

"Could you drown her? I mean, does she swim…"

"Jesus Christ, Sofia." Michael grabbed Sofia's thin arm. "What part of shut up don't you understand?"

"I'm just trying to help."

Michael's face reddened. The veins on his neck corded as he shouted, "Don't help. Shut the fuck up."

Sofia's eyes dropped to her hands. He'd humiliated her, but he didn't care. Fury building, he needed to hit her—or someone.

Teresa. That worthless bag of bones was in the back room. He finished off the beer and threw the empty in the kitchen sink on a mound of garbage. As he headed to the back bedroom, he heard Sofia ask, "Where are you going?" He felt for his sheathed knife on his belt but decided against using it. He needed her alive for a little longer.

The door was open. The stench hit him like a brick wall. Teresa had vomited and messed herself. He didn't want to get too close. Covering his nose with his elbow, he strode across the room to a window. He slid it open for ventilation. As a crisp late winter breeze wafted in, his focus fell to the human heap shivering in a corner. With hands duct-taped behind her back, she wouldn't put up a fight. He grabbed a handful of her dyed black hair. It felt like straw, but he got a good grip.

His arm reached back and shot forward to her jaw. With a weak cry, her head dropped back. His pent-up rage dictated a release, even through her stink. Then, filled with disgust, he tossed her to the floor and went to the kitchen. The drawers were empty except for dead batteries and discarded gum wrappers, but in one, he found a rolling pin. It would do the trick.

———

RELIEVED, ten minutes later, he sauntered back out to the kitchen. Sofia stood looking out the window. He threw the bloody rolling pin onto the garbage in the sink and walked to the refrigerator for another beer.

"Do you feel better now?"

Sofia's snarky tone got under his skin. "Yeah. You want some, too?"

She sat up straight, dread at his reaction stiffening her spine. "I only wanted…"

He was satisfied with the effect of his question. His temper spent, he waved her comments aside. "I do my best thinking when I'm working out. This was the next best thing."

"Oh?"

"Yeah, I know what I'm going to do next." He frowned and

nodded to the bedroom. "Go on in there and fix her up. I need her alive until I get this project done."

Michael's phone chimed an incoming text. It was from Frank: 'Woman lives at 503 Melvin Street.'

'Yes.'

Chapter Seventy-Five

Wednesday, March 14, 2:30 PM

BENNETT, DEB, AND MEREDITH STOOD IN MEREDITH'S KITCHEN. Bennett was on the phone getting information. Meredith pushed iced water glasses across the counter for them while waiting for Bennett to get off the phone. When he did, he took a long drink. He dropped to the kitchen chair and looked at the two women.

"We ain't doing so hot here."

"What?" Deb sat across from him.

"The PD only had one car in the area, and he followed the Corolla—which he lost downtown."

"And the other?" Deb leaned onto her elbows. Meredith noticed how interested she was with this. A few days ago, she wouldn't even return Meredith's calls. She hated doubting such a long-time friend. Maybe she could get some answers soon.

Bennett sighed with exasperation. "In the wind. The PD got a description but didn't get a license plate. It's an older red Jeep Cherokee. The Corolla's plate was bogus and probably cold plated." Cold plating is done by taking the license plate of a similar vehicle and putting it on another to use in a crime. It's a dead-end for law-enforcement.

"The Corolla wasn't registered to Sofia Toth?"

Bennett shook his head.

"So, we're no better off than we were before," Meredith said, more to herself.

"Not true." Bennett pushed his empty glass away. "We know for a fact that this Michael or Mikhail character is behind your girl's abduction. We're sure he's involved in simple pimping or some kind of human trafficking, maybe even some minor drug sales. What his role was in the Nuñez homicide is unknown, although Medina says a woman pushed him."

"Homicide?" Deb's eyes caught Meredith's gaze looking for answers.

Where had she been? Didn't she know her agency had a homicide? Meredith nodded. "I'll fill you in."

Bennett stood and fished in his pocket for car keys. "One thing is for sure—he knows who you are. Did you hear him say your name?"

"I did." It chilled her that Michael knew that much about her.

"I'm going back to the office. I've got to run this by Admin and set up some kind of security for you." Bennett nodded a goodbye to both detectives and left.

"Security?"

Deb tipped her head like she was talking to a first grader. "If he knows who you are, he very well could know where you live."

Meredith realized that. She nodded slowly, adding the icing on the cake. "Esme is staying with us, too."

Deb sighed.

"I tried calling to let you know." 'But you didn't answer and never called me back', Meredith thought.

"I know. My bad." Deb looked away absently. "Can you fill me in *now*?"

Meredith gave Deb all the details about the search warrant fiasco but wondered how much she already knew. The incident happened in her jurisdiction, and Bennett had notified their brass. The homicide case had been referred to Rohnert Park DPS as the incident occurred in their jurisdiction. Another detective, someone Meredith didn't know, had been assigned to work with the sheriff's investigators. Deb had to be aware of that. Rohnert Park DPS wasn't that big, and Deb had bemoaned how short-handed they were in Investigations. Meredith also found it odd that Deb's association with Esme's case seemed unimportant to her. She speculated that she hadn't shared Esme's case info with the detective working the Nuñez murder.

Deb was silent as she digested the information. "I didn't know Esme was staying with you. I figured CPS would've managed her housing."

"They planned on shipping her out of the county. She wanted to stay in school, and when this all happened, that was the plan. Now we know Michael is still after her."

Deb eyed her. "Maybe a placement out of county would be best."

Meredith shrugged but felt reluctant. She wanted to keep Esme with her. Still, this was officially Deb's case. "Maybe. But I don't mind having her here. She's a great kid."

"You have your hands full with this case. I'll call CPS when I get back to the office and see if I can find her a safe place."

Meredith sighed but bowed to protocols.

With his hair standing on end and clad in sweats, Nick padded into the kitchen. "Hey, Deb. What's shakin'?"

Deb stood and gave him a perfunctory hug. "I'll let the little woman catch you up." Then to Meredith, "I've got to go write a supplemental report and build a fire under CPS."

Meredith stood and put a hand on Deb's shoulder. "Before you go, we need to talk. Let's go out to the front porch."

Chapter Seventy-Six

THE WOMEN STOOD ON THE ROOMY PORCH, THE ACTIVITY OF THE busy Petaluma Valley a low hum in the midday. The women ignored the comfortable wicker chairs.

"We've been friends for too long to let this go without saying something." Meredith noticed Deb didn't look surprised or ready to deny anything. Meredith went on. "When I first came to you with Esme's case, you were willing to look into it. Then, I feel like you wanted it to go away. You discouraged me from following up on solid leads. Why?"

Deb looked at the floorboards on the porch. A breeze lifted a lock of her hair. Meredith waited, disappointed in her friend's lack of honesty.

"You're right. At first, well, after I got the idea that it wasn't a simple runaway case, I was enthusiastic. I wanted to find the girl and the asshats who took her." A sharp intake of breath signaled a serious admission. "But then I got warned off. The DA's task force is rotating personnel, and Rogers is going back to patrol. I'm next up to replace him."

It didn't make sense. "But why call you off a possible human trafficking case?"

"The sergeant in charge told me he'd refer the case to the state. It was a distraction. He thought they'd have resources that we don't..."

"That's BS, and you know it." Meredith couldn't go easy on her. "You wanted the task force position. You pushed a serious crime aside to serve your own interest. You weren't willing to make sure the right people were investigating a missing thirteen-year-old girl."

Deb hung her head. "Yes. I was totally self-serving."

"Dang, Deb. I never would've thought it of you."

Deb dropped to a chair, her hands covering her face. "Me, neither."

Hearing her friend's voice filled with remorse, Meredith rested her hand on Deb's shoulder. Sobbing shook her friend's body. "Everyone makes mistakes. It's just that this could've cost a girl dearly. Forced her into a life of prostitution—or worse. It can be a stepping stone..."

"I know, Meredith. You're not saying anything I haven't already said to myself." She wiped her nose with her sleeve. She looked up at Meredith; her eyes flooded with tears. "Has this damaged our friendship?"

Meredith had wondered the same thing. "I don't know. I thought I knew you."

"I can't lose you, girl."

Meredith expelled a deep breath. "I don't want to throw our friendship away either. Let's take it slow and build up trust."

Deb flashed a broad smile. "I'm glad. I couldn't bear to lose you and what's his name in the same week."

Ten minutes later, Deb left. The front door closed behind her, and Meredith went to the living room window to watch her friend leave.

Nick hollered from the kitchen. "You want a cup of coffee?"

She turned and replied, "No thanks. I'm going to get Davy and Esme at Tina's."

"I'll take a shower while you're gone. You can fill me in later."

Meredith nodded, her mind a million miles away as she headed out the back door.

Chapter Seventy-Seven

Wednesday, March 14, 4:30 PM ·

TINA'S HOUSE SMELLED LIKE AN ITALIAN KITCHEN. MEREDITH'S mind had calmed enough to realize she hadn't eaten lunch. "Wow, it smells fabulous in here."

"Spaghetti and meatballs, ma'am. Early dinner. Paul has a soft-ball game at five-thirty. Here." Tina handed Meredith a glass of white wine.

Davy trotted in, his tennis shoes slapping a beat on the laminate floor. Esme followed, but with a hand on Davy's shoulder. Dark cres-cents under her eyes didn't conceal the trace of contentment in her smile. Meredith's heart skipped a beat. The girl was obviously happy here with Tina and Davy. She seemed equally at ease at Meredith's home. She hoped Deb didn't get onto CPS's case to find Esme another placement. She wanted more time with the girl.

Tina stirred the spaghetti sauce and made a circling motion for Meredith to sit at the table. Tina joined her and sipped from her wine glass. "Esme helped me with dinner. She's darn good at putting a meal together. She even worked on the salad."

Esme bowed her head, looking embarrassed by the attention.

"In fact," Tina smiled, a conniving smile Meredith had seen before when she knew her friend was going to get her way. "I was thinking...you and Nick should join us for dinner. Esme has already been invited, and Davy, well, he's part of the family."

"Oh, I don't know, Tina. We've already imposed on you—"

Tina's palm hit the table. "No, I won't listen to that. Henry and I want you all to join us. And Paul should be here any minute."

She hadn't figured out what to fix for dinner yet and knew Nick hadn't planned anything. He'd still be in the shower. "Okay. I'll text Nick to bring a bottle of red wine." She stood in a corner, out of the way, to send the text.

"Excellent! Esme, help me set the table."

Esme beamed as Tina handed her placemats and silverware. Tina pointed out the seating arrangements, and Esme followed, laying out the settings where directed. After the last napkin was folded in place, Esme straightened, glowing with satisfaction at a job well done. Even the simplest home-oriented task seemed to delight the girl. Meredith was so pleased that her friend Tina could provide such a simple routine. The girl needed a solid home-based schedule. She would've soaked up family life at Almita's no matter how crowded. Meredith planned to provide the same as long as Esme was with them.

The girl's voice was quiet when she asked, "Were you able to find my mom?"

Meredith had dreaded the question. But she couldn't whitewash Teresa's situation. "Our plan didn't work out today." She touched Esme's hand. "We'll keep looking for her."

Esme's face flushed as she moved away from Meredith. She shook her head. "She's in trouble. I just know it."

"We're doing everything we can."

"You must find her. I think Michael has her. Otherwise, she'd be texting me. Really texting me."

It was clear the last text from the phone, tentatively identified as her mother's phone, was from Michael. Meredith shared Esme's concern for Teresa, but there were no viable leads to follow up. She still had the Nuñez homicide to unravel. That investigation was also a dead end at the moment. Without a witness, it was anybody's guess what happened to Bernardo Nuñez. Medina said that after Teresa pushed him, he'd fallen and hit his head against the hearth at 734 Burton Avenue. They knew little beyond that. They didn't even know if that was true or if Medina had been keeping more information from them. "We'll start fresh tomorrow." Meredith reached out to Esme again. "We won't give up."

Nick arrived with a bottle of wine. As he would be working tonight, Tina took the wine and pressed an iced tea into his hand. He took stock of the room, Davy and Henry running up and down the hall, Tina putting condiments on the table, and Esme helping, but her face clouded with concern. He lifted an eyebrow at Meredith, who whispered, "Later."

The next minute, Paul came in through the front door, greeted with the enthusiasm of two preschoolers and a puppy happy to see him. An electrician by trade, Paul dropped his toolbelt and hoisted Henry over his head. Henry's dad was a strong, brawny guy with a head of curly black hair. Squeals of delight rumbled through the house. Meredith heard Nick fingering keys in his pocket. It was an absent gesture that told Meredith he was savoring the pleasant scene. Tina stood with delight, observing her husband and son.

Then she yelled, "Dinner. Everybody grab a seat."

Dinner was a success. Tina's culinary prowess was in full bloom. With a cleaned plate in front of him, Nick pushed himself away from the table. "I need a nap now instead of going to work." He rubbed his belly. Paul stood, gathering his and the plates on either side of him. He rounded the table on his way to the kitchen sink and glanced out the window.

"Smoke," Paul shouted. "Jesus! There's smoke." The plates clattered to the table in front of Meredith. Spaghetti sauce dripped on Meredith's hand. She jumped up in alarm. Paul stood at the window, stuttering, "Smoke."

She reached for a napkin and wiped off the mess. Then joined

Paul and Tina at the window. "Your house. It's on fire!" Tina shouted, "Someone call 911."

Meredith and Nick were out the door before Paul could tap 911 on his phone.

Chapter Seventy-Eight

Wednesday, March 14, 5:30 PM

"FRANK, ARE YOU SURE SHE IS IN THERE?" MICHAEL'S VOICE sounded shrill even to him.

"Yes. She hasn't come out. I set the fire and can see the smoke coming from the garage."

"You're still there?"

"Yeah. I'm a block away on a hill and have an unobstructed view of the front of the house."

"And she hasn't left?"

"I swear. She's in the house. I've been watching." Frank cleared his throat. "I hear sirens."

"Okay. Get out of there. If you can see smoke, the neighbors can, too. Time for you to get back here."

Michael disconnected before the moron could say anything more. So far, he'd followed directions. He'd told him to find a way to start a fire. It was an old house, built a hundred years ago. He'd told Frank to scout around inside. He was to start in the garage and move out from there if he couldn't find any way to start a fire. Garages had the most incendiary supplies inside, gasoline, propane, paint thinner, and so forth.

Chapter Seventy-Nine

Wednesday, March 14, 5:45 PM

MEREDITH AND NICK RAN DOWN THE ALLEY FROM TINA'S TO THE back of their home. "Mere, I don't have my gun."

"I have my backup." Meredith carried a Glock 42 in an ankle holster. "You want it now?"

"Yeah."

She handed it over.

Sirens wailed through the night. Meredith and Nick burst through the back gate into their yard. Nick went to the hose bib and turned on the water. He sprayed the exterior of the garage door until the smoke thickened enough to force them back to the alley.

Smoke billowed from the crevices around the garage doors. The house sat on a slope with the garage at the deepest end. Above it was the primary bedroom. Their bedroom, where Nick had been sleeping an hour before.

There was little they could do. A firefighter relieved him of his duty with a larger, more powerful hose. They walked around the alley to Melvin Street, dodging fire trucks to get across the street.

Meredith's focus was on their home. They'd lived there two

years and were just finishing the minor remodeling to make it the way they wanted. Last week, hardwood floors had been installed in the bedrooms to match the flooring in the rest of the house. She loved that house.

Hoping the firefighters could get control of the fire, she scanned the street, looking at the apparatus. Two engines, a rescue, and a battalion chief's command car blocked the street. A complex web of fire hoses laced from the hydrant across the street.

Then, as she always did, she glanced through the neighborhood, looking for anything out of the ordinary. The cars parked in driveways belonged to residents. One or two on the street looked familiar, except one. A dark-colored Toyota RAV4 with a solo occupant caught her attention. The second car from the McNear Park attack was a RAV4.

She stared at the man behind the wheel. He stared back. Suddenly the headlights flipped on, and the car jerked into reverse. It wobbled backward over the crest of the hill and out of sight.

Meredith jabbed her husband's ribs as she started toward the car. "Nick, I just saw the guy who fought with us at McNear Park." She glanced at the Subaru in her driveway, blocked by an engine and hoses.

"He's not getting away this time." Nick turned, leaping in the opposite direction. "My car's parked in the alley." Because the flooring company had taken the front curb spaces, Nick had taken to parking his unmarked department car in the alley near the trash receptacles. After the job was done, he told Meredith that he preferred the alley, after all.

"We can get out through English Street." Meredith huffed, barreling downhill to the next-door neighbor's gate. She followed Nick through the yard and out their back gate to Nick's department Ford Explorer. From ten feet away, the door locks clicked. A second later, Nick pulled open the driver's side. Meredith barely had time to buckle up before he stomped on the accelerator.

The alley behind Melvin Street met with English Street in a perpendicular junction. To the right was an uphill 'L' connector to Hill Boulevard that looked like a dead end. Neither was more than a narrow lane. On a gamble that the suspect would try to get away toward Highway 101, Nick took a left onto English Street. A wide city street of sprawling 1960s ranchers lined with sculpted juniper bushes stretched before them.

Three blocks ahead, Meredith saw a pair of taillights. "That might be him."

Nick grunted and pressed the gas pedal. Meredith's head sank into the headrest. As they drew closer to the red lights, Meredith asked, "Do you want me to call this in?"

"It's not a pursuit. We're not sure this is the right car yet." Nick was silent for a second, then said, "Call Pet PD as a courtesy and tell them. Then call Barry at the SO. He's watch commander until I get in."

"*If* you get in." Meredith made the first call, not asking for help but letting them know what they were doing. She gave their dispatch a summary of the chase, and after making sure they knew this wasn't a mutual aid request, she disconnected.

Before she could punch in the number for the SO, Petaluma PD's sergeant called her back.

"Brad Collins, sergeant, Petaluma PD here. Did my dispatcher get it right? You're following the guy you think set the fire on Melvin Street?"

"That's right. But there's—"

"That's our case, then, Deputy Ryan. I'd appreciate you giving us his horsepower, and we'll pick up the chase."

"There's more to it."

Meredith pictured him sitting back in his flexible office chair, making decisions based on little information. He wasn't keen on this scenario. She was almost surprised when he agreed to listen. "Okay, shoot."

"First, this isn't a pursuit. We're in an SO unmarked car, so I doubt he knows we're following him. In fact, we hope he doesn't. We're not even sure he's the suspect. He looks like a guy involved in a kidnapping case I'm working on. We have to get a bit closer to the car to be sure."

"Kidnapping?"

"The kidnapping is Rohnert Park's case." Kidnapping might be a stretch, but Meredith was sure Michael was holding Teresa, presumably to catch Esme. "But this guy might be associated with a homicide case of mine. He's associated with the doer."

Nick picked up the narrative, shouting across the cab. "We're hoping he'll lead us to the homicide suspect."

"I'm in the car with Sergeant Nick Reyes."

"Oh, hey, Nick." It didn't surprise her that the sergeant knew her husband. Though the rural county was large, the law enforcement community was small and close-knit. "Okay, so no pursuit to alert him?"

"Right, Brad. Like Detective Ryan said, we're in an unmarked unit, a dark blue Chevy Tahoe. I'm keeping my distance."

"That means you can't get a good look at the guy. You don't know if he's the one."

"Correct." Nick turned right, almost two blocks behind the RAV4, onto Western Avenue. He gave the sergeant a location update. "Even so, I'm not willing to let him get away without knowing where he's heading. He could lead us to the murder suspect."

Meredith continued. "Sergeant, it's also possible the suspect is holding a woman hostage. He's trying to get a 13-year-old girl to pimp out using the mother as bait. He arranged a meet that turned out to be a set-up to snatch the girl just as we thought. The meet went south, but I got a good look at the suspect and his partner before they bailed. The partner showed up, watching our house. We're following him now because we believe he started the fire in our house."

"The fire on Melvin?"

"Yeah. Our house. The car's a dark Toyota RAV4. Just turned north on Petaluma Boulevard, South of Western. We think the main guy is holding the juvenile's mother."

The chair squeaked. Meredith imagined him sitting up at attention. "What do you need from us?"

"To stay away. It's bad enough we're following in an unmarked unit. If he saw more, he might run, and we could lose him."

"I'll take care of that. We'll keep watch but from a distance." She heard his office chair squeak. "Say, do you need me to call anyone for you?"

"I'll call our watch commander as soon as I get off the phone with you. Maybe you could call CHP and let them know?" Nick nodded in approval.

"Will do. Stay safe."

Chapter Eighty

Wednesday, March 14, 6:30 PM

"NICK, THAT'S HIM. MICHAEL'S BUDDY IN THE PARK HAD A BRIGHT yellow watch cap on. Look, this guy does, too."

"A judge could call that circumstantial, but it's enough for me. Let's keep on him. Call Barry."

Meredith punched in the watch commander's office number. "Barry? This is Meredith Ryan. You're on speakerphone with Nick and me. We're following a suspect in an arson. Nick probably won't make it in tonight."

"Jeez, nothing like cutting it close." Barry's nasal protestations would've irritated Meredith normally. But this wasn't normal. "He's due to work in less than two hours. Are you pursuing the suspect?"

"No, it's not a pursuit—yet. Petaluma PD has been apprised and will respond."

"Is it their case?"

"Yes, it will be. It happened in Petaluma's jurisdiction but—"
Barry cut her off.

"Then coordinate with Pet PD and have them take over the

follow. I want Nick here. It's too late to call in another watch commander."

"Barry, we have eyes on this guy—"

"Okay, *I'll* call Pet PD."

"Barry, wait—"

Nick shouted over her. "Barry, listen for a second. We're following the guy who set *our* house on fire. No way we're handing this off when he can get away. And he may lead us to where we believe a kidnapped woman is being kept."

Silence greeted them. Barry coughed. "Um, okay. I will call Pet PD and coordinate with them.

Meredith added, "They know everything except I just ID'ed the arsonist by his clothing, a distinctive hat."

Nick snorted. "We're staying on this guy's tail."

Chapter Eighty-One

Wednesday, March 14, 6:30 PM

NICK HAD CLOSED THE GAP TO ONE BLOCK. THE NIGHT HAD SETTLED in dark and quiet. Streetlights illuminated the roadway, so he backed off to take cover behind the roadway's upslope. Petaluma Boulevard was a long straight roadway punctuated by hills that obscured their view of the RAV4. Once over the hill, it was easy to keep an eye on the Toyota while following two blocks behind.

Meredith had cleared their activity with Jerry. They decided not to call it in to dispatch over the radio on the off chance the driver had a scanner in his car. Meredith created a surveillance service call on the car's MDT and typed in their locations every half mile. Also, dispatch had the unbroadcast information from the call if the surveillance went south. They'd know where to send an ambulance if it was needed. And when this adventure was over, she could merge this information into the homicide case notes nicely time stamped.

The RAV4 went to where the end of Petaluma Boulevard met Old Redwood Highway at the Highway 101 overpass. Nick slowed while the car ahead turned left onto the highway onramp northbound.

Two blocks behind, they had a good view of the roadway, the scant traffic, and the RAV4.

Lighting was not as good on the highway as it was in Petaluma. Still, the RAV4 was easy to follow north. Nick steered the Tahoe from one lane to another, falling in behind a car but still able to see the RAV4. The SUV gave no indication that it was being followed. Past Rohnert Park, then entering Santa Rosa city limits, the RAV4 took the Baker Avenue turn-off to Colgan. Then a turn north onto Petaluma Hill Road and two blocks to a left turn to Aston Avenue.

"The Toyota looks to be slowing." Nick held the Tahoe back. Dark swallowed the street; the few streetlights were inadequate to illuminate the neighborhood. One weak light hinted that the RAV4 had taken the dirt driveway beside it—a faint dust cloud the give-away. 1824 Aston Avenue. Nick stopped in the street, considering which way to follow.

Meredith had a thought. "Back when I was in patrol, I served civil papers on Aston Circle. There's a dead end on both sides of the development. One side overlooks the yard behind these homes. I stood on the front porch thinking, 'what an awful view.'"

"So?"

"So—it overlooks the yard behind these three houses, but mainly 1824."

"You're suggesting we drive to the dead end, and look over the fence to see what we can see?"

"Exactly."

Chapter Eighty-Two

Wednesday, March 14, 8:00 PM

NICK TURNED OFF THE ENGINE AND HEADLIGHTS AFTER PULLING THE Tahoe's bumper as close to the fence as he could. The street halted in an abrupt barricade and fence that overlooked the yard behind the Aston address.

Distant highway traffic hummed in the background, and an occasional low-rider blasted Latin hip hop as it cruised down Aston. All this felt far away as Meredith scanned the nearby homes. Most had lights on as it was evening time when most families were home. But windows and doors weren't open as they would be in the summer. It was cool outside, so Meredith had little concern that anyone would see her. The breeze cut through her sweatshirt and whipped her hair around. She pulled a band out of her jeans pocket and tied her hair into a ponytail to keep it out of her eyes. She had a corduroy jacket in the car but didn't want to go back to get it. She'd just be cold.

Glad she wore soft-soled sneakers that provided good traction, she hoisted herself up on the Tahoe's back bumper. Nick handed her his night vision binoculars.

It took her a moment to focus the binocs and acclimate to the night vision. She scanned from one end of the yard to the back house. It looked like about two acres, mostly grassy and neglected. Closer to the house, rusted lawn furniture, a barbeque, an old water heater, and two piles of scrap metal mounded at the exterior wall. Her pulse quickened when she saw the cars parked—the red Cherokee, light blue Corolla, and a dark-colored RAV4.

"Nick, all three cars are there, parked off to the side and not visible from the street."

"Good. What else?"

"No Dodge Charger."

"Okay."

A weak light shone through a back window. A man's voice was yelling, but she couldn't make out the words. Nor could she see into the room. She hopped down to the asphalt.

"I can hear a man shouting inside the back house, but I can't see any movement."

"That's not enough for exigent circumstances. We can't break down the door."

"What about a search warrant? For the arson, at least."

"Maybe," he nodded. "We can't tie them to the homicide." Nick rubbed his chin with his index finger and thumb. "But if we could get a judge to sign off on a warrant to search the house based on the arson and the RAV4 plus the other two suspect cars, we might find evidence of the homicide or the kidnapping."

"Or both."

"I'm going to call a unit to sit on the house until we can get the warrant signed. Since we're so close to the office, I'll drop you off to get your own unmarked. You can relieve the unit."

"Okay. You have everything you need for your shift tonight?"

Nick thought it over. "Yeah. I've got a spare uniform in my locker, and I have the rest with me in my go bag."

"You?"

"I have a go bag at the office, too. I'm good."

Chapter Eighty-Three

Wednesday, March 14, 9:00 PM

An hour later, Meredith had relieved the marked patrol unit. She picked up her go bag with snacks and a radio headset and put it on. She parked across the street from the driveway and settled in for a long night. Judges don't like getting up late at night. It would take an hour or two to prepare the warrant, find a supervisor to approve it, then track down the on-call judge. She figured she'd be there until after daybreak. Then, who knew what would happen?

If the judge denied the warrant, she'd stay there anyway and hope an opportunity presented itself. The possibility that Teresa was inside with Michael was too strong. She'd promised Esme that she'd find her mother. She hoped her mother was still alive when she did.

Using Nick's night vision binoculars, she scanned the property. It looked like the front house was vacant. There was no movement in or around the structure. Lights illuminated the windows in the second house, and the porch light flashed on. A heavy-set woman on the north end of her seventies shuffled out, holding a bag of garbage to put in the yard can. A perky chihuahua bounced beside her. She hobbled back inside, calling the dog, setting off all the others to barking in the vicinity.

Meredith considered knocking on the woman's door and asking her about her neighbors. But she ruled it out due to the lateness of the hour.

Dang. She forgot to text Tina. The clock on the dash read ten-fifty. She'd have to chance it. Tina might be awake, waiting to hear from her. But if she wasn't, a text would serve the purpose of letting her know what was going on. 'In Santa Rosa, sitting on a suspect house probably all night. Are you okay keeping Davy and Esme?'

Her reply came back quickly. She'd been awake. 'Yep, they're all settled in for the night. Good hunting. BTW, your house was saved, garage a mess.'

'Thank you! God Bless Petaluma Fire Department!' Was Meredith's response.

'Fire Marshall will be in touch tomorrow.'

Meredith sent off a quick but sincere 'thank you'.

Esme certainly would be awake. She'd call her next.

"Esme? It's Meredith."

"Have you found my mom?" She couldn't conceal the shaky anxiety in her voice.

She wished she had better news. "We're getting closer. We think we know where she is, but we need to be sure before we go breaking in doors."

"Okay," Esme sighed. "I wish…"

Meredith's voice softened. She almost felt she was talking to a younger version of herself. Although her childhood demons had been different, they were no less powerful. "You wish what, Esme?"

"Never mind. You wouldn't understand."

"Try me."

Esme was quiet for a moment. "I wish my mother was more like you. She doesn't think things through before she does them. It gets her into trouble."

"We all make mistakes…" Meredith thought about how commonly she heard this comment about suspects during investigations. She wouldn't lay the facts of life out to this girl. She'd already learned more than any thirteen-year-old should.

Meredith's phone vibrated with an incoming call. "Esme, I've got to answer this call. I'll get in touch when I can."

It was Nick. "No, go. We need more. I'm calling the on-call DA now to see what we can use."

Meredith chewed her lip. "I'm going to stay here on Aston. This is where they're holding Teresa; I just know it."

"Not good enough for a judge, Mere."

"I know, I know." Meredith scanned the neighborhood. "Keep me posted."

Chapter Eighty-Four

Wednesday, March 14, 9:00 PM

SOFIA NEVER RAISED HER VOICE AT MICHAEL. HE COULDN'T BELIEVE his ears. "What?"

"I hate this place. I can't even sit on the couch; it's so filthy." Her face turned a blotchy red.

"So, leave." He didn't need her. He didn't even want her around.

"You need me to keep that bitch alive." She squinted her grim intent at him. "I know you. Now that you've got the cop out of the way, you're going after Esme. Nothing's going to get in your way to outdo your brothers."

What would it hurt to move? The Penngrove house was much nicer than this one—more expensive, too. He might as well use it. He'd make Sofia work for it, though. He'd moved the four women that didn't get picked up from the raid to another house in Suisun City so they'd be alone.

"What d'you know about my brothers?"

Sofia put her hands on her hips and cocked her blond head. "I know they came over from the old country with your father when you were a baby. They inherited his businesses, and you got nothing.

You figured that daddy thought you were too young. You set out to prove them all wrong—that you're smarter than them. And Esme is your ticket to the big time."

He started to say something, but her fury rolled right over his words. "Oh, you had a small business started with my help," she spat. "But you want the big time. For that, you need the money from auctioning off a thirteen-year-old virgin online to put you in that class. That's why you had to eliminate that woman cop."

Sofia knew more than he thought. She could be dangerous. But she was a great lay. She had other uses, too, like keeping the women in line and keeping the houses running smoothly. If he wanted any action tonight, he'd have to let her have her way. "I guess you're right…"

Kirk burst through the front door, his face lined with distress. "That old lady in the house in front was nosing around."

"Did she see anything?"

"Nah. I watched her, but she went back to her house with the damn yappy little dog."

Sofia grabbed her purse. "Guess that takes care of that."

Michael tipped his head in agreement. "Let's move."

Chapter Eighty-Five

Wednesday, March 14, 11:00 PM

MEREDITH TAPPED HER HUSBAND'S ICON. HE ALWAYS PICKED UP when she called. It was no different this time. "Nick, they're moving. All three of the cars are pulling out."

"Can you follow?"

"Of course. We need to know where they're going. But I can't tell if Teresa is with them."

"No matter. If they're all moving, it's unlikely they're leaving her behind."

"Unless she's dead."

He paused. "I'll get hold of the owner to see if we can get his permission to open the house up and do a search of the place." He had little doubt the owner would agree to let them search once he or she has been told the house may be used in the commission of a crime. If Michael followed his pattern from Yulupa, he probably hadn't paid rent here either.

"Okay. I'll tail them and keep you updated. I'll put the location in the call notes." Dispatch had checked on Meredith's safety every half hour by MDT. She used the computer to keep Dispatch and Nick updated.

Meredith started the engine and turned off the parking lights. The RAV4 pulled out last after the Corolla and the Cherokee. She pulled away from the curb when the RAV4 got to the signal at Aston Avenue and Petaluma Hill Road. The RAV4 taillights were tall enough that it was easy for Meredith to see them over other traffic, so she didn't have to follow so close.

They turned south onto Petaluma Hill Road and passed through the South Park neighborhood. Traffic was scant, with only one other vehicle going south on Petaluma Hill Road behind Michael's cavalcade.

The dark played into Meredith's hand. Far enough behind not to be spotted, she felt safe turning on her headlights. She kept her speed below theirs, a steady forty-five miles per hour, ready to pull over to the shoulder or take a side road if necessary.

Michael's parade stayed on Petaluma Hill Road out into the country. On one side, former cattle pastures were being swallowed by encroaching housing developments. Taylor Mountain Regional Park was a dark hulk to the east. She and Nick had hiked the park trails a half-dozen times. Farther south, horse ranches built into the hillside dotted the road. To the right, they passed turn-offs for Snyder Lane, then the City of Rohnert Park. The cars slowed at the bright lights of Sonoma State University.

Meredith held back, slowing to the shoulder of the road. She updated her location on the MDT as she watched the three cars turn onto Curtis Drive, a middle-class tract of custom homes on expensive acreages.

The roadway was clear, with no traffic in either direction. She turned off her headlights and pulled onto Petaluma Hill Road to follow the turning cars. The map on her MDT showed Curtis Drive was a dead end. However, the middle of the block, Johnies Way, a narrow lane, connected with Chester Drive, a mirror image of Curtis. Chester led back to Petaluma Hill on one end. Like Curtis, the other was a dead end. The tract sat like a giant "H" fallen perpendicular to Petaluma Hill Road.

The three cars pulled into a circular asphalt driveway at 475 Curtis Drive. An ivy-covered island separated the road from the driveway, allowing for a clear view into the house. The light-colored one-story rancher had a pea gravel path that led to a matching shed in front. With a house on one side, there was a vineyard on the other. A dead end.

Meredith picked out a spot to park across the street and down a driveway that sheltered the car from view yet allowed her to see. Using the map in her MDT, she memorized the streets with their access and egress points. If someone took off on foot, she wanted to have a mental picture of the landscape.

The driver of the RAV4 parked and went around to the back. He opened the hatch and dragged out a lump the size of a rolled-up carpet. He hoisted it over his shoulder and, after words with Michael, stashed it in the shed.

A blond woman followed inside the shed, and Meredith saw the beam of a flashlight within. A dim light flickered on. The blond stayed for ten minutes, then shut off the light and went inside the house with everyone else. Meredith entered these observations in the call notes and sat back in the seat.

Waiting was a constant in her line of work. In the academy, instructors joked about how police officers worked long hours of boredom punctuated by moments of sheer terror. She'd been on the job long enough to know it wasn't a joke. She knew her interminable waiting could suddenly turn to incredible fear.

Last year, an overweight patrol deputy had a heart attack while wrestling with a drunk. Though both she and Nick took their physical fitness seriously, this stress-induced ailment had an impact on them. Both spent time in the department gym working with weights. Cardio used to be runs four times a week, but these days, with shift work and family obligations, treadmills had become their go-to.

Tonight, even though it felt so long ago, Tina's spaghetti dinner lay in her stomach. She felt antsy sitting in the car. She'd been stationary long enough.

She fished out her penlight, buttoned up her corduroy jacket, and quietly opened the car door. Her shoes crunched on the gravel from the road shoulder, then quieted as she moved across the more solid asphalt.

At the shed, she stood near the back wall, listening. Nothing. All quiet but for an occasional car on Petaluma Hill Road. An airplane droned overhead, and crickets chirped. A pair of frogs croaked in the distance. She sneaked around to the front. A padlock secured the door.

Frustrated with this lack of progress, she leaned against the shed door. Then she heard it. A faint cry. A cat? She laid her ear against the rough wood jamb.

No, a woman. Crying.

Teresa. It had to be her.

She couldn't risk saying anything to the woman, so she hurried back to the car. The trunk had a first aid kit, ballistic vest, a box of 9X19 ammunition for her Glock, and a box of forms and reference books.

But no bolt cutters.

Meredith went back to the car and typed in the latest information. Within ten seconds, Nick called.

"You think it's the mom?"

"I can't imagine who else it could be. Everyone had been accounted for—yellow watch cap, Michael, and the blond woman."

"Okay. We'll have to get really creative to rescue her. I'll make some calls. You add any updates to the MDT." His mind was already onto more important things, and he said, "I'll be seeing you soon."

"Wait." Trust ran deep for her husband, but she wanted to be sure he knew how exposed the shed was. "Nick, the shed sits directly in front of the house, with a double window not eight feet away. Do you think we can free the woman with that exposure?"

"I'll look it up on the map and Google Earth. I'll make it work. I won't put anyone at risk."

"I'll be waiting."

Chapter Eighty-Six

Wednesday, March 14, 11:15 PM

MEREDITH WAITED. AFTER A HALF HOUR, SHE GOT OUT OF THE CAR and walked the neighborhood, keeping the house and shed in view. When she ended her walk, she found herself outside the shed. There was no noise from inside. Meredith worried that Teresa might have fallen unconscious or worse. She didn't dare reach out and give her comforting words like 'help is on the way.'

Meredith turned her phone volume off, leaving it to vibrate in her pocket instead of ringing. That way, she felt a bit better about staying outside. She settled down on a wooden sawhorse stored next to the shed. That way, she'd hear any noise from inside the structure.

Ten minutes passed. Meredith heard raised voices from the house. A woman yelling in a strong, challenging tone, certainly not Teresa. Then a man's voice answering angrily. The argument came from a nearby room. She was sure she could hear if she got a little closer.

Finding a bare patch of ground to stand in, Meredith positioned herself beneath the window that looked out onto Curtis Drive.

Through the closed window, the pair were loud enough for her to hear clearly.

Chapter Eighty-Seven

Wednesday, March 14, 11:15 PM

MICHAEL STARED AT SOFIA. WHAT HAD COME OVER HER? WHY WAS she fighting him on every move? She used to be so agreeable and manageable. "What the fuck is it to you?"

"Are you crazy? You texted this little bitch once and got set up. And now you're doing it again? Don't you ever learn?"

"I'm going to do this for our future." Women always loved hearing that shit, although he thought she might see through it. He just needed her to get off his back for a while.

"Your future will probably be in prison if you do this."

"What d'you care?"

"You're my security, Michael." Her voice settled to a wheedling tone. "I need you."

Right, he thought. "You need my money is more like it."

"I need you, Michael." Sofia's voice softened. "Don't do this. I can't stand the thought of you in prison."

Michael ground his molars. He couldn't stand the thought either. He grabbed her shoulders. "It's never going to get that far. You just have to trust me."

Frank came into the room. "I'll take the pic with your phone now."

Michael tossed Frank the phone, then glared at Sofia. "It's on."

Kirk leaned against the door jamb. "You're leaving the twit here?"

"Yeah. I've arranged to meet Esme at the Wilco parking lot in Petaluma. She's already said she'll be there. I'll show her the picture, then bring her here so she can see her, then get rid of the twit. She'll have outlived her usefulness."

Sofia 'tsked' and turned away. "Thank God for small favors. Now I won't worry that she'll puke in my car."

Chapter Eighty-Eight

Wednesday, March 14, 11:20 PM

MEREDITH SNEAKED BACK TO THE OTHER SIDE OF THE SHED. SHE HAD to get to where she could transmit that information. Being so close to the house made keeping radio silence essential. She'd just leaned on the shed's siding when the door slammed at the house. She held her breath as the one called Frank stomped over the pea gravel path that led to the shed.

He flipped on the light. "Roll over," he shouted. "Roll over, you used up piece of shit."

A woman's voice mumbled. Frank shouted again, and the woman groaned in protest. At least Meredith knew Teresa was alive.

A flash illuminated the inside, a glare spilling onto the path. Flashes like for photos. Two pictures.

Frank turned off the light, closed and locked the door, and marched back inside.

Meredith waited for a moment, then made her way back to the car. She checked the call notes. Rancho Adobe Fire had been assigned with a rescue rig as well as an ambulance from Rohnert Park, all responding without lights or sirens. Nick had arranged a staging area on Johnies Drive. The homes in the area were far enough from the road that they shouldn't be disturbed by the noise of the truck and ambulance.

Thus updated, she called Esme. She had to warn her—and to caution her about Michael's plans. The call went to voicemail. She tried again and got the same. She texted, 'Don't go with Michael. He's got your mom, but we're going to get her soon.'

No reply. Meredith wasn't even sure she had received the text.

Next, she called Nick to fill him in on the new developments. There was too much info to add to the call. She'd abbreviate it later. "Nick? I overheard Michael saying he was going to meet Esme at the Wilco store in Petaluma."

"Shit. How the hell did she get out of Tina's house?"

"No clue. I tried calling and texting her but couldn't get through."

"Shit. That messes everything up. I'll call Petaluma PD to get a unit over to Tina's and see if they can catch Esme."

"Thanks." Meredith released a breath while Nick went to another phone to make the call. When he returned, she said, "I saw you've got rescue coming. Teresa is surely going to need an ambulance. I haven't seen her, but she sounds pretty rough."

"The rigs are pulling out of the station now."

"Hold them up a minute. I don't want them to cross paths with Michael and his crew."

"Hang on." Nick put the phone down and called dispatch to tell the rescue to hold up for a few minutes. "Okay, that's done. What's going on?"

Meredith briefed him on what she'd heard. "It sounds like she's hurt. Or coming down from drugs. But debilitated, for sure. She's not putting up any resistance when they manhandle her. She's groaning from pain, I suspect." She stopped. "Wait." Meredith used the binoculars to look across the street. "Michael and both of his goons are getting into the Cherokee. They're pulling out."

"Damn."

"Nick, I'm going to follow them. If the PD doesn't get to Tina's quickly, Esme could already be on her way. Michael's going after Esme…well, I can't let him get her."

"Jesus, Meredith. Anything can happen." He shifted gears. "I've got PPD on the way to Tina's. Do you want another unit at the Wilco parking lot on the north end of Petaluma?"

"Yes, one unit would help. A marked unit."

"Okay, I'll call Petaluma PD and get another car over there."

"You have the license plate of the Cherokee?"

"No."

"I got it." She repeated it to him. "Okay. I'm on the road." She pulled out when she saw the Jeep Cherokee's taillights disappear on Petaluma Hill Road. "Send rescue and fire."

Chapter Eighty-Nine

Wednesday, March 14, 11:40 PM

NICK PULLED ONTO THE STAGING AREA AT THE NORTH END OF
Johnies Way. The fire rescue truck idled nearby, with an ambulance
behind it. Nick's SUV became the incident command center, and
senior sergeant Quint Masimo, a muscular Filipino who'd just
arrived, took over command. He'd remain in place, directing
resources should any extra staff be needed. A tablet with the Google
Earth version of the neighborhood gave them all a good sense of
place. In a quick briefing with the sergeant, Nick told him what
needed to be done. The team included a mustachioed Rancho Adobe
fire captain with salt and pepper hair, a beefy blond medic, and Nick.
The three left, trotting silently to Curtis Drive. Nick tucked a
penlight into his pocket, the fire captain carried bolt cutters, and the
medic clutched a collapsible nylon litter. Planning for the worst, they
anticipated the woman wouldn't be able to walk.

It was almost midnight, and a light breeze shook the tree limbs
nearby. The air temperature was cool, and the stars shone brightly in
the glow of the three-quarter moon. The ambient light illuminated
the area enough for them to navigate to their target. On Curtis Drive,

their feet crunched on the road's gravel shoulder. From behind a house, a dog barked, rousing another pair of canines. The three froze at a human-sized juniper shrub and waited until the barking quieted.

Nick glanced around for any signs of life. No lights, no doors opening and closing, and no human voices. He gave the signal to move out.

They were at the shed door within three minutes. With Nick standing in front to buffer any noise, the fire captain clamped the bolt cutters onto the lock's shank. The lock popped free and fell to the pea gravel path with a crunch.

The captain stood aside, and Nick pulled open the door slowly. He flicked on his penlight and pointed it at the shed floor. A low moan rose from a pile of—rags—in the middle of the shed. Hoses, garden tools, gallon bottles of pesticides, and long-abandoned bags of fertilizer sat on the floor, thrown in without thought of organization. In the middle lay a mound of clothes—moaning.

Nick stepped inside. "Teresa?"

The pile moved, an index finger raised, then dropped.

"That's her." He stepped back so the medic and captain could take over. Nick heard the medics whispered questions and the subdued grunts that answered. She couldn't walk. Cautiously, and with as little noise as possible, the captain and the medic straightened her out and rolled her onto the litter. Gripping the hand holds at head and foot, the two men carried her out. They waved off Nick's offer of help as he'd offset their balance. Teresa was light. The medic estimated she weighed ninety pounds.

Nick closed the shed door and looped the cut padlock on the handle. From a distance, it would appear to be undisturbed. They needed just a few more minutes.

Nick reached his SUV in time to watch the driver close the ambulance door. A uniformed deputy accompanied Teresa. Nick felt this was a necessary precaution. No one knew for sure what part she played in Nuñez's death, but if she was responsible, as Medina said she was, he wanted her secured by a deputy. If not, she may still be in danger, and the deputy would provide security.

Nick turned up the volume on his radio. Meredith was giving

another unit directions over their private channel. She would run whatever scene would develop in Petaluma.

Sergeant Masimo hunched over against the cool evening. "What next?"

"We wait for word that the bad guy and his goons are on the way back here. If so, we'll be here for them. I want all three men in custody."

"How do you see this playing out?" Masimo's forehead creased with worry.

"I'd like to do this with the minimum of hassle for everyone. When the Cherokee gets here, we surround them and take them into custody. How many units do we have here?"

"Twelve. Two double SO units, two Rohnert Park patrol cars and a detective, one Sonoma State PD, and two Petaluma PD, plus you and me," Masimo answered.

"We won't need SWAT," Nick said to himself. Then, to Masimo, "I'd like to deploy units in pairs around the property at entrances and exits. And have dispatch send another ambulance to stand by."

Masimo nodded and went about assigning deputies and officers to their positions.

Chapter Ninety

Thursday, March 15, 00:00 AM

MICHAEL TOLD FRANK TO PULL THE CHEROKEE OVER BEHIND THE IHOP at the far north end of the lot. He had Frank and Kirk get out, and he'd take the wheel. The two men were to walk down to the Wilco Farm Store and hide until he called them out. He'd make sure Esme got out of whatever car she arrived in, and between the three of them, they'd grab her. That was the plan.

Michael drove over and parked in the lot directly across from the Wilco front doors. He turned off the engine and waited. It was just past midnight, Thursday. He had a fleeting concern about how Esme would get to their meeting, but he figured she was a smart little girl. She'd figure something out.

Ten minutes later, a battered Toyota Altima with a small Uber sign in the front window pulled up. The back door opened, and Esme got out.

She was even lovelier than he remembered. Tall for a thirteen-year-old, long brown hair, flawless skin, and full, red lips. In snugly fitted jeans and a denim jacket, she looked the picture of provocative innocence.

When she turned to close the door, he glanced to where he expected Frank and Kirk to be. They were concealed. He'd have to warn them not to touch her. Although, if he were honest, he wouldn't mind a bit of that either.

After the Altima left, Michael got out and sauntered toward Esme. No need to let her think he was in a hurry. She waited near the store's front door, her face impassive. He knew what she was thinking, though. She worried about her mother. She wanted her mommy.

When he stood six feet away from her, he stopped and nodded to the Cherokee. "Get in the car."

She shook her head. "Where's my mother?"

"She's safe."

"Safe where?"

"A special place. All to herself. No one bothering her."

The girl's eyes narrowed. "How do I know you're telling the truth?"

He reached into his pocket and scrolled through his pictures. He'd already sent her one photo to prove he had her. Now was the time to show her the second. He used his thumb and index finger to enlarge the picture of Teresa lying on a pile of tarps next to a lawn mower.

"She's hurt. You beat her up. You left her in a barn." Esme slapped the phone out of his hand, revealing the child in her. "She's in a barn." She turned and ran out the driveway towards North McDowell Boulevard.

And right into Meredith's arms.

Chapter Ninety-One

Thursday, March 15, 00:10 AM

A MARKED PETALUMA PD UNIT AND A SHERIFF'S PATROL CAR screeched to a halt behind Meredith's detective unit.

Michael had been on the girl's heels, but he stopped at the sight of Meredith. She hugged Esme to her and then shoved her behind. To Meredith's right, a dark blue-clad officer skulked toward her gun drawn. "Detective Ryan?"

"Yeah," she answered, keeping her eyes on Michael, frozen in place. She pushed Esme toward the officer. "Take her. Keep her safe." Then to Esme, she shouted, "Go with him."

The officer reached for the girl's hand and took it. As he led her away, she cried. "Find my mother, Meredith. Please, don't let him hurt her anymore."

With the girl's cries ringing in her ears, Meredith stepped a foot closer to Michael.

He stood transfixed. "You're supposed to be dead."

"You gave the orders then?" It was more a statement than a question.

Michael glanced over her shoulder, taking stock of his chances.

He wheeled around and, at a run, yelled at the two men now standing in front of the store. "Get the car. Let's get out of here."

Meredith debated whether to chase Michael on foot or to get to her car. He was far enough away that the car was the only way to get close to him. She jumped behind the wheel and got on the radio to the Sheriff's unit parked behind her. This deputy was a rookie with whom Meredith had never worked. She tried to remember his name —Wade something.

"I'm going to follow this red Jeep Cherokee. It may lead us to a kidnapped victim. Take the lead because you're marked. But hold back enough to not push the driver into a pursuit." As in all things currently in the blue world, the first thought had to be of safety with the next being liability. Police chases by unmarked cars were too often discounted by the courts. Defense attorneys used the argument that the innocent driver might not know he was being pursued. Meredith wasn't sure this would result in a pursuit, but she had to think that far ahead.

Meredith gave Wade an update as he pulled in front of her. "They're pulling out now—a right turn onto Redwood Highway."

Over the radio's private channel, Wade said, "I recognize the RO of that vehicle." RO was shorthand for Registered Owner. "Frank Jacox. I know him from the jail. He's a real loser, but I never saw any violent behavior from him."

Meredith acknowledged and watched the deputy as he pulled in. Past the stores, Wade followed at a safe parking lot speed. He showed admirable restraint for a rookie. Much like a K-9, when someone fled from a cop, the instinct was to chase.

The Cherokee accelerated north on the two-lane country road that in years past had been the main traffic artery of Highway 101. Relegated by California Department of Transportation engineers to a county road, it was empty of vehicles in the middle of the night. Residents tucked in early to get up with the birds to work on dairy and horse farms. The drunk drivers and others intent on keeping a low profile were the usual motorists.

Lunging forward, the Jeep Cherokee picked up speed under the driver's lead foot. The Sheriff's patrol SUV kept back with Meredith behind. Past the Twin Oaks Roadhouse, Meredith noted a half dozen cars in the gravel parking lot awaiting drivers after last-call. It was twelve-thirty. Another hour to go before the serious drunks were on the highways. The country road had few streetlamps after the Rancho Adobe Fire House in downtown Penngrove. A right turn began the main artery of Petaluma Hill Road that skirts Rohnert Park and dead ends in Santa Rosa.

The Penngrove population was 2368, mostly scattered around the hub of the fire station, post office, and market. The most notable item about passing through Penngrove was the train tracks bisecting it.

Without brake lights, the Cherokee thumped over the tracks, up the hill, and through a stop sign, a solid half mile ahead of Wade and Meredith.

Staying straight on Petaluma Hill Road, Meredith firmed her speculation that the Cherokee was heading back to Curtis Drive. Petaluma PD dispatch had relayed that Esme was in safe hands at their station. Relieved that she was secure, Meredith re-directed her focus.

What would happen if Michael and his crew got back to the Curtis Drive house? She hadn't had a moment to check her phone for a message from Nick. Looking for notes about the rescue at her MDT while driving wasn't smart, either.

She considered a felony car stop. With only two units—herself and Wade—it could be difficult to contain. With suburban ranchettes on one side and open fields on the other, it could get messy. She couldn't endanger residents or risk losing Michael and his crew.

She used her voice command to call Nick.

He answered with a question. "Are you okay?"

"Yes." She took a breath to normalize her voice. This wasn't a pursuit, but she was following the guy who was responsible for a kidnapping at the minimum. She hoped Teresa survived her abduction. "Did you get Teresa?"

"She's at Sutter Hospital now. She was pretty beaten up. They'll be doing tests to see about internal injuries."

Meredith blew out a breath of relief. Another concern put to bed.

"Okay. Do me a favor. Call Petaluma PD and get word to Esme that her mother is safe in a hospital. Talk to her yourself if you can."

"Good idea."

"We'll figure out how to get her to see her mother later. Right now, we've got Michael for kidnapping with no direct tie to Bernardo Nuñez's homicide."

"That's okay. It's enough to hold him while we stack up the charges."

"I want to do a felony stop on these jokers, but I need another marked unit or two. Can you get another deputy or Rohnert Park?"

"I've got ten units surrounding the house. I can call off two and have them meet you on Pet Hill somewhere." 'Pet Hill' was cop shorthand for Petaluma Hill Road.

Meredith's breath caught. "No, check that. There won't be time. Curtis Drive is right up ahead. I'd have to wait for those units. The timing is bad. We'll do it at the house." She heard Deb's voice on the radio advising dispatch she was on scene.

"Deb just got here."

"Okay. The units are here in place. I'll apprise the SWAT commander. This may go south, and we want to be prepared."

"Okay. I'll do the radio while Wade takes point." Meredith would communicate on the radio to dispatch and incoming units where she and Wade were. "Wade, don't turn into Curtis. Drive past. Take the next right to Chester, then Johnies."

Nick said, "Stay safe," and disconnected.

Chapter Ninety-Two

Thursday, March 15, 00:25 AM

Michael directed Frank to pull into the Curtis driveway. He'd watched the sheriff's car behind them, and though they made no move to stop them, he'd broken out in a sweat. When the Cherokee turned onto Curtis, the sheriff's car had stayed on Petaluma Hill Road. Michael wanted to believe his trouble was over, but his life lessons had taught him that as soon as he thought he was out of danger, his problem got worse. Sure enough, a pair of sheriff's patrol cars came from nowhere and cruised down Curtis, parking behind him diagonally across the road.

The Cherokee had lurched to a stop, and Michael bailed out of the passenger seat. He ran to the shed. When he grasped the padlock to insert the key, the whole mechanism fell off. The door swung open. No one inside.

Fuck.

Shadows to his left moved, then more to his right. Frank jumped out of the Cherokee and ran into the vineyard. *Asshole.*

Michael yelled at Kirk. "Get the girl and bring her out." The front door squeaked open.

Chapter Ninety-Three

Thursday, March 15, 00:35 AM

MEREDITH WAS IN POSITION BEHIND A SO-MARKED SUV. SHE shouted, "Michael Fedorov, sheriff's office. Put your hands up."

"Fuck you," Michael yelled.

She kept at him. "Michael Fedorov, you're under arrest for kidnapping.'

Michael raised his hands to his ear height, a feint to buy time. "I can't hear you."

The front door squeaked open again. Kirk stumbled out of the house holding Sofia by her hair, her wrists bound in front with duct tape. In Kirk's hand was a small automatic pistol tucked under Sofia's chin. He dragged her over the path and then pushed the woman over to Michael. Now the three of them stood at the shed, the whimpering woman in the middle and Kirk holding his pistol at Sofia's temple. Michael poised on the other side.

"Wade, watch the guy holding the girl," she said, across the hood of the SUV. Then, she pressed the transmit button on her radio headset, "Someone get a spike strip up here." Though the sheriff's SUVs blocked the roadway, the multitude of driveways could still allow the Cherokee to leave.

Meredith heard the acknowledgment and then shouted at Kirk, "Put the pistol down." He continued to ignore her, his eyes riveted on Michael, whose attention jetted from one distraction to another. Meredith swept her focus to both men. She watched Michael's volcano of arrogance erupt at the indignity of it all. She could hear him thinking, 'How dare they think they could make me do what they wanted?'

Michael got a grip on himself. He glanced at Kirk. "You got the car keys?"

She barely heard his muffled voice but understood enough to realize one of her worst-case scenarios was coming to life. *That spike strip better get here soon.*

"Yeah," Kirk answered, his voice filled with a loud bravado.

"Get in the car. Start it up." Kirk handed Michael the gun and hurried toward the car.

"No, Michael." Sofia wriggled away from him but not out of his grip. "What are you doing? Michael, please."

"Stay where you are. Freeze." Wade yelled loudly. Like volume would stop him. Then to Meredith, "I got this one."

"Check," Meredith acknowledged, relieved he'd keep eyes on Kirk. They couldn't be permitted to leave in the car.

Michael clutched a handful of Sofia's hair as she squirmed to get away. "Michael, NO!"

Chapter Ninety-Four

Thursday, March 15, 00:40 AM

"SHUT UP, BITCH." HE GLANCED AROUND AT ALL THE COPS. MUST BE a dozen of them. "You're my ticket out of here."

"Michael, I loved you." Sofia's voice trailed away like she finally figured out where she ranked in this whole deal. She slumped against him.

He felt a tug at his belt. He heard a different woman's voice shout, "No!" The cop.

Then a pain sliced through his side. He shoved her away and clasped his rib. His own pocketknife protruded from a wound. The pain ripped through him like a thousand knife blades instead of just one. He dropped to his knees.

It was over in a second. He didn't see much but felt the cops descending on them like piranha on a handful of ground beef. He heard Kirk's face hit the concrete with a deputy on top of him while that bitch cop laid out Sofia beside him. Someone must have taken Frank down in the field.

Then the cop jumped over to Michael, rolled him over, and

secured his hands before he could get a grip on his Ruger. There was no more fight in him. He felt his energy draining out. He was too tired. Beaten by a woman. Two women.

He saw Frank being marched back to the cop cars with his hands cuffed behind him. It was over.

Chapter Ninety-Five

Thursday, March 15, 00:45 AM

MEREDITH SLAPPED THE HANDCUFFS ON MICHAEL FEDOROV AND attached him to the gurney. He was bleeding profusely, and the medic working on him elbowed her out of the way twice before he got the wound staunched. Deb stayed in the ambulance and at the hospital with Michael until security was set up for his stay.

Deputies took Kirk into custody at the scene. On his way to the county jail, he'd have to be treated before he would be admitted for booking. He needed his road rash cleaned and bandaged on his forehead from the arrest. Frank was on his way to county jail. Directly.

Sofia sat in the back of a patrol car. She was uninjured physically but shattered by Michael's betrayal. Her chin jutted out in a defiant nod. "What d'you want to know? I'll tell you everything."

"About Michael Fedorov?" Meredith was surprised at this about-face of her loyalty. Usually, it took more convincing. But, Meredith thought she wouldn't be too loyal to a guy who pointed a gun at her head and planned to use her as a pawn.

"Everything," Sofia repeated.

"Sofia, I'm going to read your rights to you first, just in case you're held culpable for any crimes. Do you understand?"

Sofia met Meredith's gaze clear-eyed and with a firm jaw. "I need you to say yes or no."

"Yes, I understand."

A half-hour later, Meredith had Sofia in handcuffs and on her way up to the sheriff's office. Sofia had told her story—once. Meredith decided to move her to the office for both their comfort. The night temperatures had dropped, Sofia was shivering, and there were more questions.

Chapter Ninety-Six

Friday, March 16, 11:00 AM

MEREDITH HAD SPENT THE ENTIRE MORNING AT THE DISTRICT attorney's office in Santa Rosa. Wrung out from the meeting, she was glad it was over. While they were on the same side, the deputy DA wanted to be sure there were no surprises in court. An in-depth interview was the way to ensure it.

There were several loose ends in this case that required Meredith to tie up. Gustavo Medina had been arraigned for Isaac Santiago's murder, and Hardy was managing his case through trial.

Meredith would do the same for the Nuñez homicide. The autopsy report had been straightforward. Bernardo Nuñez had suffered blunt force trauma and bled out from exsanguination. The District Attorney planned to charge Teresa with Murder One because she took the screwdriver into the house to confront Bernardo. The DA felt he could prove pre-meditation. Her arraignment would take place next Tuesday with a public defender to speak for her.

The general opinion in the office was any good defense attorney would be able to plead her down to voluntary manslaughter because she was trying to save her daughter from a pimp.

Nick scheduled security in the hospital for three days at the doctor's recommendation before Michael would be transferred to the county jail infirmary. He would recover and stand trial for human trafficking.

Meeting with Raul had been another huge hurdle that challenged Meredith's college sprints. She could've sent him a letter but felt an in-person visit would be best, as much as she hated to face him. Even with this news, she'd always be his victim. The prison had made special arrangements for Meredith to meet with Raul that day.

The room was the same as before. The light was different as this was afternoon, and she'd previously met him in the morning. Raul, however, was the same. His face drawn and a bit pale, his fingernails bitten to the quick, he studied Meredith intently while the guard brought him in. Shackled and subdued, he sat before her, waiting.

She couldn't find it in her to smile. "Good news. Esme is home and safe."

Raul sighed, and his chin dropped to his chest. He murmured, "Is she okay?"

"She's fine. She's with her Auntie and is back in school."

"Was I right? Did someone try to snatch her?"

"Yes, you were right." Meredith nodded. "But we got the guy for a minimum of kidnapping. The DA's working up further charges as their investigators find more women he forced into servitude."

"Pimping?"

"Yes." She had to talk over him to finish her answer. "But she wasn't violated."

Raul rubbed his eyes with thick, rough fingers. When he finally met her gaze, "What else?" A cop through and through, he believed the worst of people. He knew there was more.

"She may have witnessed more."

His eyes were dark and flinty, believing yet not wanting to hear it. "Go on."

"Teresa busted out of her rehab to chase after Esme. The girl had a misguided idea of getting a job to support her mother and found someone that would put her to work."

"Misguided is right…"

She waved away Raul's comment. "Teresa broke into the house to free her daughter. We don't know exactly what happened yet, but your niece was in the house. Teresa isn't talking, and neither is Esme."

"Jesus."

"It gets more complicated, but the end result is we have Esme safe at Auntie Almita's, and Teresa is in custody."

"Teresa did something. I bet she took the guy out. Esme saw it and is protecting her." Raul nodded. "She won't be able to get Esme in trouble from prison. And the girl will be safe from predators like the guy who took her." His mouth curled in hesitant approval. "Auntie will take care of her."

"Right."

"Will she have to testify in court against her mother?"

Meredith shrugged. "The DA's waiting for the arraignment. Teresa has been wobbling about which way she was going to plead."

"It wouldn't be in her nature to spare her daughter the trauma. I mean, reliving in a courtroom the death her mother caused would be brutal for anyone, especially for a thirteen-year-old." Raul shook his head at the depths to which a person could fall.

"It's up to her and her lawyer. We've done what we could."

"You did." Raul's eyes softened, a look Meredith had never seen. "You probably did a lot more than you're telling me. But the bottom line is the girl is safe. For that, I thank you."

They were each in their own cubicle with plexiglass separating them. Touching was impossible, but Meredith had the feeling if he could, he would've shaken her hand. His thanks had an impact on her. She nodded and stood, not wanting to give in to any emotions. "Are we square now?"

Raul's thin lips curled in what could pass for a smile. "We are," he said into the receiver.

Chapter Ninety-Seven

Friday, March 16, 3:30 PM

FRIDAY AFTERNOON—MEREDITH AND NICK TOOK ESME TO SUTTER Hospital to see her mother. In the hallway outside the room, Meredith eyed the girl's stoic exterior but glimpsed vulnerability in her eyes. She'd already been through so much. But now wasn't the time to soften the news. She had to know the truth.

"You know your mother is under arrest for murder, right?"

Esme nodded.

Nick folded his arms across his chest. He didn't like this any more than Meredith did. "With the evidence we have, she'll go to prison. Maybe for a long time."

Esme shrugged. "My dad was in prison." Meredith waved away her nonchalance. It didn't apply here. This girl cared about her mother. Esme's father was a mere photograph in her mother's wallet. Esme was a toddler when he'd been put away.

The hospital room was spartan, with a bed and nightstand the only furniture. The deputy standing guard had moved the only chair out of the way into the corner as a nurse and an aide were prepping Teresa for transport to the jail. Teresa had a cast on one arm and bandages on the other. Her face was purple and swollen, with small cuts where a knuckle had busted open the thin facial skin. An IV stand and monitor were off to one side but not hooked to the patient.

Meredith had a glimmer of recognition for the deputy as he nodded to her and Nick. He'd be the deputy to take Teresa to the jail infirmary. A northern beat deputy, one who she rarely saw, and Meredith had to read his name tag to greet him.

"Ah, Chaz. Nice to see you again." She gestured to Esme. "This is Teresa Alfaro's daughter."

Chaz nodded politely and kept his attention on the nurse. "Is the patient ready to go?"

The aide replied, "Yes, but we need your name and signature on the discharge papers."

Meredith interrupted. "Can we have a moment, then? The daughter would like to say goodbye to her mom."

The three retreated to the corner to complete paperwork, and Esme walked over to the hospital bed. Meredith stayed beside her, with Nick at a respectful distance a few feet back.

"Hi, momma." Esme's voice was frail, like it would break from the slightest pressure.

Teresa's bruised face turned to her daughter. She squinted, and her eyes squeezed out a tear. "I never wanted you to see me like this." Skinny and pale except for the bruises, the woman's cheekbones were sharp enough to cut glass.

Esme took her mother's handcuffed hand. "It's okay, momma." Her voice thickened, trying to sound brave.

"I did what they said, you know." Little spots of blood broke out on Teresa's chapped lips when she talked.

"You mean the guy who fell? I was there, Momma. I saw it."

"I thought of it as self-defense." Teresa squeezed her daughter's fingers. "He came after me, so I had to defend myself."

The two talked in muted tones while Meredith glanced at Nick. His face was impassive as usual. Neither of them had known for sure that Esme had witnessed the man's death. Esme hadn't admitted to it, and Meredith hadn't asked if she was there. Teresa's brain must have been fried to not remember that her daughter was in the room

—or banked on Esme to protect her. Meredith knew she could've pressed Esme—but hadn't. The girl was stronger than any of them thought. Teresa wouldn't have volunteered that her daughter was there, either.

Meredith wondered about this hospital bed declaration that she wasn't intended to hear—she happened to overhear the admission about killing Bernardo Nuñez while Teresa had been talking with her daughter. She'd let the DA know and let them figure it out.

She glanced at the wall clock, stepped out of the room, and made the call. There was someone in the DA's office who could conduct Esme's interview. They promised they'd have the public defender sit in to protect the girl. But it was Friday afternoon, and they'd have to hurry.

The transport deputy hovered behind Meredith when she returned. "We're ready to move her."

"Esme, time's up." Nick moved near the girl.

"Nick, we have to take her to the DA's office right away for an interview."

He grimaced, anticipating their next stop. "Esme, we have to go." Meredith saw that Nick had put his hand out to touch Esme, then pulled it back.

Teresa's sinewy fingers tightened on her daughter's. "Wait, no. I..." But Teresa's words failed her just as she had failed her daughter.

Meredith put her arm around Esme's shoulders as Chaz and the attendant wheeled her mother out, handcuffed to a wheelchair.

Esme whispered, "Will there be a trial?"

"I'm not sure." Meredith looked to Nick for an explanation.

"It sounds like she's going to plead guilty," Nick explained. "So, it could be a sentencing appearance only. But we don't know what her attorney has advised her. If she pleads not guilty, that will prompt a jury trial."

Esme sighed. "So, will I go back to my auntie's?"

"It looks like it." Meredith's voice softened. "But we need to go to the District Attorney's office. They need to hear what you saw when Bernardo Nuñez fell."

Esme was silent for a moment, then looked into Meredith's eyes and nodded. "Thank you for all that you've done for me."

Meredith's heart lurched for the heartbreak of those left behind when a loved one chose a life of crime over family. Esme, an innocent in this drama of addiction, human trafficking, prostitution, and much more. She had no choices and had almost made a huge mistake by innocently seeking to work for Michael. But she'd seen the immorality he offered soon enough to get out.

Nick smiled. "This isn't goodbye, Esme. We're not going anywhere. We'll help you through this. This doesn't have to be the end of our friendship. Davy will be asking about you."

Esme's face broke into a smile. "I'd like to spend time with him, too."

"And Tina asked about you, too." Meredith grinned. "Looks like you are part of the family already."

Chapter Ninety-Eight

Saturday, March 31, 09:00 AM

ESME AND DAVY DOZED IN THE BACK SEAT OF NICK'S CHEVY TRUCK as he drove up Highway 101 northbound. He glanced in the rearview mirror at the two and couldn't help the smile that spread across his lips. "We may need another vehicle to carry our brood. It seems to be growing."

"You mean trade in the Subaru, right? I know you won't sell your truck."

"Yeah." He shrugged. "By the way, you mentioned that Deb had an expensive car, and that fueled your suspicions about her."

"We talked it over. I don't know about the car, but she told me that she dropped the ball on the missing case because the sergeant told her to. She wanted the next spot on the county drug task force, and the sergeant told her to refer it to the state."

"About that expensive car that Deb drives..." Nick inhaled deeply. "What I'm going to tell you is classified." He hesitated, considering the wisdom of disclosing this information. But he trusted his wife. "There's another task force operating on the QT. It's from the state Department of Justice. They've been looking into one or two Sonoma agencies with ethics questions that have come up."

"Ethics? Oh no."

"Before you flip-out over this, I want you to know that I took your issues about Deb to someone I trust—the lieutenant in charge." He raised his hand at her protest. "Wait, let me finish."

"Okay."

"He did some checking. You were right to have qualms about the expensive car, but not for reasons you may have entertained. Deb is in debt up to her eyeballs."

"Debt? Like credit card debt?"

"Exactly. The car is leased, the bank foreclosed on her house, and she owes tens of thousands on her credit cards."

"Oh my God."

"Apparently, the jackass she lived with had a gambling problem and used her name to get credit, then more credit."

"They split up." Indignant that someone would use another like that, she snapped. "That day she rescued Esme and me behind the school, that guy was moving out. How could Deb not see it? She's a cop, for God's sake."

"She didn't catch on soon enough to prevent damage to her credit."

"She should've known. She knows about fraud and gambling and stuff like that." Meredith shook her head, looking out the window at the vineyards. She should have known.

"The bottom line is Deb is guilty of bad decisions, not bad morals."

"Some consolation, I guess."

"Whatever you do, you cannot say anything about this to anyone. Especially her. This task force is totally secret."

His wife sighed and reached over to him, touching his hand. "Thanks for checking."

"I saw how it grieved you to see your friend in a potentially compromising situation."

Meredith squeezed his hand and smiled. "Thank you."

Thank God it wasn't what she'd thought.

Chapter Ninety-Nine

Saturday, March 31, 4:00 PM

"NOW GRAB THE HORN AND SWING YOUR LEG OVER THE SADDLE. Just settle into the seat. I'll get your boot in the stirrup." The afternoon sun glinted through the scrub oak leaves playing a wild pattern on Raymond Cavanaugh's Stetson. Budding trees and newly sprouted grass announced that spring had arrived in Geyserville. The day had warmed despite the fresh breeze warning them not to become too used to the sun.

Cav stood in the center of the wood fence pen, straightening after giving his guest a leg up. Meredith and Nick leaned on the outside of the railing watching the scene. Filomena watched from the back deck while Davy raced around on a scooter.

Esme looked at Cav like he'd told her to stick her head in a lion's mouth. "Really?" she mumbled. It wasn't a question. Meredith smiled as the city girl squinted with skepticism. She was surely doubting the wisdom of staying at the Cavanaugh's Ranch.

But Meredith wasn't. She knew this was just what Esme needed. Something to take her mind off Teresa's troubles and to be around people who knew what family affection was all about. The last two weeks had been horrible on Esme, enduring the drama surrounding her mother's arraignment. The proceedings had been fraught with delays and distractions. The public defender assigned to Teresa had suffered a medical emergency, and a substitute appeared in court to ask for a continuance. But in the end, Teresa appeared yesterday and pled not guilty to murder. The trial date was set for next month. Her daughter could breathe for a few weeks until she had to testify against her mother. Witnessing Bernardo's death was bad enough, but now Esme had to swear in court about what she'd seen—against her own mother.

To add to her tension, she had been interviewed a half dozen times by the sheriff's detectives, DA investigators, the public defender, as well as Rohnert Park and Petaluma Police detectives, and the Petaluma fire inspector. That, at least, was in her past.

Aunt Almita had given permission for her to stay with the Reyes family. In an already crowded apartment, it was a relief to send her off, even though she loved her niece. Esme was in favor of it as long as she could go to school at Lawrence Jones Middle School in Rohnert Park. Meredith took her to school each morning on the way to work and picked her up from Almita's in the afternoon.

Now, while she was staying with Nick and Meredith, the family had to move out for a week while the contractors worked on the garage and the primary bedroom above. The family bunked at Tina's temporarily. The fire had damaged the garage, but there had been water damage upstairs. The new flooring that had just been installed had to be replaced. Staying at the Cavanaugh Ranch for the upcoming three-day weekend was a no-brainer. Tina was welcoming to the Reyes family but put up little fuss when they told her they were going to the ranch for the weekend. Tina needed a break, too, it seemed.

At Cav's encouraging nod, Esme turned her weight in the left stirrup and swung her long leg over the cantle. Cav slipped her boot into the stirrup and smiled up at her. "Now, you're set. Take hold of the reins in one hand, look at where you want to go, and press your calves into the horse's flank." He took a step back.

"Wait, he's moving!" Esme choked.

"That's what you just told him to do." Meredith stood at the railing of the corral with Nick and Jake.

"I did?"

"Yes. You're doing fine." In jeans, a blue T-shirt, and borrowed boots, Esme sat tall in the saddle, soon captivated by the motion under her. The sorrel pony was fifteen and a half hands tall—enough size for her long legs but not so tall as to scare the first-time rider. The horse, Jasper, was a mature gelding that Cav kept for Nick. He was an easy goer, not given to bad habits, and the perfect mount for a beginner.

Esme settled into the saddle, her hips moving with Jasper's slow walk. Cav showed her how to make Jasper turn and stop. After three circles around the corral—stopping, turning, and returning, a smile broke out on her face. "This is awesome."

"I knew you'd like it." Nick's hand covered Meredith's. Jake made a curious chuckling sound.

Esme turned in the saddle to look at Meredith. Jasper stopped, his head bobbing with confusion. "I want to go faster."

"We'll do that tomorrow." Cav squinted at the house up a slope a hundred yards away. "Just what I thought. Dinner time."

Filomena's dinner bell rang from the back porch.

"You go on up to the house and wash up." Cav helped Esme dismount. "I'll put Jasper away."

Chapter One Hundred

Saturday, March 31, 5:30 PM

THE CAVANAUGH DINNER TABLE HAD EXPANDED OVER THE PAST FEW years. First, Nick and Meredith joined Cav and his grandson, Jake. Then came Filomena, the housekeeper, just in time to take new addition Davy under her wing. Lately, Manuel, a neighbor, had begun to drop in to enjoy Filomena's fabulous Mexican cooking. Jake suggested her cooking wasn't the only thing Manuel came by for.

And now Esme.

The food was on the table, and Nick had said grace, then Jake stood. "Everybody. I'd like you all to raise your glasses to Esme, our newest ranch hand."

With the welcome toast easing into her heart, Esme gave a shy smile. "Aw, shucks, dude."

Laughter erupted at the table and then died down as food passed around. "How long are you here for?" Filomena looked from Nick to Meredith to Esme. Esme looked to Meredith for the answer.

Meredith swallowed. "It's a three-day holiday at school, and Esme needs to be back by Tuesday."

Esme frowned. Meredith's heart swelled. She doesn't want to go back. As much as she loves school, she was enjoying this more.

"Back where?" Cav asked. He'd been briefed on what the girl had been through but with several details up in the air, Meredith couldn't comment on everything.

"My auntie's." Still frowning, Esme put her fork down on the plate. Then she looked around the table at everyone. "I love my auntie. She's my only family left, and she takes good care of me." There was an unsaid 'but' hanging on to the end of the sentence.

Nick provided the rest of the comment. "But there are nine people already living there. Esme sleeps on the couch."

Jake groaned; the kid who had always had privilege and didn't know about missing meals or sleeping on a couch. He'd had his rough patches, but under Raymond's guidance, had grown into a hard-working, compassionate, moral young man. He stared at Esme as she picked up her fork and resumed eating.

After a glance at Nick, Meredith cleared her throat. "That's why Nick and I have submitted our application for foster parents."

Esme jumped up from the chair. "No? Really? Can I come live with you?"

Nick answered. "We've been talking to your social worker about that, and she's not anxious to take you away from your family. And your auntie wants you there, but she can see how difficult it is for you."

Esme sat down and stared at her plate. Meredith imagined the gears turning in the girl's head. Seeing the Reyes' and Cavanaughs gathering together and saying grace at the table, gave her a new version of what being a family could be. Meredith saw the glint in the girl's eye at their easy laughter, how they loved each other and showed something she probably hadn't seen much of before her stay with Almita—respect.

"We're not sure how it will play out, Esme." Meredith said. "But you surely know that you are wanted and loved by two families."

Cav's weather-lined face broke into a smile. "And when she says two families, she means us, too."

Tears appeared in Esme's eyes, and she put her hand over her heart. "I'm so sad that my mother is in such a mess. But you all are my silver lining. Thank you."

Meredith grasped her hand and pulled her into a hug.

If you like this, you may also enjoy: Catalyst
Cat's Crusade Book One by Nik Morton

A fast-paced thriller with never-ending threats and sexy suspense...

A catalyst is a person who precipitates events. That's Catherine Vibrissae. Orphan, chemist, model, and crusading cat.

Seeking revenge against Loup Dante, the Head of Ananke—and the man responsible for the takeover of her father's company—Cat will stop at nothing to uncover his wicked agenda. A trained chemist and an accomplished climber, she is not averse to breaking and entering. So, when she crosses paths with an attorney for the bloodless organization and uncovers a mysterious product called Catananche, Cat risks injury and death to learn more.

Ranging from South England to Northeast, from Wales to Barcelona, Cat's quest for vengeance is implacable. But will she be able to escape the clutches of an unexpected and whip-wielding enemy?

The first in the Cat's Crusade series, Catalyst follows a strong female character who has a thirst for action.

AVAILABLE NOW

About the Author

Thonie Hevron is a retired 35-year veteran police Community Service Officer, Records Supervisor and 911 dispatcher who grew up in Mill Valley, California. She now lives in Petaluma, California with her husband, Danny, two rescue dogs and a cat. For ten years, she lived in the High Desert town of Bishop, California, working as a dispatcher and writing monthly columns for the *Inyo Register*. Returning to the Bay Area in 2004, she worked for a local law enforcement agency and wrote a regular column for the *Tri-Valley Times* and the *North Valley Times*.

Thonie's writing includes four award-winning mystery novels and short stories. She is a member of the California Writers Association/Redwood Writers Chapter, SistersinCrime/NorCal Chapter and the Public Safety Writers Association.

Her work has appeared in the *Beyond Borders: 2014 Redwood Writers Anthology* and the *Felons, Flames and Ambulance Rides: Public Safety Writers 2013 Anthology*—along with recently releasing in *Cops Writing Crime Fiction: To Serve, Protect and Write*. She is the author of four award-winning mystery thriller novels, re-edited and published by Rough Edges Press. Her website, www.thoniehevron.com, includes a blog with law enforcement guests as well as a writers' column.

When not writing, Thonie rides horses, actively participates in her parish church community and enjoys traveling.